BLUE BLOODED

Jessica McClain:
Book Six

AMANDA CARLSON

BLUE BLOODED
JESSICA MCCLAIN: BOOK SIX

Copyright © 2016 Amanda Carlson

ISBN-13: 978-1541001831
ISBN-10: 1541001834

All rights reserved. No part of this book may be reproduced in any form or by any electronic or mechanical means, including information storage and retrieval systems—except in the case of brief quotations embodied in critical articles or reviews—without permission in writing from the author.

This book is a work of fiction. The characters, events, and places portrayed in this book are products of the author's imagination and are either fictitious or are used fictitiously. Any similarity to real persons, living or dead, is purely coincidental and not intended by the author.

Other Books by Amanda Carlson

Jessica McClain Series:
BLOODED
FULL BLOODED
HOT BLOODED
COLD BLOODED
RED BLOODED
PURE BLOODED

Sin City Collectors:
ACES WILD
ANTE UP
ALL IN

Phoebe Meadows:
STRUCK
FREED
EXILED (*coming Spring 2017*)

For Billy. My always.

1

"I don't sense anything." Rourke turned from his place in the front seat. All eight of us gazed out at the apartment building, situated on a quiet street in Baltimore, trying to figure out if we were walking into a trap. The only thing wrong with this undercover operation was our current ride. We'd been forced to do our recon in a bright orange van with the charming words *Everglades Tours. See Dem Gators Up Close* emblazoned across the side in bright green letters. It was less than ideal if we wanted to keep a low profile, but it couldn't be helped.

We'd just driven up from Florida, with a brief pit stop in Georgia, where Juanita had instructed me to head to Baltimore. There hadn't been time to swap the van out for a new, less conspicuous model.

"I don't sense either," I said.

"Anyone else picking up on anything?" Rourke asked.

"My window's cracked and nothing seems amiss," James commented from the driver's seat.

"I got nothing," Marcy quipped from the backseat. "Enid's

magic is as stealthy as a ghost and leaves no residue. Dang, I wish I had a pair of magical cojones like hers. If I did, I'd be spelling the crap out of everything. Those stuck-up witches would never know what hit 'em."

"Does everything look normal to you?" I asked Kayla, the necromancer we were currently trying to help. Her younger brother was in trouble, possibly taken hostage by the Hag who was trying to kill me. The location of this apartment building was the only information we'd managed to glean from her on the ride today from Georgia to Maryland. "Can you see or detect anything out of the ordinary?"

"Everything seems fine," Kayla answered in a flat tone. "My brother should be at school, but we won't know until we get inside." She made a move to open the door.

"Wait," Rourke ordered, his voice firm enough to still her hand. "We're taking this slow. Enid has left us alone thus far, but that's only because she knows where we're heading. We have no idea what's waiting for us inside."

I'd recently learned that Enid was Juanita's sister, and she was after me for killing the host who would've given birth to her long-lost sister, Bianca. It was a tangled web, which I was trying to untangle. I'd taken away the potential for her sister to be reborn, via an incredibly evil host in the Underworld by the name of Ardat Lili, without knowing it.

Now Enid was out to get me.

"I don't care if it's a trap," Kayla huffed. "I need to know if my brother is safe. I've waited long enough."

"You're not going to help anyone if you *die*," Marcy pointed out, leaning over the seat. "Listen, we all have family. We know what you're going through. My aunt, and possibly my baby cousin-niece, are missing right now. It's driving me batty. But we have to be smart about this. If we're stupid, Enid wins, which is what she wants. We have to outsmart the smarty. That means you can't go in there with both guns blazing. We have to go in stealthlike. Think puma under the cover of darkness. Not elephant in broad daylight."

I peered at my friend. "Pumas and elephants?" My voice cracked.

Marcy sighed. "Pumas are stealthy predators, elephants just stomp around and make annoying noises." I made a face. "Never mind, it makes total sense in my mind, and that's all that matters." Marcy swished her hand, dismissing me. "We go in like predators, not elephants."

I refrained from pointing out to her that most of us *were* predators.

"Pumas are wusses," Rourke muttered from the front seat.

"Fine," Marcy huffed. "We go in like big cats and wolves. Better?"

"Much," I agreed. "And vampires and witches."

"Way to get technical on my awesome analogy," Marcy said.

Kayla shot us both searing gazes. "You don't understand. We have to get to him right now, before it's too late."

There was no doubt Kayla was hiding important details. "Too late for what?" I prodded. "You're going to have to be more specific, Kayla. What's going on?" None of us wanted to go into the apartment cold if we had a better option.

Her amber irises danced, color shooting every which way, but she refused to answer. Her skin had gone from pale to light bronze since we'd plucked her out of the cemetery, where she'd been using her necromancer skills to raise the dead against us, on Enid's orders, to protect her brother. She'd been close to death before I infused her with a jump-start of power. Now she was as good as new.

"Ray," Rourke ordered. "Go check it out from above. See what's on the roof. We'll meet you on the ground."

"Got it." The van was so beat-up that when Ray opened the door, it sounded like metal crunching on metal.

"What floor do you live on?" I asked Kayla. "Surely you can tell us that much."

"Fourth," she answered.

"Can you see your windows from here?"

"No, our place faces the alley."

"Once we exit, we fan out in groups, just like at the cabin," Rourke instructed, coming up with a plan. "Irish, Marcy, and Nick, take the street in front. Jessica, Tyler, Kayla and I will take the back. Everyone is on high alert. Move slowly."

We nodded as we piled out, the doors creaking to various degrees. It was hard to be "stealthlike" in a van that screamed, *Look at me!* I didn't think anything could be worse than a canary yellow Hummer. It appeared I was wrong.

"Marcy, can you detect any spells?" I asked once we were clear of the van.

"Nope, but that's not saying much. Like your mate growled earlier, Enid's not giving away anything if she can help it."

I turned to Rourke. "We should all enter the building at once. Strength in numbers is all we have."

"Agreed," he said. "We split up for now, examine the building from the outside, and wait for a signal from Ray."

We broke into two groups, and the four of us circled around, Kayla in the lead. We cut into an alleyway halfway around. There was a large parking lot situated behind the building.

As we neared, I grabbed Kayla's shirtsleeve, tugging her to a stop. "Which is your window?" I asked in a low voice. "Point it out to us."

She gestured toward the middle of the top floor. The shades were drawn.

"There's a fire escape near their unit," Tyler said. "I can climb up and check it out."

"Do it," I said. "But don't enter the building. Once we get an all-clear from Ray, we'll decide what comes next."

Tyler made a move to leave, but before he could go, Kayla placed a hand on his arm. He stopped immediately, giving her his full attention. "If he's in there," she whispered quietly, "you should be able to sense him. If he's in distress, please call me first. I will have to...calm him down before we can enter." Her voice held urgency. "*Please*."

Tyler nodded. "No problem. If he's there, you go first."

My eyebrows rose as I glanced at Rourke. *Calm him down? This kid has to be a serious threat. That's probably why she's so protective. She's worried we're going to freak out when we find out what he is.*

I understood protective siblings.

She's going to have to come clean sooner or later, my mate reasoned. *Either way, once we catch a good scent of him, we'll figure it out. Her secret will be out soon enough.*

Somehow I don't think it's going to be that easy, I answered. *It almost never is. Juanita said I had to find this kid to fulfill my destiny. But is my destiny really located in a tiny apartment in Baltimore? My guess is he's not here.*

Rourke shrugged, his eyes pinned on Tyler as my brother climbed up the ladder. *Stranger things have happened. Maybe there's a portal up there? Who knows?*

Hah, I laughed. *Well, if there is, we're not going through it.*

Famous last words.

If the kid went through a portal, chances were we'd follow him.

Tyler made it to the top in less than a minute. He crouched low as he investigated, trying to seem like he wasn't casing the joint. It didn't work. He stuck out like a loitering thug up to no good. He turned to us, his hand up in a wave. *I don't sense anything,* he told me internally. *No movement or sounds coming from inside.*

Ray landed next to me in a whoosh, so fast no human could track.

I startled, like usual. Dammit. "Feeling a little jumpy there, Hannon?" He chortled at my discomfort. He was never going to give up calling me Hannon, the name he knew me by on the police force all those years ago. I'd made peace with it.

"I hate it when you do that," I grumbled. "It's unnatural to be able to do what you do. I know you revel in sneaking up on me, but you need to control yourself. There's going to be a time when my fist reacts before my brain does, and I hope, for your sake, your neck is not in its path when it happens."

"If I went any slower, I'd risk being spotted. And, please, shifting into a wild animal is normal?" he scoffed. "You're right up there with me on the list of things that go bump in the night." He crossed his arms, legs splayed, steel-gray flattop unmoving, looking the picture of a cop.

"What'd you find?" I asked, watching my brother as he continued to search for any signs of supernatural life.

"The roof's clean. There's a door, but it's locked from the inside and doesn't seem to have been tampered with lately. I didn't smell anything fresh. But"—he raised an eyebrow—"something's been up there on more than one occasion, and its scent is strange as hell. Smells like an animal—but not really. Definitely supe. Like a cross between an animal and a rock or something. I couldn't figure out what the hell it was, but that's not saying much since I haven't scented that many things. But whatever it is, it hasn't been up there in a few weeks."

"You don't say," I said. Switching to internal, I told Tyler, *Ray smelled something strange on the roof. An old scent trail. Head up and see what you think. When you're done, come down and we'll meet the others.*

Will do, Tyler answered. We watched as he scaled the rest of the ladder to the top, jumping cleanly from the fire escape to the roof.

"Where's he going?" Kayla asked, turning toward me.

"He's checking out your brother's scent signature on the roof. He goes up there sometimes, doesn't he?" I said. "Maybe to get away from it all?"

"That's none of your business," Kayla answered, her face set, her long black hair swaying in agitation.

I sighed. "Kayla, we're here to help you." This was the seventeenth time I'd reiterated that particular fact. "I get being a protective sibling, I am one, too, but we need information so we know what we're dealing with. It's obvious you're keeping his identity from us on purpose." She turned away. "But with all the clues we have, it's not that hard to put the pieces together. Tyler is known for his nose. He's going to find what we need up there. Your brother is young and likely unstable with his magic. When it goes wrong, or he gets upset, he puts people at risk, right? Your fear is apparent. You already told us your mother was from Iceland and your father was Greek. We've deduced you got your necromancy from your father. Rourke mentioned in the van that Iceland was known for two things: elves and trolls. Elves don't smell like animals or stone, as far as I know, so that leaves trolls. Would you like me to keep going?"

She whipped around to face me. "You can't hurt him! Promise me!" She grabbed on to my forearm with both hands. "He's just a kid. He'll get the hang of his abilities soon enough, and once he does, he can and will destroy anyone who seeks to harm him. But for now…he's vulnerable."

Ray whistled. "So, a troll, huh? That sounds intense. Does he morph? Or is he always in his troll form?"

Kayla looked like she wanted to ram a fist into Ray's face, so I gently restrained her, walking her backward a few paces. "I need you to calm down. No one is hurting your brother." I put as much emphasis on my words as possible, hoping my power would have some kind of effect on her. "None of us care what he is, or what he can turn into. He's an innocent pawn, caught up in a very complicated game. We will find him—alive—and once we do, we will keep him safe. You have my word, Kayla. I'm not sure why you're choosing not to trust us after all this, but it would be beneficial for you to start doing so now. We're standing in front of your apartment, and if this isn't proof enough of where our loyalties lie, I can't do much better."

She openly assessed me, her heartbeat elevated as she tried to gauge how much of what I was saying was true. I spread my arms wide to show her I wasn't hiding anything. She and her brother must've been on the run for some time, subsequently building up a lot of trust issues. "He's not a regular…troll," she finally conceded. "He's an…ice troll. But he hasn't fully come into his powers yet." The rest of her words came out hasty and rushed. "He can only shift sometimes, but it's unpredictable, and when it happens…it's messy."

Messy? It sounded chaotic.

"It's okay, Kayla. We're going to help him."

2

"Ice troll?" Rourke commented after Kayla was done. "I don't think I've ever heard of one before." That was saying something, because Rourke was old. His Pride had died out long ago, leaving him the sole survivor.

Kayla stuck out her chin. "The proper Icelandic term is *blár risastór*, which translates to 'blue giant.'"

"So, are you telling us your brother turns into a blue Hulk?" Ray asked incredulously, ending on an appreciative whistle. "That might be the single-most-awesome thing I've ever heard."

"I'm not familiar with a shifter who turns into a giant either," I said.

"He's not technically a troll or a giant." She rocked back and forth on her heels, agitated. "Once he shifts, he resembles…a large gargoyle, his body coloring slate blue."

Rourke nodded. "I've met a few gargoyle shifters in my time. They're among the strongest and most powerful of any shifter, their skin tough as stone. Though, I haven't seen one for centuries. I thought they'd died out."

Kayla shrugged. "My mother's ancestors were giants, said to be interbred with gargoyles. My brother's abilities were...a surprise." She cleared her throat. "We were told his genes...are unusual. He's not a troll or a giant, he's a *blár risastór*."

A necromancer married a giantess with latent gargoyle genes.

It was actually quite astounding.

It made me wonder how many other intermixed supernaturals were out there with strange and wonderful abilities. "Kayla, this doesn't change anything," I assured her. "What I said before stands. It doesn't matter to us what he is. I'm certain he's a great kid who just needs some guidance and help with his powers. We will find him, and once we do—"

"He's in trouble," she interrupted.

"I know," I said. "That's why we're here—"

"No, not because of all this," she said. "We were...on the run for another reason. I'm telling you this because I've decided to trust you. If you choose to go in there and help him, I want—I *need*—you to make me a promise"—she took a deep breath—"to take us both somewhere safe so they can't get to him. Our location here is compromised now. We've lived in ten different cities in four years. I'm running out of options."

"Who exactly is after him?" I asked.

Kayla glanced at Rourke and then back at me. "Your mate is partially right. The gargoyles are almost extinct. There is only one pack left in the world. They are extremely secretive and live in Eastern Europe—Czechoslovakia, I believe. Their numbers are small, and they've been actively seeking to grow for the last fifty years. When they found out about Jax, they decided they wanted him." She bowed her head. "My family refused to give him up."

It was common for shifter fathers to take their teenage sons away from their mothers and raise them in a pack lifestyle. But in this day and age, it was a little archaic, especially if the parent *wasn't* the shifter. It would've been frightful for Jax to go against his will, especially if he wasn't full gargoyle.

"Are either of your parents still living?" I asked gently.

She shook her head. "No. They were killed by this same pack four years ago. Jax and I have been on the run ever since."

Tyler walked up to us.

He'd heard our conversation, and without even glancing at me, he stated evenly, "We give you our solemn oath, Kayla. We will find your brother and make sure you both remain protected."

Kayla turned, appraising Tyler with quiet apprehension, finally nodding.

"Everything clear?" I asked my brother. "Do you think Jax is inside?"

He shook his head. "My best guess is no, but he might be sleeping or—"

Kayla bristled. "Jax is not dead. There's no way he could be dead. He's too strong for that."

"I wasn't going to say dead," Tyler said, "but Enid might've knocked him out or is keeping him quiet."

"It's time to find out," Rourke said. "How many staircases are inside?"

"Two," Kayla answered. "One in the middle and one at the far end."

Rourke turned to Ray. "Go tell Irish we're ready. They enter from the front, we'll take the side. Tell them to be ready in five. We meet on the fourth-floor landing. Nobody goes any farther until I give a signal."

"Will do," Ray said as he shot into the air.

We walked around to the side and entered the building. Smells from the other tenants—garbage, takeout, and pets—were all over the hallway. As we ascended, I couldn't detect any sign of a struggle, and there were no strange supernatural scents permeating the air.

Once we reached the fourth floor, we spotted James down the long hallway. He was waiting at the top of the stairs as directed. Rourke nodded. We all crept forward, following Kayla's lead until she stopped at the door in the middle. I hovered over her shoulder, reaching a single finger out to press it against the wood.

Nothing buzzed back, so it wasn't warded or spelled.

I nodded the all-clear, and she grabbed on to the handle, turning it. It swung wide with no resistance.

We all paused at the entry and peered in.

The living room was in shambles, everything overturned.

Kayla made a move to rush in, but I held her back. I scented nothing, but tossed my power out to check. It came back clear. After a few moments, I whispered, "Okay, but move cautiously. We're right behind you."

"Jax!" Kayla called as she made her way through the wreckage. "Can you hear me?"

We picked our way through the debris, shifting wood and scraps of furniture out of the way as we went. There'd been a massive fight here. Jax had not gone with his kidnapper willingly. The lack of police presence or any concerned neighbors milling around meant that Enid, or whoever she'd hired, had warded the area until they'd had the boy under control.

I didn't think he was dead. Lifting my head, I took air in and filtered it over my tongue. There was no scent of death, and Enid would've left him behind like trash to rot. "Is anyone picking up on any strange signatures?" I asked. "This place had to have been magically locked down while this was going on, or it would be crawling with cops, yet I scent nothing. Marcy?"

"Nada. Not even the smallest whiff." Marcy stood behind me. "This place is totaled. Whoever did this was massive. The dents in the wall are eight feet high, and things are crushed to smithereens." Marcy and the others hadn't yet heard what Kayla had told us about her brother.

There'd be time to explain later.

We followed Kayla down a narrow hallway. She paused by a closed door, stretching her hand out tentatively. "Jax," she called quietly. "Are you in there?" Her fingers curled over the knob. She closed her eyes, angling her head toward the ceiling. I knew she was praying to someone—*anyone*—to give her strength to open that door. I prayed right along with her.

She swung the door wide, and we all gasped.

If the living room had been ruined, the bedroom had been demolished.

There wasn't a thing left standing.

Most of it was broken to dust. Giant holes marred the walls, and the mattress was in tatters, springs poking out everywhere. There was nothing resembling a dresser or any furniture anywhere to be seen. There wasn't even room to walk.

The wreckage was three feet high.

"Your brother put up quite a fight," I murmured. "Anyone can see he's a force to be reckoned with. Whoever took him is likely ruing their decision to do so right this instant."

A quiet sob issued out of her throat. She covered her mouth with her hand and bowed her head. A long curtain of her dark hair fell, blocking her emotions from us.

I didn't know her well enough to physically comfort her, and it likely wouldn't have been welcome, so I didn't reach out. Instead, we stood shoulder to shoulder, and when she was ready, I would be there.

Rourke made a small sound. "Look, there's something sticking out of the wall."

"Where?" Kayla's head shot up, hope breaking in her voice.

Tyler saw it too. "It's tucked into one of the holes on the far side." Tyler gestured to the wall.

Sure enough, a rumpled piece of paper, barely visible, was stuck in a remnant of obliterated sheetrock near the window.

Kayla went forward to claim it, picking her way over the obstacles carefully, stumbling and sliding as she went.

Rourke rested his hands on my shoulders, gripping them tightly, leaning over to whisper in my ear. "Whatever that note says, it's not going to be welcome news."

I nodded.

That note wasn't going to contain anything we wanted to hear, but hopefully it would lead us to Jax.

A sudden feeling of déjà vu washed over me, and I shivered. Rourke, sensing a change, rubbed my arms, a small growl issuing from the back of his throat.

We were all gathered in this place, at this time, for a reason.

I knew it for certain, and foreboding flooded through me.

Juanita had told me I would find my destiny once I found Jax, and whatever was in that note would lead me to him. Whatever it dictated, I had to do, without fail.

We watched as Kayla plucked the scrap of paper from the wall and read it to herself. She glanced at me, meeting my gaze. "It's for you." She brought me the note, her face set.

Once it was in my hand, I spread it open, so we could all read it. It was printed in pristine block letters:

> I HAVE THE BOY, THE WOLF, AND THE FEMALE VAMPIRE.
> IF YOU WANT THEM TO LIVE, THERE IS ONLY ONE OPTION.
> YOUR LIFE FOR THEIRS.

It wasn't signed, but we all knew who it was from.

Three words were written in the bottom right corner: THE PONTE VECCHIO.

"She has Danny and Naomi," I said, anguish filling me.

Enid knew there was a possibility I wouldn't trade my life for Jax, someone I'd never met, but she knew there was no question I would for Danny and Naomi. I'd allowed them to leave Florida on their own, after Danny had almost been killed. It had been a mistake. One that I would now pay dearly for.

I fisted the note in my hand, crumpling it, fury blinding me. I didn't trust myself to speak.

"The Ponte Vecchio is a bridge in Florence, Italy." Marcy was the first to comment, her voice filled with quiet contemplation. "That's an odd place to send us, but Florence is the epitome of old magic. It swirls around that city like a thick carpet of smog. Tons of places to hide three strong supernaturals against their will."

Tyler added, "Florence is also home to the Mediterranean Pack. This is no coincidence."

Of course it wasn't.

There were no coincidences.

"It's also where the Romanian witch told me there had been recent disturbances when I called about my missing aunt," Marcy added. "Tally might be there too." Her voice shifted to hopeful. "When we find that old bag of bones, and those responsible for kidnapping her, heads are going to roll, and when I say roll, I mean they are literally going to come off the shoulders and bump down those cobblestone streets."

Everyone's eyes landed on me.

"So what are we going to do?" Tyler asked.

Without pause, I replied, "We're going to Italy."

3

Getting to Florence safely was another question altogether. We'd found a dive bar by the harbor and were sitting around a table discussing our options. Other than the bartender and one random customer who was too sauced to notice us, we were the bar's only occupants.

"Let's throw out a few more options," I said. "After we're done, I'll talk to my father. As Alpha, he'll have the final say about how we get there."

I'd spoken to my father briefly last night, after I'd had my mind interlude with Juanita, to inform him of what had gone on at the cabin. Juanita had told me to head to Baltimore. My father had given us the okay to come here, and he was now awaiting an update.

"I say we hitch a ride across the Atlantic with someone powerful," Marcy said. "Enid can't kill indiscriminately, or the fabric changes too much. Preferably a witch of some sort who can keep the plane spelled with me. You know, in case I get knocked out or something." She drummed her fingers against her chin. "Lemme think."

The thought of getting on a plane made my head pound. The last ride hadn't turned out very well for us. We'd gone down in the middle of a swamp. I wasn't eager for a repeat performance.

I hadn't had adequate time to process the fact that Enid had taken Danny and Naomi. She'd definitely hit me where it hurt. I told the group, "We can't forget that Enid wants us to make it to Italy. If we don't, her evil plan can't take shape. She's kidnapped our friends, and she knows we're invested. I don't think she'd take a plane down, but that doesn't mean I want to get on one." I turned to Nick. "Are the phones operational?" We'd stopped briefly to get new ones.

"Yes, I've set up five," he told me, holding one out.

I reached for it. "Great—"

The door to the bar burst open.

We all leaped out of our seats, ready to face the threat. It was almost comical, each of us positioned in a different way. Marcy had her hands out, fingers twitching. Tyler was crouched, ready to spring. Rourke had his fists on the table, teeth flashing. James's shoulders were drawn back. Nick had his hands out to the side. And I was down, knees bent, ready to launch myself forward.

We looked like the mismatched Avengers.

The only person who remained seated was Kayla.

Two seconds later, Eudoxia strode in, her gown flowing out behind her like it had its own wind. This one was a deep, rusty orange. Her delicate features were precise and perfect, her pale blonde hair piled on top of her head in its typical mass of curls. The only detectable difference since I'd seen her last was her pallor.

Instead of being a chalky, dead white, she glowed rosy pink.

She'd taken my blood in the Underworld, and it'd brought her fae side to the forefront. Apparently, it had stuck.

I righted my stance.

She was the last person I'd expected to walk through those doors.

"What—" I cleared my throat. "*What* are you doing here?" I began to make my way toward her, but Rourke gave me a look before I rounded the end of the table.

He bent down to murmur in my ear, "I'm going to have Marcy spell the humans."

I nodded. Having them witness this encounter wouldn't be wise. I hadn't seen Eudoxia since the day we'd left the Underworld and she'd flung herself through the portal without looking back.

My power stretched out ahead of me, testing her signature, trying to assess how strong she was after ingesting my blood.

We shared a connection now, but it was muted.

That wasn't surprising, as she survived on blood, and had likely drunk from many since then, diluting what she'd taken from me.

"Stop probing me," she scoffed in the irritated voice she reserved just for me. "That's not how you greet someone of my stature, ignorant wolf. And, yes, I'm strong. More so than before. No need to further investigate." Before I could formulate a response, she strode forward, slapping a note on the table. The fragile wooden top threatened to break as it wobbled under the impact of her strength.

Everyone gathered around. It was lettered exactly like the one Enid had left behind in Kayla's apartment. It read:

> IF YOU WANT YOUR PLACE ON THE COALITION, FAE QUEEN, BE AT
> 1928 FLEET STREET, BALTIMORE AT 5:00 PM TOMORROW.
> IF YOU FAIL TO SHOW, YOU DIE.
> GO ALONE.

The address was this very bar. Eudoxia crossed her arms, her red lips pursed in her perpetual frown. "Care to explain?" she asked, giving me a *what have you done now?* face.

"Um. It's complicated," I answered, hedging. The fact Enid had known *yesterday* that we would be at this exact place at this time was unsettling enough. But it was a clear indication that she wanted us to arrive in Italy. "The supernatural world is in an uproar, if you haven't noticed. Things are happening around the world as we speak, and people we love are in danger. We're on our way to Italy as soon as possible." I left out who exactly was in danger, because Eudoxia wouldn't give a rat's ass about helping Danny or Naomi. She considered her former vamp a traitor anyway, since Naomi was now bound to me, instead of her, by blood. Naming them wouldn't compel her to join us, but clearly Enid wanted her to go with us, or she wouldn't have sent for her.

"It doesn't matter if things are unsettled here or in Europe," Eudoxia huffed. "That doesn't mean we need to get involved."

"How can you say that?" I said, stunned. "That's exactly what it means. We *are* the next Coalition. Our job is to intervene. All the time. In fact, I think that's pretty much all we'll be doing from now on—getting involved." We'd discovered we both had a place on the Coalition not that long ago.

The Coalition was made up of five of the biggest supernatural Sects—werewolf, vampire, fae, demon, and witch.

The Power of Five.

My job was Enforcer. I had no idea what would be asked of me, only that I was taking my team with me.

"We are not the Coalition *yet*," she countered, her eyes narrowing. "Until we take our vows, what happens is of little interest to me." So very Eudoxia. If it didn't concern her, it was inconsequential.

I pointed to the note. "Enid certainly thinks it's of interest to you, or she wouldn't have dragged you all the way here."

"Enid?" Eudoxia's delicate eyebrows drew inward. "The Hag?"

"One and the same."

"That can't be right." Eudoxia snatched up the note and held it to her nose. "There is no signature residue, no hint of magic." She waved the offending piece of paper in the air like not having a scent solved everything.

I moved around the table to face her. "Why would you come all this way if you thought that was a random note left by no one of consequence?"

The Vamp Queen shifted, looking mildly uncomfortable. She raised a hand to twirl an errant curl that had dropped near her face. "Because of its location."

"You're going to have to be a little more specific than that."

She abruptly turned and waltzed away. "I found this note in an area that only I can reach. No one else has access to it." I immediately pictured a dirty cell filled with death and despair. "Also," she added, "Alana advised me, 'When you get a special note, you must do as it says.'" She turned and glared. "But no one told me you'd be at the end of this missive." She glanced around the dive bar with disgust. "Nor that I would be leaving the country." Alana was a seer and Eudoxia's fae aunt. I'd encountered her during extenuating circumstances not too terribly long ago. I would be happy never encountering the likes of Alana again.

"Well, you're here now," I pointed out. "And this place isn't *that* bad." The bar was called Bad Decisions, which sounded a bit ironic at the moment.

Eudoxia snorted. "This note said to meet here"—she gestured around the room—"it said nothing about going anywhere with you. I have a Coterie to run with vampires who eagerly await my return."

"Enid wouldn't send you all the way to Baltimore for no reason," I countered. "She must want you to accompany us to Italy. And the note says if you don't show, you die. Are you willing to risk death by being stubborn?"

Eudoxia crossed her arms, her lips curling into a sneer. How was I going to deal with this woman for an eternity? It was a puzzle I wasn't anxious to solve. "There is nothing in that note that states I must accompany you anywhere. It only states that I come to this address."

There was a noise, something between a throat-clearing and a cough.

We all turned toward the bar.

The bartender held something in his hand.

My head snapped to Rourke. *I thought Marcy was going to spell them?*

He shrugged. *She did.*

Before I could question why the bartender was interacting with us, the man said, "This was left for the lady in the orange dress. I was supposed to give it to her at exactly this time." He glanced down at his watch. I could see from where I stood that his eyes were glazed over. Apparently, Marcy's spell did not trump one from Enid.

I met Eudoxia's gaze. "Are you going to get that, or shall I?"

Without answering, the Vamp Queen paced forward, her shoes clacking angrily as she stalked to the bar, her dress billowing out behind her. She walked straight up to the bartender and plucked the note out of his hand. The guy didn't move, or seem to register the interaction.

"Marcy," I murmured. "Is this bartender going to be a problem?"

"I don't think so," she said. "Enid is one sneaky witch." Marcy went over and snapped her fingers in front of the bartender's face a few times just to be sure. He didn't respond. He didn't even blink. She glanced over her shoulder. "We're good to go. He's not going to remember. This other guy looks comatose, so no worries there." The other patron had one hand on his drink, his eyes gazing off into nothingness.

I nodded.

Eudoxia stomped back to the table with the new note in hand. She yanked out a chair and sat like she owned the place, swiping her dress beneath her. She read it to herself and then took time to glare at me before stating the obvious. "This is all your fault."

I took a seat across from her. "Tell me something I don't know," I muttered. "At this point, we have to do whatever that note says. We're not in a position to push back. We play this out and see where it takes us. What does it say?"

She tossed it into the middle of the table, folding her arms and sitting back in her chair.

Rourke picked it up and smoothed it out. It said:

GO TO ITALY WITH THE SHE-WOLF.
OR DIE.

"Well that settles it, then," Marcy said. "Now we're back to our original discussion, which was, how do we get ourselves to Italy safely? I vote we magically morph there. Please tell me teleporting is a possibility. If I remember correctly, there's an old wives' tale—or make that an old witches' tale—about transcendental transportation where your body goes along with your mind across physical time and space. Or maybe I'm thinking of trans-*meditational* transport where you have really high-quality virtual reality goggles and crazy ambition? Either way, I still vote we beam ourselves there."

Eudoxia glanced at Marcy like she had three heads. "There is no such spell, witch. If I must go to Italy, I go my way."

"Which is how?" I smirked. "Via your broomstick?"

"Very funny, impertinent wolf," she answered. "I will use my personal jet."

My eyebrows rose. "You have a personal jet?"

"Of course. How do you think I arrived here?"

"Um, spread your arms and took to the air?" Stating the obvious, since all vamps could fly.

"I don't fly on my own unless there are no other options available to me. I am not a masochist." She smoothed down her hair in an effort to appear like she didn't enjoy pain and suffering, which we all knew she did.

"Amen, sister," Marcy said. "I've only flown Vamp Air one other time, and it was awful. Bugs stuck in every possible orifice, hair like a rat's nest, fingers like ten sticks of ice. I'll never do it again if I can help it."

Ray snorted. "You two are crazy. Flying is like alcohol. Never met a drink I didn't like. Soaring through the air is liberating. Nothing like it."

Eudoxia cringed. She was on the verge of ordering everyone out of her immediate area, so I preempted her with, "Am I going to have to beg you for a ride?" I cocked my head and slapped on my sweetest smile. "I shouldn't have to point out that we should all stay together. It's safer that way."

Eudoxia laughed, which sounded all kinds of wrong. It was maniacal mixed with raw, sugary sweet. "There is nothing that can harm me, so safety is of no consequence. I will take you and your"—she glanced around the table with a sour look—"cohorts with me, but only under one condition."

"And what is that?" I asked.

"You give me more blood."

4

Are you sure about this? Rourke asked.

Yes, I replied. *If I give her more blood, I don't think it will change anything. When we swear vows to take our place on the Coalition, we all share power anyway. What difference does it make?*

I don't like it, he growled in my mind, which felt funny, kind of like internal goose bumps. *The Vamp Queen takes her advantages where she can, regardless of the consequences.*

Well, it's too late to change my mind now. I glanced around. We were already seated on her luxury jet, every need attended to by two vampire flight attendants. Leave it to Eudoxia to have a Learjet. It was almost like she was trying to channel Wonder Woman. We'd ditched the gator van at the airport and taken off not an hour after she'd walked through the doors of the bar.

The estimated travel time from Baltimore to Florence, Italy, was a little more than ten hours. The deal I'd made was to give Eudoxia my blood *after* we arrived safely across the pond. It wasn't much of a negotiation, but it would ensure we landed in one piece and that she would help us fight if something did happen.

I'd talked to my father briefly on the phone on the ride to the airport. He'd agreed with the plan and was going to book a plane himself, along with some of his wolves, to join us for whatever was going down. He assured me he'd be in touch with Julian de Rossi, the Alpha of the Mediterranean Pack, and that he'd have him meet us at the airport in Florence.

I'd met Julian only once before, staying with him for a short time when I'd first left the Compound at eighteen. After my time there, I'd come back to the States under the alias Molly Hannon and enrolled in the police academy. From what I remember, Julian was very much the quintessential Italian—dapper, suave, and regal. He ran his Pack with an iron claw and razor-sharp teeth. He had not been my favorite host of all time, but he had been nice enough.

My father stayed in contact with him regularly and had commented that the last time they'd spoken, Julian had mentioned there'd been trouble in Italy recently. Wolves had gone missing, and random acts of magical mishap were on the rise.

"Dang it," Marcy muttered from the seat in front of me, tossing her phone into her purse. "Nobody's answering. I have a literal laundry list of Coven numbers in my cell, and no one will pick up my call. How am I supposed to find out what's going on with my aunt when no one will answer their phone?" Marcy's nervousness about being on a plane so soon after our recent close call was right at the surface. James, her mate, laid a firm hand on her thigh, trying to comfort her.

I leaned forward, grabbing on to Marcy's headrest. There was plenty of space on the Learjet—big gaps between the seats, which made for easy communication. "Why aren't they answering?" Tallulah Talbot, Marcy's aunt, was the leader of the witches and had been missing for a while now. The entire

Coven had been empty upon our return from the Underworld. Tally had mysteriously disappeared right before she was supposed to guide me back through the portal the witches were in charge of keeping open. It was not in her character to leave a post like that.

Not to mention, Tally wouldn't have left me trapped down there, which was what would've happened if the Princess of Hell hadn't gained power from Lili's heart and become the ruler of the Underworld.

Marcy twisted in her seat to face me. "I wish I knew," she answered. "I can't believe they'd all be incapacitated. There were at least thirty of them living at the Coven. But that's what I'm beginning to think. When I went over to the house to investigate, there hadn't been any evidence of a fight. It was just plain empty. That doesn't mean much if the supernatural who took them was as powerful as Enid." Marcy grimaced. "I hope they're not all dead. They aren't my favorite people in the world, but being dead is final. And if they died, they did it trying to protect my aunt."

I patted her shoulder. "We're going to find Tally. She's alive, and so is Maggie." Maggie was Tally's toddler daughter, who happened to be a powerful oracle. "Whoever took the leader of the witches isn't going to succeed in killing her. They wouldn't be that foolish, nor would they have the strength."

Marcy smiled, her expression thoughtful. "That old bat would be hard to kill, that's for sure."

"Would you know if she was dead?" There was no easy way to ask.

"Yes," Marcy replied. "We share the same bloodline. It's a powerful bond for witches. I would know. She's alive. But I have no idea what kind of shape she's in. She's been missing for a long time." A frown showed her concern. "I would only know if she ceased to be."

"That's good enough. I'm happy she's alive." I sat back in

my seat. Rourke slung his arm around my shoulders, pulling me close. "If I had to guess, Tally's in Italy, along with everyone else. This is where it's all going to come down, for better or worse."

Shivers raced up my spine, and my wolf howled in my mind. Ever since she'd received her whole soul back, thanks to our creator, Marinette, our relationship had shifted. She'd become more calm and easygoing, fading into the background.

I wasn't complaining.

All the regular everyday stuff would be handled by me, and she would be in charge of the supernatural crises. It'd been a seamless transition, one that I'd barely been aware of. My wolf and I had finally melded, getting along in the way that I assumed other shifters did with their animal sides. There was less anxiety for both of us this way.

She howled again. *What's wrong?* I asked, the hair on my arms at attention. *The plane isn't going down, is it?* In response, she showed me a vision of us engaged in combat. It wasn't a clear picture. It was grainy and foggy, and our opponents kept changing. *We're going to be fighting more than one person?* That wasn't really a shocker. I expected as much. The vision morphed once more, but this time it was a still shot.

One side of the photo was dark and bleak, the other sunny. Both had me, standing alone, bruised and bloodied.

"What is it?" Rourke asked, sensing my unease.

"I'm not sure," I answered. "My wolf is showing me visions of us fighting. It looks like there will be attacks from a few fronts, which is not surprising. But the last thing she showed me was a picture with two sides. One dark and bleak, the other sunny and bright." I glanced at my mate, comforted by him. He grabbed my hand. "There's a lot at stake waiting for us in Italy. My wolf is showing me two outcomes, one good and one bad." I had to make sure the outcome was sunny and bright. The other option was unacceptable.

"Jessica, we will prevail," he assured me, leaning over to nuzzle my neck the way I loved. "You have to believe that. You're not going to be fighting this alone."

Ray piped in from the aisle. No conversation on this plane would go unheard, as supernatural hearing was both a blessing and a curse. "Hannon, there's no way we're not winning. We've come too far. The bad guys don't stand a chance against our force."

"I want to believe that too," I agreed, turning to address him. "I have to make sure I follow my heart. If I don't, Juanita said it would go badly." She'd told me that if Enid got her way, and I died, there would be years of chaos before it finally turned around. I couldn't let that happen. "I just wish I knew who we were fighting, so we could better prepare for the threat."

Eudoxia sauntered up the aisle, emerging from a seat that looked suspiciously like a throne. "The way to avoid fighting at all is to say our vows as soon as we can. Once the Coalition is united, no one would be foolish enough to engage us directly."

I eyed her. "Yeah, that sounds great, except who else is on the Coalition? We know of two for sure. Me and you. Possibly the Princess of Hell. Who's slated to take the witch slot? Who will take the vampire place? These questions have to be answered before we can swear any vows."

Jebediah Amel, the warlock with the big book, would likely know this information, but I had no idea how to get a hold of him.

"I will take the vampire slot," Eudoxia stated with finality.

"I don't think so," I told her. "You can only fill one spot, and my guess is you're supposed to fulfill the fae spot. There are only a few fae left in the world, and you have to be the most powerful one, right?"

"I am both the most powerful vampire and the most powerful fae," she said in her haughtiest tone. "So naturally I will take both positions."

I shook my head. "That's not how this works. And as much as you desire it to be true, you don't get to decide." Thank goodness. "The decision is made by Fate, and you know it. There are five of us. Or it wouldn't be called the Power of Five. It would be called the Power of Four. So, if you're slated to take the fae position, who takes the vampire spot? Who is the most powerful master under you?"

She appeared stymied, and I tried not to laugh.

Seeing Eudoxia unsure of herself didn't happen very often, and I thoroughly enjoyed it. "There are eight masters under me, scattered all over the world." She paused. "But they are all male."

The plot thickened.

"How can you not have a single female powerful enough to rule under you?"

She shrugged, turning to pace the aisle. "I do not decide these things, the power does. Masters, by nature, are the oldest living vampires. For thousands of years, there have been males in places of authority." She turned back, her orange skirts swishing around. "So males they are."

"And you can't think of a single female with enough power to take a place on the Coalition?"

"There are a few," she said. "But they are meek in comparison to the males."

"I can think of one," Rourke muttered under his breath.

I turned to him, surprised. "Who?"

"Naomi."

I gasped. "Naomi? But she's bound to me, not to Eudoxia." When Naomi took my blood, her allegiance shifted, much to Eudoxia's dismay.

"That may be so," he said. "But when you gave her your blood, you made her extremely powerful. And she's still a vampire. Eudoxia's right, the power decides, and there's a chance it will choose Naomi."

Eudoxia huffed. "I will not share my space at the table...with that thing. She is no vampire, at least not to me!" The Vamp Queen's tiny fists struck out at the seat in front of her, and the leather burst open. "She is not worthy of a place on the Coalition."

Had I unwittingly created the most powerful female vampire?

Ignoring Eudoxia's tantrum, I turned to Rourke. "Do you think that's why Enid took her?" I'd been wondering why Enid would take Danny and Naomi. She was trying to get to me, and it worked, but it would've hurt even more had she taken my brother or my father.

"Could be," he replied. "If Enid has control over when and where the Coalition gathers, she can manipulate things. That makes the most sense."

"I don't believe it!" Eudoxia exclaimed. "That little imp doesn't have as much power as I have in my pinky finger." She held up her smallest finger and wiggled it, in case we needed a visual to the size of said pinky. "How can she possibly be strong enough to sit on the grandest jury of them all?"

It was hard not to laugh. "Ah," I chuckled. "But she is incredibly strong. I've given her my blood twice, and that's one more time than you've gotten it." Well, until the end of this flight. "Plus, she's old. You should've promoted her over the years. She's extremely capable. But she's always been your faithful tracker. Sounds like it's your fault. You overlooked a diamond in your nest. After all, she escaped from Selene *and* one of the Hags, using only her wiles. That takes talent."

"Nonsense," Eudoxia said, sticking her nose in the air as she paced back to her throne. "I would bet my life it is not her."

"If only we could take you up on that," I muttered.

5

The wheels bounced roughly, shaking us in our seats. We'd just touched down in Florence. It was eight a.m. We'd flown through the night. I'd gotten some spotty sleep, but not much. I glanced out the window and realized we hadn't landed at a regular airport. "Where are we?" I asked. It looked like a field of some sort.

I hadn't thought to ask what the flight plan was. I'd just assumed Eudoxia knew what she was doing.

One of the two vampire flight attendants answered, with some distaste, "We have landed at the Mediterranean Pack airport, a few miles outside of Florence."

Before the flight attendant could add anything more, Eudoxia replied tersely, not bothering to look around, "There are only a few options when one is in need of a supernatural landing place. It was either here, or farther south with the nymphs, who have taken over an entire town. I figured this would be preferable."

"You thought right," I said. "My father said Julian would be here to greet us. I hadn't questioned how we'd find him, but this makes it convenient."

"That's why he's the Alpha, and you're not," Eudoxia huffed, meaning it as a burn, but I took it as a compliment. My father *was* Pack Alpha for a reason. It was a job I wasn't even remotely interested in. Looking after my small group was more than enough. Tyler and Danny had sworn fealty to me, with a blood oath, and I'd given my blood to Naomi and Ray. I'd sworn a childhood oath with Nick that had involved a blood swap. I'd given my essence to Marcy to heal her. That, in turn, had bound these people to me. It was more than enough.

The flight attendants moved to the door, both of them covered head to toe in black. Only the oldest and most powerful vampires—and vampires who had ingested my blood—could walk in the sun. One of them opened the door, tossing the set of steps down, hissing. They both retreated quickly.

I had no idea what to expect once we got outside.

Tyler deplaned first, then Kayla, followed by Nick, then James and Marcy. Rourke took my hand, and we went together. Ray brought up the rear, and Eudoxia, who was busying herself with some task, would come when she was good and ready and not one second before.

"Is that the son of Callum McClain I see?" The accented voice erupted from the small group of wolves situated a few feet away from the plane. "The Northern Territory Alpha in training? Or, should I amend that to the *U.S.* Territory Alpha in training?" Julian referred to the fact that my father had fought, and killed, Redman Martin, the former Alpha of the Southern Territories, effectively joining the Packs together as one.

The comment was meant to let us know that the Mediterranean Pack was well aware of what had happened in our neck of the woods—or, more precisely, our neck of the swamp—since my father had defeated Redman in the Everglades while we'd been down there trying to deal with the Made wolves and a possessed bokor.

"Hello, Julian," my brother answered graciously. "It's good to see you again." They clasped hands.

Julian de Rossi looked exactly the same as when I'd last seen him, around eight years ago. His jet-black hair was slicked back in his signature style. His expensive button-up shirt was popped open at the top, and a gold chain hung loosely amidst a thick nestle of dark chest hair. He affected a casual stance, looking every bit the debonair Italian he was, but I detected a slight change of expression as he took in the rest of the group as we proceeded down the steps.

Apparently, my father hadn't informed him about the motley crew who would be accompanying me. Wolves were devoted pack animals, and they rarely interacted with other Sects. It was highly unusual for a wolf to travel with so many different supernaturals.

Julian recovered himself quickly, reaching his hand out to James. "It's good to see you, James," he said. "I've never seen Callum travel without his second, but times in our world are changing."

"Indeed, they are," James replied. James was indeed my father's second-in-command, but since he'd found his pairing with my friend Marcy, and considering all of the dangers I'd faced over the last few months, it'd made sense for James to travel with us. It was risky for my father to be without his second, in case a challenge arose, but for now the wolves were occupied with the common threat to Pack, so it was safe enough. "I'd like to introduce you to my mate. This is Marcy Talbot." James steered her toward Julian, grinning at her with a pride that made my heart swell.

They were a perfect match.

Marcy stuck her hand out. "Pleased to meetcha," she said. "I've heard a lot about the Mediterranean Pack over the years. Nice to finally meet the wolf in charge."

"Well, I hope for my sake what you've heard has been favorable," Julian replied with a grin.

"Yes and no," she deadpanned. She paused just long enough to make it awkward and then expertly followed with, "I'm just joking. Honestly, I know next to nothing about you or your wolves, but I'm sure things run like a top around here. What I'm really hoping is that you're in contact with other supernaturals in the area. My aunt is missing, and my first priority is to find her, hopefully with your help."

Julian recovered nicely, smiling to reveal a set of perfectly straight teeth. "Of course." He bowed. "I am at your service. Callum informed me that someone close to you was missing." He glanced over Marcy's shoulder at me. "Or more than a few, from what I gathered. I have many contacts. I'm happy to share them with you."

I walked forward, extending my hand. "It's nice to see you again, Julian. Thank you for meeting us here. Sorry if this put you out because it was so last minute. And, yes, you are correct. We are here to track down a few of our friends who are missing. That's our top priority." I left out the Enid hunting us part. I didn't know how much my father had shared with the European Alpha, but it was best to be strategic and keep as much information as we could to ourselves, releasing it only if we were forced to.

Julian's gaze flicked past me, landing on Rourke, who stood behind me.

The two Alphas held eye contact, and I felt Rourke tense.

If he wants a fight, he's got one. Rourke's words filtered through my brain.

I was about to answer my mate when Julian broke contact first, pretending to hear something over his shoulder. That was big in the Alpha world. Breaking eye contact first was akin to giving up.

In order to allow him to save face, and to keep the peace, I said, "Julian, thank you for being such a gracious host. We've clearly invaded your turf uninvited. We are happy to defer to your lead while we're here."

No, we won't, Rourke growled in my mind.

Be nice, I warned. *We're here to retrieve Tally, and find Danny, Naomi, and Jax. We're not here to war with the Mediterranean Pack. Plus, he just dropped eye contact. That was a willing submission.*

He's dangerous, Rourke said. *I can smell it. We can't trust him.*

Luckily for us, Julian's attention was diverted as Eudoxia made her grand exit, striding down the short set of steps like she owned Florence and everyone in it. "I forget how much Europe smells like the backwoods," she sniffed. "It's not pleasing at all."

Julian brushed by me. "Ah, Vampire Queen, I am delighted you have graced us with your presence. It's been far too long between visits. You look ravishing, as usual." He swept her hand up to his mouth, kissing the back of it reverently, his head bowed.

I had no idea if it was an act, or just how people did things in Europe, even if they were from opposing supernatural Sects. I desperately hoped it was a show for our eyes only and that when he'd mentioned the word *ravishing*, he'd meant *good enough to eat*—as in ripped apart by a wolf.

Wolves and vampires notoriously did not get along. I was curious what their background together was, because it was apparent Julian and Eudoxia had a past.

For once, I was glad Eudoxia had monopolized the situation.

It had diffused the incident with Rourke.

Julian turned back to the group, Eudoxia's small hand tucked under his elbow. "We have a few cars waiting." He gestured toward two SUVs parked at the edge of the field. "If you will follow me, we will be on our way."

Ray met my gaze. I nodded. He stepped back from the group.

He would follow us by air and make sure Julian delivered

us to our destination as planned. Rourke was right that we didn't know Julian, or what his agenda was. We had to stay vigilant.

As we made our way to the waiting cars, I said to my mate, *We don't have to trust him to take advantage of his resources. He and my father have always been on good terms, but they run their Packs differently. It's been a lot of years since they've seen each other in person.*

They ran them *very* differently.

Over the years, stories had trickled in about torture and forced submission. The Mediterranean Pack had the highest number of defectors, contributing to a rampant Stray problem. A wolf had to be part of a Pack. It wasn't okay to be a lone wolf. It led to issues, and eventually mania, as wolves were meant to be social animals, not loners.

If he tries anything, it'll be the last breath he takes, Rourke replied.

What exactly do you think he's going to do? I asked. *My father's on his way. I can't believe Julian would be stupid enough to jeopardize his life by crossing us. He already brought up Redman. He's well aware of what happened.* In a wolf-to-wolf Alpha challenge, my father had Julian, and they both knew it. That's why they didn't come in contact very often. It was risky. If Julian's wolves felt that my father was the superior Alpha, it could cause more chaos than it was worth.

I have no idea what he'll do, Rourke said as he opened the door, ushering me inside. *But my guess is he'll do whatever serves his own needs. And if that means selling you to the highest bidder, he wouldn't blink twice. Plus, he has to feel your power. It's off the charts. A guy like that will be threatened by it.*

You may be right, I said. *But I'd like to believe that wolves have some loyalty to each other. We are a common race, after all.*

Well, he's no cat. I owe him no loyalty.

Nick climbed in after Rourke. Tyler and Kayla were already in the backseat. Marcy, James, and Eudoxia had entered the other SUV. Julian walked up to our door, and Nick rolled down the window. "The Compound is only a short distance from here," he told us. "You will be safe there, and we can talk more. I will ride with the others."

I nodded as Nick brought the window up. I was a little puzzled as to why he thought I was in danger. I'd mentioned nothing of the sort, but I let it go. My father might've said something to him when they talked.

As the SUVs pulled out, my wolf sent power out ahead of us to see if anything was amiss, which had become second nature to us both.

After a mile on the road, it pinged back with something strange.

"Stop the car," I ordered the driver, one of Julian's wolves we hadn't been introduced to. He glanced in the rearview mirror, a questioning look on his face.

Rourke didn't need me to explain anything. He already had his window down, his nose angled out the window.

The wolf sitting in the passenger side turned. "We haven't arrived at our destination yet. It's a few more miles down the road. It won't be long."

"No, stop the car right now," I insisted, this time more firmly. "Pull over here." Once the driver complied, I looked out the back window. Our vehicle had been in the lead, and as it'd pulled over, the other had pulled in line behind us.

Tyler sat up, using his nose along with Rourke's to see what they could identify from the air. My brother had awesome scenting capabilities. "I know you picked up on something, but I don't scent anything, Jess," he said. "Nothing's coming back as a red flag."

"It's not a threat," I assured him. "The power signature was aimed specifically at me. It's odd, almost cloaked, yet not. Just enough to let me know it's there." My wolf barked and then flashed me a picture. I smiled. "I know who it is."

"Who?" my brother asked.

"Jebediah Amel, High Ambassador of the Coalition," I said. "He must have some news for me." I reached for the door handle.

Rourke growled, "I'm coming with you."

6

Rourke and I stepped out of the SUV. Julian was already out of the second vehicle, coming toward us. "Why did you stop? This is my land, and it's well protected. You are safe here. If there was a threat in my inner sanctum, I would know about it." He made a show of scenting the air to prove his point.

"This isn't a threat," I assured him. "Someone has come to see me. If it's okay with you, Rourke and I will meet him, and then we'll head to the Compound."

"I don't understand," Julian said. "I just told you that no one can access this land without me knowing about it." He narrowed his gaze, consternation on his face.

"This is no ordinary someone," I replied, trying for a casual tone. "He's a very powerful warlock and very old. He's my assistant, of sorts, and he can cloak himself really well. If he didn't want anybody to detect him, they wouldn't be able to." I didn't want to divulge too much. This wasn't the time or the place to talk about the Coalition with Julian. To put his mind further at ease, I added, "He likely just arrived. He can materialize at will." I said it like it was commonplace that everybody could pop in and out of time and space. In reality, very few supes could achieve such a feat. I actually knew of no other.

Rourke crossed his arms. He had nothing to add, but was showing the Alpha of the Mediterranean Pack that if he didn't grant us our wish for a private meeting with Jeb, there would be a fight.

Julian's gaze was intense as he looked between us. Finally, he bowed his head. "Very well," he said. "I will send a car back to pick you up. I will instruct them to stay on the road and wait for your arrival."

"Thank you," I said. "We appreciate your willingness to help. I apologize for any inconvenience this may have caused. Like I said, this is no ordinary supe. And please don't blame any of your wolves for the intrusion. There's no way to guard against someone who can beam themselves into the middle of a forest."

Julian's grin faded. "I see we have much to discuss. I'll leave you to your meeting, and we will talk later." He turned back to his waiting SUV. Once he was inside, the vehicle pulled forward, stopping beside us.

Marcy rolled down her window. "You got this? Or do you want us to stay? You know, because mayhem follows you like a vulture to roadkill."

"No, we're good. We'll handle this ourselves," I told her. "You guys go on to the Compound and get settled. We shouldn't be too long." I had no idea how long Jeb would keep us, but I couldn't imagine he'd stick around for any length of time.

Eudoxia sniffed from inside, "We've been on Italian soil for less than ten minutes. Leave it to you to find something wrong." I hadn't told the Vampire Queen about Jeb yet. I wondered for a moment if he would want us to bring her along. He was the High Ambassador of the Coalition, after all, and Eudoxia had a place on it.

I decided not to extend that offer just yet.

But I was curious about what the warlock had to say. I'd left him only a short time ago, so something interesting must've been written in that big ol' book of his to warrant contacting us so soon. "It's nice you have my back, Eudoxia," I told her. "You make the world a safer place."

"If you get yourself in trouble, keep me out of it," she warned. "I don't have the time or energy to bail you out again." She was referring to the fact that she had traveled to the Underworld to help rescue me. Something she was loath to do. "I swear I will leave you to rot if you dig up something disastrous right now."

"That's reassuring," I said, refraining from making a comment about her having absolutely zero things to do in the next few hours, except drink my blood. I knew she hadn't forgotten about the feeding. It was a top priority for her, but she wouldn't speak about it in front of Julian, which was smart. "I'll be sure to take care of myself. I'm also taking a big cat with me, so have no fear. I'm certain we won't be needing your stellar rescue services." Rourke growled his agreement that one big cat was more than enough to protect me from danger, as Marcy winked and pointed upward. I gave her a slight nod. She was not-so-subtly letting me know she knew Ray was there, or she would've stayed. "We'll see you at the Compound."

Once both vehicles drove away, it didn't take long for Ray to make his landing.

This time I was ready.

"What's up?" he asked. "Why'd you get out?"

"Did you notice anything strange from up there?" I asked. He shook his head. "No weird colors or auras or magic signatures?"

"No. Should I have?"

"Jeb's out here somewhere," I told him, turning in a circle. "I was just wondering if you detected anything. If he leaves any kind of magical imprint, we might be able to spot him sooner than later next time."

"Are you talking about that short dude with a porcupine hairdo?" Ray mused. "He's powerful as hell. Last time, his magic damn near burned my skin. I don't think anybody would detect him if he didn't want them to. I'm good, but not that good."

"What he says is correct." The sharp voice sounded from the base of a small junction of trees not twenty feet away. "If I had wanted it, no one would have ever known I was here."

Jeb hadn't worried himself with trying to appear normal this time. He wore a long, flowing white robe, which dragged comically behind him as he paced toward us. He was even shorter than I remembered—four and a half feet at most. He held the same golden leather-bound book in his arms, which looked enormous, his brown hair still spiked at attention all over his head. His bushy eyebrows and beard completed the confusing look. I imagined that under the sleeves of the robe his arm hair was carpet-thick. I suppressed a giggle.

"I hadn't expected to see you again so soon," I told him. We'd parted ways not more than a day ago. "You could've given me a heads-up that we'd be meeting here."

He sniffed, "Well, I couldn't very well predict our next meeting, as I wasn't sure you were going to make it through the cemetery ordeal. But once you did, it was written that you would arrive here, at this time." One of his thick fingers began to trace over a page. "Since we last saw each other, you have increased your odds of survival by fifty-three-point-four percent. That's fairly impressive, especially in such a short amount of time." He nodded approvingly, eyeing me over the massive tome in his arms. "But we must do better. As you know, your survival is imperative. With your death would come great loss. The supernatural world would be unable to recover itself for a millennium. We must not allow that to happen."

No pressure. "Yes, you've told me." I moved closer to the strange little man who'd declared himself my assistant the last time we'd met. Rourke and Ray followed. "Juanita wants me to survive as well. She arranged a meeting after you and I saw each other and told me that finding Ajax would lead to my destiny."

"She is mostly correct." He nodded, his spiky hair not moving an inch. "But there are other things that must be completed before you are able to find your way back to your true path. We will get to that in a moment. But first, according to what's written here, if you follow Enid's instructions blindly, you will not survive. So you mustn't do that. She is shrewd and knows that you will risk much for the people you love. You have to outsmart her without her knowing, which will be tricky."

Trying to outsmart a powerful seer sounded a little more than tricky. "You mean like we did with the wendigos?" I asked. By changing my mind for a split second and going with my heart instead of my rational brain, I'd managed to reverse the outcome of what could've been a horrific death for all of us, not to mention an innocent town full of humans.

"In simple terms, yes," he agreed. "But this will be much more complex than defeating a pack of flesh-eating zombies. It will take finesse."

I coughed. Defeating a horde of reanimated bodies that had had the power to change a living creature into a mindless, deadly killer had seemed like a pretty complex ordeal at the time.

Rourke interrupted, "Can we trust Julian, the leader of the wolves?"

Jeb frowned, glancing at Rourke with distaste. "That is undecided." Jeb seemed pained to have to answer my mate.

Before Rourke could argue or give Jeb a verbal smackdown, I asked, "What do you mean it's *undecided*? I think it's important to know who we can and cannot trust." I would let Jeb know later that my team was an extension of myself and that he needed to treat them as such. The warlock was going to have to get used to doing business a new way—like dealing with those he thought inferior to himself, which was likely everyone on the entire planet.

"Julian de Rossi is a man after his own interests," Jeb answered, confirming what we already suspected. "It is unclear exactly what he will do next, because he changes his mind to suit himself."

Rourke had been right in his first assessment of Julian. "Does that make it harder to predict what his future choices will be?" I asked.

"Yes and no."

"Jesus, man!" Ray piped in, disgruntled at Jeb's obtuseness. "I thought you were an all-powerful supe who knew what was up? Telling us if we can trust Julian should be a no-brainer."

Jeb visibly bristled, his spiky brown hair vibrating with anger. It was the first time I'd seen his hairdo move. "You are incredibly lucky I decided to include you in this meeting at all," he huffed. "I could've very well kept you both out." He glared at Rourke and then Ray. "The only reason I've allowed it is because Jessica has informed me she will be doing things differently, so I have given her the benefit of the doubt. But this is not how I'm accustomed to working, and I will *not* have my authority challenged by a mere *infant*." His nostrils flared. "You may be a reaper as well as a vampire, which is highly unique—in fact, you are the first of your kind. But you know nothing about this world." He paused dramatically, before adding, "I would love to answer every burning question you have, but unfortunately, Fate is complex and it doesn't work that way." He turned his gaze on me. "To answer your question, Julian is hard to scry for because he changes his allegiances often, *but*"—he raised a hand in the air—"the final outcome will never change, because he will continue to do things for his benefit only. So I say *yes and no* because we won't know every detail until he makes up his mind." His finger went back to tracing the page. "I can tell you that on this night you are safe. He is interested in learning about what has happened to you. He's curious about your power and genuinely wants to protect you, as his allegiance is to your father, Callum. But it won't stay that way for long. He will be tempted away."

"By Enid?" I asked.

"No, by someone else," Jeb answered after he read a few more lines. "Julian de Rossi has a very dark side, one that he's fed for much too long. His lover will prevail. He will be faced with a choice, one that will have severe consequences. He will choose wrong."

"A choice between Pack or a lover?" I asked.

"No, between power and the chance at greater power," Jeb answered.

I rubbed my forehead.

The warlock was tiring me out.

I wasn't going to pull a Ray and insult him to his face, so instead I asked, "Why is it that you can't be more specific? I feel like we're dancing around extremely important issues, and we don't really have time to waste. Enid's note said we had to get to the Ponte Vecchio or my friends will die. I'd like to know if we're supposed to go there right away. Or find Tally first? It's time for some real answers, Jeb." I refrained from adding *quicklike*. I didn't know my new assistant well, but I had the distinct feeling that after working with me for a while, he was going to be at his wit's end.

"I understand your frustration, and it would be wonderful if I could give you all the answers." He nodded his agreement. "But I cannot do so without significantly altering Fate's fabric. I am only allowed to give you what is written, but not everything is contained in this book for a reason." His tone let me know that I should know such things. "For instance, I can see here that Julian's lover will interfere and that she is very powerful, but she is unknown to us." He glanced over the book. "But there are ways of finding out that information. Some simple sleuthing should allow you to figure out who she is." He lifted a single, thick, bushy eyebrow at me. "You do have a background in sleuthing, isn't that correct?"

Score one for the warlock.

"Yes, I do," I said. "It shouldn't be hard to find out who she is. I'll put Nick and Marcy on it. Can you at least tell us what comes next? You said earlier that if we follow Enid's directives, I will die. How do we get around that?"

"The key word here is *you*," Jeb answered. "You will die, no one else. So, while you must not follow them, someone else may. Enid will be able to anticipate some of your moves, but she cannot see us right now, which is making her very, very agitated. By having this meeting, we have already put a rent in her plans for the evening. She will have to scramble to make new ones, which will have a ripple effect." He grinned, clearly proud of himself.

I examined the warlock before me, all four and a half feet of him. "Are you the only one who can mask us from Enid?" It would be handy if we could cloak ourselves as often as we liked.

"Myself and Juanita," he confirmed before bobbing his head down and rifling through more pages in his book. "Wait, there is one other. It was written here"—his eyes bugged in surprise, tracking up to meet my gaze—"only yesterday. A powerful supernatural lives in this city and has the capabilities you're looking for." He closed the book with a loud clap. "This is a sign. If you find this supe and convince them to help you, you may very well survive."

"I don't get it," Ray complained. "Why can't you just hang with us? If you're so powerful you can keep us cloaked, what's the problem? Aren't you supposed to be Jessica's assistant or something?"

If Jeb could've struck Ray down where he stood, he would have. But the warlock knew I would not be pleased.

"Do you take me for a common supernatural?" he sniffed. "I am no such thing! If I were to 'hang around' any longer than necessary, my power signature would alert every supernatural in the world to my location. I risk much by coming here before the Coalition is confirmed and certain protections are put in place. I do this for Jessica's well-being only."

I didn't feel like reminding Jeb that no one knew who he was. It was clear he thought supernaturals would try to kidnap him for his power or some such thing. But since the time of the last Coalition, it had been too long, and supernaturals were not the same as they used to be.

I did have one question, however. "So, once the Coalition is formed, then you'll be able to stick around?"

"Yes. The Power of Five will bind to protect me from interference in this realm, and I will be able to come and go freely. But most of my affairs will be done outside of this realm. I prefer to work in my own home."

Sounded good to me.

"Okay," I said. "So how do we go about finding this powerful supernatural?"

Jeb opened the book, and we watched the pages arrange themselves. He laid a single finger down and said, "He can be found, and I quote, 'Where the statues stay, he will play.'"

I sighed. "That's it? That's all that's written? Only that it's a he, not even what kind of supe he is?"

"It specifies only that he is old and has kept his power in check for a long time. His help might not be easy to acquire, because if he decides to show himself, he will become a target like myself. But you must try." Jeb shut the book with a flourish, indicating he was done. "Now I must take my leave. Enid searches for you and is close to uncovering your location. Julian's wolves are up the road. They will take you back to the Compound. Search for this supernatural this day and then head to the Ponte Vecchio for Enid's next clue. You will be safe there for the night. If you can convince the supe to accompany you on the next task, tomorrow morning, he will guide you and keep you cloaked. If not, send someone else in your stead." Before I could respond, Jeb popped out of reality with an audible crack.

It was disconcerting to see him go like that.

Ray shook his head. "That is one weird little dude."

My sentiments exactly.

7

Julian's wolves were surprised to see us walking up the road. The SUV's hood was up, and they stood scratching their heads. It was a brand-new vehicle.

But, like magic, once we came within five feet, the engine started.

Jeb had lots of tricks up his big, baggy, white sleeve.

The drive to the Compound was short, up a long, winding driveway lined with beautiful trees and a rolling vineyard as far as the eye could see.

I'd forgotten how beautiful it was here.

The old villa was typical for Italy, built out of big blocks of buff-colored stone, with enormous terraces that wrapped around the entire estate and big floor-to-ceiling multipaned windows that could be opened twofold to let the beautiful outside in. The grounds were enormous, with several outbuildings in the distance and many more we couldn't see.

Julian stepped onto the veranda to greet us as we arrived. "I take it your meeting went well." He made a sweeping gesture with his arm. "Come, we are enjoying some breakfast. I am sure you are hungry."

My stomach rumbled on cue.

I'd finally learned how to keep my constant craving for sustenance in check—by blocking it out of my brain so I could function—but I wasn't about to turn down a free breakfast. "Thank you," I said. "We are starving."

"I don't need breakfast," Ray commented. "Instead, I think I'll head into Florence and take a look around." He glanced at me pointedly. "Get a head start on things."

I nodded. "Agreed. We'll be ready to head out in about an hour. Meet us there." He didn't linger, shooting up into the air immediately.

Julian appraised us, but said nothing as we followed him inside.

It was clear to anyone who paid attention that Ray and I were closely bonded. I was happy Julian hadn't asked any questions. My relationship with the reaper vampire was a hard one to define.

Ray, Rourke, and I had briefly discussed matters after Jeb had vanished. Ray was going to snoop around the city and see what he could find about a supe who played with statues, while Rourke and I informed James, Marcy, Tyler, and Nick about everything in private. Then we were going to have to make some polite inquiries about who Julian's lover was. I was confident we could figure it out without a lot of hassle.

I was hopeful that once we found the powerful supernatural who could cloak me, he would help us. I mean, what kind of creature would want the world to fall into chaos if they could be of service?

I didn't think many.

Unfortunately, Florence was the home of statues. There would be many places to look.

Julian ushered us through an ornate foyer, complete with a huge crystal chandelier and a set of double spiral staircases, each leading to a different wing of the house. We walked under an archway and into a massive kitchen.

A long, ornate table was the centerpiece of the room. It was positioned in front of three sets of French doors, overlooking a balcony and the vast expanse of the vineyards. The table could seat at least twenty. The parquet floors were honey-colored, and the table appeared to be made of reclaimed wood. Off to the right was a fully functional, modern kitchen, with marble countertops and big stainless-steel appliances.

It was a gorgeous setting.

"Hiya." Marcy waved from the table. "Have a seat. The croissants are to die for." She held one out as I pulled out a chair.

"Did the meeting go well?" Tyler asked. In my mind, he asked, *What's up? Did Jeb have any important things to share? You weren't gone that long.*

I took the proffered croissant from Marcy and sat down. The pastry was warm, indicating it was just out of the oven. The buttery crust flaked as I broke it in half. I held my moan inside. "The meeting went well," I told the group. "Just some routine stuff he wanted to tell me now that we've arrived in Italy." My tone was light. In my mind, I told Tyler, *We're going to have to track down a supe today who works with statues. We need to feel Julian out about where to go without alerting him that we're on a mission. Oh, and we also have to find out who he's sleeping with.*

Got it, Tyler replied. It was hard to ruffle Tyler, which I loved.

Julian sat at the head of the table. He picked up a fork and knife and began to cut into what appeared to be an omelet. Eudoxia was nowhere to be found.

A chef bustled into the kitchen, complete with a large white hat. He came up to the table. "Welcome, what may I offer you? In addition to the fresh fruit and pastries on the table, we have anything your heart desires. French toast, pancakes, soufflés, bacon, sausage, you name it." He was a wolf and didn't appear to be older than thirty human years, which meant he was at least fifty immortal years. He had dark hair that curled under the hat at the back of his neck. His skin was a warm olive tone, and his voice was heavily accented Italian, but he looked to be of mixed heritage of some kind.

By his scent he was a wolf...but as I inhaled I found it was mixed with something else.

That got my attention.

"French toast and bacon sound wonderful. Thank you so much," I told him. I refrained from asking him to bring me a bucket full of bacon. I figured he knew how to serve a pack of wolves, so he wouldn't skimp. He took Rourke's order, but before he left the table, I couldn't help asking, "Are you a hybrid wolf?" It was rude to ask, especially after just meeting him, but I had to know. Something told me it was necessary. My wolf barked her agreement. I added hastily, "I'm sorry if I'm prying, please forgive me. But your scent is so interesting, I had to ask."

His expression reflected he was a little shocked that I'd been so bold, but it warmed quickly. It was clear he was a good-natured guy. "Yes, I'm a hybrid. I'm half wolf, half fox. Not many pick up on that."

I raised an eyebrow.

Fox was the last thing I thought he'd say, as shifters usually inherited their supernatural genes from their fathers. So that meant his father had been both fox and wolf, or his mother had fox genes of some kind.

He seemed to anticipate my next question and preempted with, "My mother was Japanese. In Japan, there are female fox shifters, called—"

"Kitsune," Nick finished from across the table, grinning.

My eyes flashed to my friend. Nick was a fox, but his shifter genes came from his father, who was Inuit. I smiled, turning back to the chef. "That's so interesting. Thank you very much for telling us," I said. "I apologize for being so brash. I know it's impolite to ask. My only excuse is that I'm new and very curious. It seems you have some things in common with my friend here. Nick is a fox shifter as well."

The cook blushed. "I picked up on that. My Kitsune genes have given me a *very* enhanced sense of smell. I can detect almost any supernatural by their scent alone."

My eyebrows shot up again.

Nick pushed back his chair and rose, reaching his hand across the table. "It's a pleasure to meet you. I'm Nick Michaels. I look forward to sharing stories. Being a fox in a wolf's den is a precarious position. I've never met another fox before—Kitsune or other."

The chef leaned over the table and shook Nick's extended hand, grinning widely. "I'm Lucas Mancini, and I look forward to swapping stories. You are correct, it's not for the faint of heart."

Julian cleared his throat.

I glanced up. It was clear the Alpha was trying to contain himself. Lucas should be beneath our notice, and this entire interaction had taken too long. A hybrid wolf was not a true wolf, especially not to a leader like Julian. Lucas's place was likely at the very bottom of Pack hierarchy.

Lucas didn't take offense to his Alpha's interruption. Instead, he smiled, bowing his head graciously before heading into the kitchen to prepare our breakfast.

"Julian," I said amiably, getting us back on track while popping another piece of delicious croissant into my mouth, "I'd forgotten how absolutely gorgeous your estate is. It's stunning in every way. You must entertain a lot." To my mate, I said internally, *We have to find a way to bring Lucas into town with us. We need him to sniff out the supe we're looking for. Try to think of something that doesn't seem too suspicious. I'll talk to Nick as soon as I can.*

Julian's demeanor relaxed as he smiled proudly. "Yes, this villa and the grounds around it have been a work in progress for many years. I inherited it all from my father, who failed to keep up with all the needed repairs. These villas were built hundreds of years ago and need a lot of upkeep, especially one of this size. The renovations are finally complete."

In what I hoped was a casual tone, I changed the subject with, "Are there a lot of supernaturals in the area? I mean, Florence is a big city with old magic. It would only make sense that there is a large population of creatures living here." I reached for some apricot preserves.

Julian appraised me for a moment, settling back in his chair. "Yes, there are many who live here. Florence is a thriving city, full of magic."

Judging from how he'd handled seeing Eudoxia, it made sense that he might interact more regularly than my father did with other supernaturals. "Back in the States," I told him, "we tend to stick to our separate Sects. There isn't a lot of commingling going on. Is it the same here?"

He shook his head. "No, we Europeans tend to be more relaxed about most things. As I told your friend, I have a lot of contacts. We've learned over the years that different species, who have different magic, can be an asset, so we've managed to get along for the good of everyone."

My brother cleared his throat. "Because of that, are there a lot of interspecies couplings? If everyone is hanging around each other, it makes sense that they would be drawn to one another." Tyler immediately turned red, reaching for his water glass and taking a long draw.

That was very smooth, I told him. *Interspecies couplings? Why didn't you just come out and ask if he was banging a nymph and get it over with?*

Julian chuckled. It was the sound of indulgence. "Yes, it does happen. In my opinion, another supernatural is a much better match for a wolf than any human could possibly be."

I kept my face passive. Humans, as far as I knew, were the only species genetically matched to give birth to a wolf outside of a mated pair. So a supernatural was not a better choice if you wanted to procreate. Fated matches were another thing altogether, but we weren't talking about those.

Julian smoothly changed the subject. "What are your plans for today? Other than hunting for your missing friends."

"We're planning to head into Florence after breakfast," I said. "Two of our friends, Daniel Walker and Tallulah Talbot, are missing. If they're near here, we're hoping some of the supernaturals in town might've seen or heard something." I watched Julian's face closely to see if either name registered. "Tally is a very powerful witch and Marcy's aunt." I inclined my head toward Marcy. "She's been missing for a while now. It's baffling, since she's incredibly powerful. Whoever took her has to be her equal or greater. Either that, or they had help. Whatever the case, we plan to get to the bottom of it, starting in Florence."

Julian folded his elbows on the table. "It's strange that your friends have gone missing recently. The city of Florence and the surrounding areas have been in an uproar these last few weeks. I don't understand it." He shook his head. "It was fine one day, and then almost like a switch had been flipped, our world changed, fights breaking out, supernaturals going missing. Honestly, it's threatening my capabilities to keep it under wraps from the humans, since I'm the prominent leader in the area." He glanced at me pointedly. "Do you know anything about that?"

Julian knew more than he was letting on. But I wasn't about to get into it with him right now. I would wait and talk face-to-face with my father so we could come up with a plan. My place on the Coalition would create a power rift between Julian and me, as I would technically outrank this Alpha on his own turf. Julian wasn't a wolf who would stand for that very long.

"I don't know anything about it. That's strange—" I was blissfully interrupted as Lucas delivered our food to the table. His cheery demeanor was exactly the distraction I needed.

Marcy picked up on what we were trying to do. "Hey, Lucas, what are some places to see in Florence? While we're trying to locate some supernaturals to question, we'd love to see the sights."

"We're particularly interested in seeing some of the sculptures," Rourke added, digging into his food. "It's been a long time since I've seen any great works of art."

"Oh," Lucas answered readily, "then you must to go to the Galleria dell'Accademia. You can't miss seeing Michelangelo's masterpiece David with your own eyes. It's the greatest statue in Italy. There are also great works there by Botticelli, Andrea del Sarto, Alessandro Allori, and others." It was clear Lucas was an art aficionado. "There are other museums, of course. But the Accademia is my very favorite."

I made my move. "Would you mind accompanying us? I think it might be easier if we had a guide who knows Florence." I hoped asking Lucas wouldn't raise any red flags for Julian. After all, it wasn't uncommon for a lower-ranked wolf to be a chauffeur. I shot a glance at Julian, who didn't seem to be paying much attention to the conversation anyway. "Julian, you don't mind if we steal Lucas away for a few hours, do you?" I asked. "We'd love to head into Florence as soon as possible. We'll be back before my father's plane arrives at six."

Julian blinked. I had a hunch he'd been having a conversation in his mind with someone else. "Yes, that's fine." He took his napkin from his lap and crumpled it up, dropping it on his plate as he pushed his chair back. "I have a driver who will take you all, of course. But if you'd like Lucas to accompany you in addition, that's fine. There are others who can cover his lunch shift." He stood and gave us a small bow. "Now if you'll excuse me, some business has come up that I must attend to. I will meet you back here later this afternoon. Enjoy your day."

As he left the room, Marcy leaned forward. "Was it just me, or was he a little distracted there at the end?"

"He was totally distracted," I said. "Let's finish up our meal and head outside. I have to see Eudoxia first, and then I'll fill you in on what Jeb had to say. We have some business of our own this morning."

8

I'd found Eudoxia exactly where I thought she'd be—lounging in one of the suites, complaining that things weren't quite up to snuff. As I walked in, she spun around. "Exactly how long do we have to stay here?" she asked, wrinkling her nose.

I shrugged, looking around. "This isn't a house made for peasants. The accommodations are pretty cushy. But I didn't come here to chat about the decor or time frame. I came to fulfill my end of the bargain." I pulled back my sleeve to expose my wrist. Her teeth snapped down as she stalked toward me. It was a horrid sound. "I'm going to let you have a thirty-second draw, nothing more."

She glared at me, but said nothing. She latched on, taking her full thirty seconds. When she was done, she dragged her sleeve over her mouth, smearing my blood as it trickled down her chin. Classy. The only thing she'd refrained from doing was smacking her lips.

I rolled my shirtsleeve down. "We're heading out, hoping to find answers about Tally's whereabouts. We'll be back later this afternoon."

"I will not be here," she stated, turning around and walking back to a large window that overlooked the vineyards. "I have business to attend to. In fact, I will be spending as little time as possible here."

"It's not an issue," I said. "I'm sure we will run into you at some point."

She huffed, but didn't answer. I was certain she would've loved to have said something along the lines of, *Not if I can help it.*

Her back was to me as I started for the door. Her monotone rang out, "There is danger here."

My face showed my surprise. "Are you trying to keep me safe by telling me that?"

"No, insolent wolf," she said, glaring over her shoulder. "I'm simply stating a fact."

"Got it," I said. "I'll be sure to keep an eye out." I left the room, shutting the door behind me. My wrist was already healed. I had no idea how I was going to work with that woman for an eternity.

I sighed.

The entire group was standing by an SUV parked in the drive when I walked out the front door.

I filled them in on the basics of what we learned while you were gone, Rourke said.

I joined them outside the vehicle. "Everybody ready?" I asked. "We're on the hunt for statues. We didn't get very clear details, but since Florence is the city of sculptures, it shouldn't be that hard to find some. Accademia sounds like the right place to start."

"So this supernatural has the ability to cloak you?" Nick asked. "That's pretty powerful stuff. What kind of a supe can do that?"

I shook my head. "I have no idea, but I'm hoping Lucas's nose can help us out. Between him and Tyler, we should be able to figure out if there's a supernatural in that art gallery. If not, we go elsewhere until we find what we're looking for."

"When are we going to the bridge?" Kayla asked pointedly. I'd seen her holding on to Enid's note earlier.

"As soon as we find this supe," I told her. "Without his help, I won't be able to rescue anyone. Jeb said that if I followed Enid's directives, I would die. Kayla, I know you're worried about Jax, and we are too. He is our priority, as well as our other friends who are missing. Enid isn't going to kill him. If she did, she'd risk not getting what she wants—which is me. She doesn't want your brother. I'm the one she's after."

"I get that," she replied. "But the note said to go directly to the Ponte Vecchio. We're not doing that, and if we don't follow what she said, my brother could be harmed." Kayla's voice was carefully measured. She'd obviously been waiting to say this since we'd landed on Italian soil.

I walked over and settled my hands on her shoulders. She didn't brush me off, which was good. "Kayla, you have to believe me, your brother's going to be fine. He's an ice troll and, by the looks of it, an incredibly strong one. He put up a huge fight when he was taken at your apartment. He's braver than you think. I know waiting is hard, but if we can't convince this supernatural to help us, our chances of succeeding in this mission go down dramatically. I need your head in the game. You can help us." I dropped my hands. "We're not the enemy. You have to believe that."

She bowed her head. "I do," she replied softly. "I see now that you're the good guys. But you have to understand that I haven't trusted anyone since my parents died. All I care about is getting my brother back alive."

"I promise we're going to do just that." Rourke yanked open the door of the SUV as Lucas came rushing down the steps. "Help us track down this supe," I said, "and we're that much closer to finding your brother."

She nodded. "I'm pretty good about sensing supernaturals. I will try my best."

"That's all we can ask for." Lucas was almost to us. "Nick," I murmured to my friend, "I want you to feel Lucas out to see if we can trust him. See how happy he is with his position here, how he's been treated, and where his allegiances lie."

"Will do," Nick answered. "If he's anything like me, he's not that happy." He grinned as he climbed into the front seat, making room for Lucas.

"I'll take anything in our favor right now," I said as I climbed into the backseat and shut the door, taking my place next to Rourke, who draped his hand around my waist. I nuzzled his shoulder.

He growled, "How'd it go with the Vampire Queen?"

"As good as it could, I suppose. She's not going to be spending a lot of time here, so we've got that going for us."

A wolf I didn't know got into the driver's seat. "Matteo is going to bring us into town," Lucas said, turning from the front seat. "The parking is difficult, and I figured time is of the essence."

I nodded. "Sounds good."

There were nine of us, including the driver, but this was a custom SUV. There were three large rows in back, each big enough to hold four adults.

The driver and Lucas chatted in Italian about our destination as we took off. Once the car began to move, Lucas turned again. "I was able to procure us tickets. I have a friend who works at the museum, and luckily, she was there today. She will meet us out front and guide us in. We will be able to skip the line," he said with a wink. "Many flock to Florence to see our beautiful museums, but waiting can be tedious."

"That sounds perfect," I told him. Supernaturals weren't used to waiting for much of anything, but we would be forced to if there were too many humans around. It would be futile for Marcy to try to spell an entire street full of people, or for Nick to use his persuasion on that many. "Is your friend, by chance, a supernatural?"

He chuckled. "Alas, no. She is the daughter of one of the bakers I buy from frequently. We've gotten to know each other over the years. She's a very sweet girl."

I didn't want to say too much in front of the driver, so I held my tongue, even though I was dying to ask Lucas a dozen questions about supernaturals in the city and where they congregated.

The roads were ridiculously narrow and full of curves. It took us roughly forty minutes to get into town. I was certain Ray would know exactly when we entered the city. The streets were bustling. After a few twists and turns in a densely populated area, the driver slowed, pulling over to the side. "This is as far as I can take you. The streets ahead are restricted."

"This is fine," Lucas announced. "We're only a few blocks from the Accademia." As we piled out, Lucas told the driver, "I'll call you when we're ready to be picked up." The guy didn't even bother responding. Lucas didn't seem to mind, which was a testament to his character.

I liked Lucas immensely, even though we'd known him only a short time.

Once we were on the street, smells swirled everywhere. My nose was bogged down with all kinds of tantalizing aromas, but in particular garlic, onions, and tomatoes—all the delectable scents you would conjure when you thought of Italy.

I couldn't imagine how Tyler was faring with his sensitive nose. Lucas was likely used to it, but Tyler looked as overwhelmed as I felt.

How's it going, bro? I asked. *I haven't smelled this much food in one place in a long time. If we lived in New York City, being here would be easier. Are you going to be able to the channel it away so you can pick out the supernaturals?*

Of course, he answered. *It's just gonna take me a minute...or two...or three.* He grimaced. *There are just so many open air restaurants.*

We followed Lucas down a side street. He gave us a brief history of Florence. My wolf was parceling away the smells as quickly as she could, and I was grateful. After a moment or two, things began to calm down and I could focus again.

"The statue of David was originally located in the Piazza della Signoria for all to see, but it was moved inside in 1873, and a replica was made—there have been a few since then—that stands in the piazza today."

This piqued my interest. "Who is in charge of building replicas?" I asked.

"I'm not sure," he answered. "They should have that information at the Accademia. I'm sure there have been a number of people in charge of different things over the years."

Or one person, if that person is supernatural, Rourke said. *I think you're on to something. If statues need replicas made, they need a master craftsman to do so. They wouldn't entrust that task to anyone.*

That's what I'm thinking, I told him. *It's lucky we have Lucas with us. Do you think we can trust him? It's going to be hard to keep him in the dark with all the questions we need to ask. If he runs back to Julian, however, it will be a problem.*

I don't smell any malice on him, Rourke said, grabbing my hand. I loved feeling his warmth encircling my fingers. I let myself enjoy it for a moment. *Seeing how Julian treated him, I think it would be easy to break his alliance, if he even has one. But before we decide to let them in on our plans, let's let Nick speak with him alone. I trust him to get a good bead on Lucas.*

Agreed.

After a few more turns, we came upon a street that was

more crowded than the others. People were queued in front of an unassuming tan stucco building. The only thing giving the location away was a single banner that announced we had arrived at the Galleria dell'Accademia. A red plastic sign jutted out from beside the door that read *Entrance Reserved*.

A young girl waved at Lucas. She looked pleased to see her friend. He embraced her, giving her a kiss on each cheek. "Maria, so good to see you." He stepped back. "I'd like you to meet some friends of mine. This is Jessica, Rourke, Marcy, James, Tyler, Kayla, and Nick."

"And I'm Ray," Ray said.

Lucas's eyes widened at the sudden appearance of the vampire, whom he had not met at the Compound, but he recovered nicely, which made me smile. Lucas definitely had some hidden talents. "And this is Ray," he finished smoothly. "We are so grateful you could get us in today. It's a large group, so I'm thrilled you can accommodate us."

"Of course," she answered gracefully, her English a little broken, but easy to understand. "This is the reserved-tickets line, but it will be easier to take you in via the service entrance. I've gotten prior approval already. Follow me." Without hesitation, she led us around the building. "I apologize, but we have to go all the way around to access the employee entrance."

"We don't mind at all," I told her. "We are happy to get this opportunity. We won't be in Florence long, and we didn't think of purchasing tickets ahead." To my brother, I said, *Keep your nose on high alert. I'm hoping the service entrance means we will get better access to the scents of those who work here.*

Any idea what we're looking for exactly? he asked. *Shifter, vamp, witch? It would be helpful to know at least what type of supe I'm searching for.*

I have no idea. All we know is he's old and powerful. I'm

thinking it won't be anything typical, so keep your nose open to anything strange.

Nick picked up the conversation with Maria. "If we're going through the service entrance, does that mean we might get a peek at the curator's area? I'm a huge museum buff. I would love to see a little behind the scenes, if we're allowed." I wasn't sure if Nick was using his persuasion on this sweet girl, which was his special gift, but hey, whatever worked.

"Occasionally, we're allowed to bring tours into the secure areas," she admitted. "But we usually have to request prior approval." Her eyes lit up. "But you're in luck, as our main curator is in attendance. He only arrives from Milan once a month." She took keys out of her pocket to unlock a small, unassuming door. "If you stay here in the vestibule, I will go ask permission to take you through."

"Thank you so much, Maria," Lucas said as we crowded in. "Tell him I'm here as well. He and I are old friends. We will await your return."

My nose was on high alert, but I wasn't picking up anything unusual. Just a lot of paint, plaster, dust, and people. No power signatures from any supernaturals. I wasn't the one with the super scent, however. I casually glanced at my brother. "Finding anything of interest?"

He shook his head as he turned in a circle. "We're only a few feet inside the building. Give me a minute."

"Picking up on any magic?" I asked Marcy.

"Nada. This place is dry. But I am getting a rather creepy sense of foreboding. That could be the nature of the building, though. These old places are ghostly hideouts." She rubbed her arms as James pulled her to his side. "I hate specters. They're so incorporeal and rude."

Maria came back a few minutes later wearing a bright smile. "You've been approved! I can take you through. Please follow me."

Lucas grinned as we began to walk. "It *is* your lucky day," he said.

My eyebrows rose. "Why's that?"

"Because Leonardo Russo doesn't agree to see just anyone."

9

"Leonardo Russo?" I asked as we followed Maria through a long, narrow passageway. The name had no meaning to me. The back rooms of the gallery were how you'd expect a museum to look: art on shelves in various degrees of rehab, tools, clutter, stuff stacked in corners.

Overall, a calculated mess.

It was interesting, but my mind was occupied elsewhere.

"Of course," Lucas answered. "You're here to see Leo, aren't you? That's the reason we came to Accademia in the first place. You're not actually interested in the art. You wanted to find a powerful supernatural, and he's likely the one you're looking for."

"Er…" I quirked an eyebrow, both wanting to divulge our mission, and not. It seemed Lucas was cagier than he'd let on, and I'd underestimated him. "It might be? I guess it depends on who exactly Leo is."

"I understand your trepidation and lack of trust. We just met," Lucas said. "But it's misguided. I am completely trustworthy. I mean, it's not every day that I get to be in the company of Jessica McClain." He grinned, giving me a saucy wink. "I won't betray you."

I stumbled and had to grab on to his arm to steady myself. "What do you know about me?"

"Quite a bit," he replied casually. "Every time something new happens in our world, we gather around to hear the latest. Word travels fast. When you took out that powerful supernatural in the Underworld, Lili something-or-other, everything changed here, and supernaturals became fearful of what's to come. Julian is both excited by your arrival and very anxious. He is hoping to glean information from you, so he can decide what needs to be done. You weren't exactly forthcoming at breakfast." He smiled. "Good strategy."

I'd had no idea people were talking about me on such a large scale.

I was a little aghast. "Do you know why I'm here in Florence?"

He shook his head. "No, not exactly. Obviously, you have friends missing and hope to find them here. But your arrival happened so quickly, and with so little notice, no one knows your true intent." I was relieved he didn't have more specifics. It would not be good if everyone knew our day-to-day business.

I asked, "What did you mean when you said so Julian 'can decide what needs to be done'? Is his Pack allegiance compromised to the other wolves?" Ahead, Maria stopped. Lucas and I had dropped back, everyone hearing our conversation and letting us be. Nick asked Maria a question, so she was occupied for the moment.

"Julian's allegiance has always been to Julian alone," Lucas replied, trying to be discreet. "I expect him to make wrong decisions regarding you moving forward."

I appraised this hybrid wolf in a new light. "Why are you trusting me with this highly sensitive information? It's risky for you to go against your Pack. Your Alpha will not be happy if he finds out."

Lucas shrugged. "I've lived my entire life at the bottom. Julian has not been kind to me. He let me accompany you today because he feels I'm worthless and know little to nothing about Pack proceedings. Even if I had something to share, he feels it will be of no use to you. I owe my allegiance to the Coalition, as does every other supernatural in the world. You are the higher power, not Julian." He inclined his head. "You have my trust and my fealty." I was happy he didn't drop to one knee. That would've alarmed the human.

I was overwhelmed.

Maria tapped softly on the closed door in front of her. "Signore Russo, may we enter?" She smiled over her shoulder. "This is the main sculpture room. It's a place where most of the statues are stored, repaired, and replaced. It is quite a sight to see and is as big as a warehouse. When Signore Russo is in the building, he usually resides here."

"You may enter," a voice intoned.

As Maria turned the handle, I leaned into Lucas. "How do you know Leo?"

"I am an art lover," he whispered. "I was here many years ago admiring the statues, and I caught a strange scent. I was curious, so I followed my nose. Leo was the end result. I am certain it is he who you seek."

"How can you be sure?"

Lucas shrugged once again. "Because it makes sense you would want to find the most powerful supernatural in the city to aid your cause, whatever it may be. And Leo is that supe."

It *did* make sense.

I had to hand it to Lucas. "Does Julian know Leo?"

Lucas shook his head. "No. There was no reason to tell my Alpha about this particular supe. He is of no consequence to wolves and poses no threat. Plus, not many would be able to detect him, especially if he didn't deem it so. There is no worry that he will be uncovered. He chooses to live in peace, and I respect that."

We moved into a big, cavernous room.

The walls were a few stories high and whitewashed, and old paned windows were lined up across the top. Platforms and scaffolding were scattered here and there, holding various busts and full statues, some covered with sheets, some not.

In the middle of it all stood a real-life Adonis.

He was easily over six feet tall, had a full head of wavy brown hair, bronze skin, and a face that looked like it'd been chiseled out of stone.

The man was flawless.

Rourke growled low. *What is he? I can't make out his scent.*

I have no idea, I answered.

"Holy beautiful man," Marcy muttered. "The Greek gods forgot this one down here." James made a disgruntled noise, but didn't comment further, other than to put a protective arm around his mate.

As we came closer, Leo gave a small bow, his hands clasped behind his back.

He wore expensive slacks and a black dress shirt. "Welcome to my inner sanctum." His English impeccable, only a slight Italian accent was detectable. "This is where I feel most at home—among the artifacts and relics of times gone by. Feel free to take a look around."

Leo appeared no more than forty human years, if that. I didn't want to push my power out to investigate his signature, even though my wolf kept urging me to do exactly that. *We have to be polite,* I told her, reining her in. *People don't like it when we examine them. What does he smell like to you? I can only scent dirt, stale plaster, and dried paint.* She flashed me a picture of Leo illuminated by blinding white light. *I don't know what that means. You're going to have to be more specific.*

I'm coming up short, Tyler said, interrupting us. *He doesn't smell like much, just wet soil, outside, and some old paint. He's hiding his signature, and he's damn good at it. He must be powerful if none of it leaks around the edges. Maybe this isn't the guy we're looking for.*

Oh, it is. I was sure of it.

By the look on Leo's face, he knew it too. If he was as powerful as Lucas said, he knew what kind of a supe each of us was instantly, likely before we'd even entered the building.

But we had to play the game. So it was small talk and no feeling him up for power. "Are you a sculptor by trade?" I asked as we all began to meander around the room to investigate things.

"You sure got a lot of stuff in here," Ray commented. "It's like a bank vault of art and stone sculptures and stuff." *Eloquent, Ray. Really smooth.*

Leo nodded, a small smile forming. "Yes, sculpting is my trade. Try not to touch anything. These artifacts are priceless. Most people have no idea how much worth lies in this room." He nodded to indicate a large pallet to his right where a half-completed statue stood. "This is a work of Michelangelo's, but none believe it to be true, as it can't be properly authenticated. It was done when he traveled abroad to the South Seas and is atypical of his other works. So here it stays."

"How do you know it's a true Michelangelo?" Nick asked curiously.

"Because I was there when he started it," Leo answered nonchalantly.

My head jerked around to locate Maria, curious to see if she knew her boss was a supernatural. But Maria was nowhere to be found.

By admitting that tidbit, Leo had let the proverbial cat out of the huge elephant-sized bag, opening up our conversation to the real reason we were here. I decided to play it cool.

"You've been an art lover for a long time, then," I said. "Have you held this job long?"

"Yes, dear wolf," he replied, casually letting me know where we stood. "Art has been my passion since the day of my birth. Many of my very own works are in this museum. Produced under pseudonyms, of course, because I could not continue to create art under the same name for centuries at a time. That would become a bit suspicious."

I tried not to gape. "You're Michelangelo, aren't you." It was a statement, not a question.

Marcy gasped, her palm thumping over her heart. I was glad I wasn't the only one having a moment.

"Indeed," he answered, inclining his head. "My birth name is truly Leonardo. But during the time of Michelangelo—some of my greatest years—Leonardo da Vinci had already claimed that moniker. There could not be two famous Leonardos who hailed from the same city. So you see, I was forced to pick a false title. But it has served me well."

I didn't really see at all. It shouldn't be as surprising as it was, but I was shocked by the news that he was *the* Michelangelo and we were standing in the room with him. "May I ask what kind of supernatural you are?" I couldn't hold back my curiosity any longer. "I apologize for asking so bluntly, but we're having a hard time deducing it."

Leo glanced over at Lucas, who stood quietly to my right, smiling. "My friend, the Kitsune, had no problem identifying me. In fact, it was a pleasure to meet such a skilled supernatural, as I had not immersed myself in that world for a very long time."

Lucas appeared a little flustered by the praise. "It is in my nature to be curious. Although, to be fair, you do not smell like a supernatural. I just knew you were *other*."

Kayla surprised me by speaking. "I agree," she said. "You don't smell like a supernatural, but you do smell odd."

"Odd?" Leo chuckled. "Do explain."

A low growl emitted from the back of Tyler's throat, but it was so low I wasn't sure others had heard, or if it had been only in my head. He took a protective step toward Kayla.

Leo was a charmer, that was for sure.

Kayla appeared flustered by the attention. "You smell...like the earth and the sky combined," she finally answered. "Like they met in the middle to create you. My magic comes from deep within the earth, so I'm familiar with how it smells. The air scent is distinct, crisp, like a fall day."

"I agree," Marcy chimed in. "My magic also comes from the earth, but to me you smell celestial. I've never scented anything like it. Like how I would imagine a star to smell."

Tyler nodded. "It smells like dirt in here, but I took that for the clay, not the man. You fooled me."

"Don't worry, young wolf. It's much harder for shifters to scent me," Leo said. "You smell of the earth yourself, so it's harder to discern. But the women are correct. I was made from the earth, the sky, and the stars."

"You're an angel, aren't you?" Kayla said in a tiny voice.

An angel?

I was blown away.

Leo made a full bow, complete with an arm crossing his midsection. "Indeed, I am." As he stood back to his full height, which was at least six foot five, he directed his gaze solidly on me.

It held weight.

I knew, without a doubt, that if Leo decided to unleash his magic, the entire city of Florence would be obliterated.

I hadn't known angels existed until right this second. There was mythology surrounding them, but no one I'd ever known had met one. "I..." I cleared my throat. "I mean, we...are pleased to make your acquaintance. Thank you for allowing us to come into your private space." I had no idea what else to say to this spectacular being. "We were lucky to catch you on a day you were in town."

Leo tossed his head back and laughed. It was a vibrant sound, like bells chiming. "There is very little in the world that has to do with luck. Or in any of the worlds, for that matter."

"Do you know why I'm here?" I asked. That would save some time. I had no idea what kind of abilities angels had, if they were oracles or not.

"In general, I know why you seek me," he replied. "But I am not a seer or a predictor of the future. And, unfortunately, I'm very out of touch these days. I have not lived as a true supernatural in too many years to count. My life is very simple here, among the art and the statues." He gestured around the room. "This is where I am content to live out the rest of my days, and I have many of them left."

"If you know why I'm here, will you help us?" I asked.

Leo walked over to a stool next to a cluttered workbench and sat. He picked up a chisel that lay on the worktable and spun it idly. "You must state your case to me, and then I will decide. Helping you means I must reveal myself to the supernatural world, and doing so would put me at risk." That's exactly what Jeb had said. "Other powerful supernaturals of my stature have died out or left this plane long ago. There are very few, if any, left. Exposing myself would alert all races and creatures that I exist. But I will listen to what you have to say. If anything, I've learned to have an open mind after all my years of interacting with humans."

I had to convince him.

Walking over, I pulled out another stool and sat facing him so I could plead my case. "Are you familiar with a warlock named Jebediah Amel?"

Leo nodded, his brilliant blue eyes flashing. They were disconcerting compared with his otherwise bronze complexion. And they weren't just blue—they were clear, like two crystals reflecting the bluest sky. "Yes, I am familiar with the warlock. I have not seen him in centuries. He lives outside this realm, because of the things I already mentioned."

"Yes," I said. "He's my assistant—or will be my assistant soon—and the one who alerted me to your presence here in Florence. I'm not sure how much you know about what's happening in the supernatural world, but a new Coalition is forming."

"I'm aware."

"I'm slated to sit on that Coalition as the Enforcer," I told him.

"I'm aware."

I fidgeted on my stool. "I recently killed a powerful supernatural, Ardat Lili, and in doing so, I ended the chance of Bianca, the third Hag, being reborn, which has altered my true path." I tried not to rush, but it all poured out, words tumbling over my tongue as fast as they could get out. "In order to set things right, one of the Hags, Enid, believes I should die. And another one of the Hags, Juanita, believes I should live. If I were to die, chaos would ensue before the world righted itself again, which could take a thousand years. There would be a huge loss of life. I've been told that if I live I would have to sacrifice something dear to me, and if I did, all would be right, and I would assume my seat on the Coalition." As I spoke, I tried making my expression imploring, hoping that would help my cause. "I can't give up on that chance. I desperately want to survive, and I want everyone else to keep on living as well. I don't want innocents to die or the world to dip into chaos. That's why I need your help. Without you, I believe my chances are slim to none. Jeb said you alone have the capabilities to cloak me from Enid, who sees my every move. Right now, she has the upper hand, and if I follow her missives to the letter, Jeb says all is lost."

"Are you prepared to make a great sacrifice?" His voice was so intense, it caught me off guard, his brilliant blue eyes boring into me.

I leaned back. Was I?

If he wanted an honest answer, I had to search my soul.

It scared me that I had to go in blind, not knowing what I had to give up ahead of time. I answered with the truth. "If the sacrifice doesn't involve me killing an innocent, or someone I love, I'm ready. Honestly, I don't think I'd be able to murder anyone in cold blood, especially someone I care about. Other than that, yes, I'm ready."

Leo picked up the chisel and twirled it in his hands. Then, looking resigned, he tossed it down with a clatter and stood. "I believe you're sincere. And if you're willing to sacrifice something for the greater good, it would be silly for me not to as well. I will help you."

10

I leaped off the stool, but stopped short of embracing the angel. That would've involved getting into his personal space, and neither of us was ready for that. "Thank you!" I gushed, relief flowing through me. My wolf howled her joy. "You've given us a chance to succeed, and I'm so grateful."

Leo walked over to some scaffolding that held a bunch of busts. "This will not be without error. Enid is very powerful. When she finds out, she will resent my help, and there may be damaging consequences. But if you're willing to pay the price, I believe I should help you." He reached out to run his fingers over the face of a woman carved into white stone. "I have not encountered an unselfish supernatural in many centuries—if ever. You are willing to risk the unknown, and that is commendable. In my experience, supernaturals are out for themselves, not others." He turned to face me. "It would also go against my being to let harm come to millions of innocents if you were to die."

"I appreciate that," I said. "So where do we go from here? Enid has instructed us to go to the Ponte Vecchio. I believe that's where we'll find a note with new instructions. Enid wants me to swap my life for the hostages she's taken. I'm willing to do it, if that's the only option we have."

Leo paced to the worktable. "I have the power to cloak you, but I cannot mask all of you." He glanced idly around the group. "Three will be enough. You and two others. Go to the bridge when you leave here and pick up what is waiting. I believe you're right, and she has left instructions. Then meet me in the Piazza della Signoria in front of the statue of David at dawn tomorrow. We will proceed from there."

"I'm sorry to interrupt, but Enid is a seer," Marcy said. "Won't she know we had this little meeting today? And won't she be able to change things accordingly?" When Leo's gaze landed on Marcy, she discreetly coughed, muttering, "Hell's bells."

"As a precaution to any and all prying eyes, I spelled Accademia long ago. If I was going to be spending a great quantity of time here, I had to make sure it went undetected from those who would scry. Since then, this museum has been off the supernatural radar. So when you entered, Enid could no longer see you. She does not know what went on here today. It would behoove you all to scrub your brains of this meeting. Once you leave through those doors, instead of remembering our conversations, lament about how you were unable to find the supernatural you were searching for as you head to the Ponte Vecchio. Your time outside of her ability to see you should alter some of her earlier plans, and she will not be able to do much in broad daylight with many humans around."

"Will that be enough to cover our tracks?" I asked. "Scrubbing our brains?"

He shrugged. "It certainly won't hurt. Enid is savvy, but she will not be able to solve the mystery without more clues. Once I unleash my power, she will know, but not until then. Spend some time in the gallery before you go, look at the art, and admire the statues, and when you leave, think of those things. Think of Michelangelo"—he grinned—"and how beautiful his art continues to be. I will see you tomorrow."

We made our goodbyes and headed out. Maria came bustling up to us in the hallway, saying, "Pardon me for leaving. I had some pressing business to attend to. If you follow me, I will take you into the main gallery now." It was hard to know if she was in on it, or had had a mind trick played on her.

It didn't matter.

We followed her into the gallery, and as we walked among the paintings and statues, admiring the beauty, which wasn't hard to do, we talked about the next step. "The note just says show up at the Ponte Vecchio," I said to the group. "Enid has to know we're coming today. I'm hoping the note will be easy to spot."

Rourke shook his head. "I don't care if it's easy to spot. I don't think you should go. You can wait on the street while we take a look."

"I disagree," I said. "I don't think Enid will leave the note for anyone but me."

"I agree with Rourke," Tyler said. "Jeb said you would die if you followed Enid's plan. Why not play it safe and wait on the sidelines? We can pick up a note, no problem."

"Yeah," Ray chimed in. "I can fly over that bridge in a few minutes and scout it out. There's no need for you to set one foot on that structure."

"I don't think so," I said, shaking my head. "I have a feeling that note is for my eyes only, and it won't show itself unless I'm there. Enid is crafty, but I don't think this is a snatch and grab. She wants me to come willingly, to forfeit myself by choice. That will be her coup de grace. Forcing the wolf to come with her tail between her legs. I have to be there." We were nearing the exit of the museum. "Once we get on the street, everybody has to think we failed this mission. You can allow the name Michelangelo to filter through your head, but nothing else. We have to come off as disgruntled. Got it?"

Everyone nodded.

"If you want," Marcy said, "I can spell everyone to temporarily forget the last hour until sometime tomorrow. My memory spell is a twenty-four hour thing. I haven't mastered the quicker version yet, sorry. I've been a little preoccupied lately and am behind on my spell mastery list, which is about two miles long."

"Thanks, but we can't risk it," I said. "Twenty-four hours is too long." I looked around the group. "We're all adults, as well as talented supernaturals. It shouldn't be hard to keep this out of our heads. Like Leo said, once he unleashes his power, Enid will know. We just need to keep it under wraps until tomorrow at dawn."

We filtered out of the gallery onto the street. "The bridge is this way," Lucas said. "It's almost a straight shot from here." We began to walk down the quaint streets. "Man, it's too bad we couldn't find who we were looking for. I'm sorry I couldn't help. Maybe next time?"

"That's okay," I answered. "Once we have the note, we can keep looking. There have to be other places with statues around here."

"We can head back through the Piazza della Signoria on the way back," he suggested. "There are several statues there. Perhaps they will give us some clues."

"That sounds perfect," I told him. "I'm confident we will be victorious. We just have to keep looking."

We covered the blocks quickly. As we neared the bridge, everyone was on high alert. "I'm going to check it out from above first," Ray said. "Wait for me across the street."

"Good idea. And, by the way, when did you get so bossy?" I joked.

He snorted. "The day I was born, Hannon. The day I was

born." He took off before I could get in a snappy comeback. He had been bossy since birth, but I was just learning to appreciate it. It was what had made him an excellent cop. Ray and I had finally achieved a bond, and I was grateful for it.

After the next block, the bridge came into view, and we all slowed.

"So, do you think this note is just going to be sitting right there in the open for us to grab?" Tyler said. "Or are we going to have to search for it?"

"I have no idea," I answered. The bridge wasn't that big, but it was thick with people. It was a unique structure. It was wide and there were parts where it stood three stories high to accommodate living quarters. It was built on massive pilings sunk deeply in the Arno River and was painted in vibrant yellows and golds to give it that eclectic Italian feel.

"This used to be a bustling marketplace back in the day," Lucas informed us, "full of merchants, mainly butchers and larders. They would throw their waste into the river, thus polluting it. Now the big draw is gold. There is jewelry store after jewelry store crowding this bridge. It's prime real estate for tourists, not so much for everyday Italians."

He wasn't kidding. There wasn't even a gap where you could see the sidewalk.

That was a good sign. I didn't think Enid would risk doing something in the middle of a horde of humans. I could be wrong, but I didn't think so.

What do you think? I asked my wolf. *Is this a trap?* She gave a low growl, but showed us walking across the bridge with no issue. *I agree, I think we should try. Something tells me they won't find the note if I'm not there.*

Rourke's voice rumbled his dislike. "Let me go first. You stay here. If I don't find the note, then I'll come back and get you."

"There is not much you like when it comes to my safety being in question." I chuckled. "If we all go together, we'll have strength in numbers. Let's wait for Ray to get back and see what he finds. If he's uncovered something suspicious, we can talk."

It didn't take long for Ray to return. He landed behind Lucas, who startled. I grinned, glad I wasn't the only one with the vampire-landing problem. "I couldn't sense anything amiss," Ray said. "There weren't any weird signatures, and I didn't pick up on any creatures lurking. But I didn't sense anything back at the apartment building either. I don't like it. It feels too easy."

"Join the club," I cracked. "There's no way around it. This entire mission is going to be full of danger. Jeb said that I couldn't follow all of Enid's missives, and I won't, but we're just picking up a note. The chances of her wanting to do a swap right here on this crowded bridge are next to none. We all walk together, keep our eyes peeled, find the instructions, and get out."

Tyler nodded. "I think Jess is right after all. Enid can't take us all out, and she knows we're all together anyway. We go as one, and if we detect danger, we haul ass out." He glanced directly at Ray. "If shit hits the fan, grab Jess and get out. We'll meet you back at Julian's."

Ray nodded before I could protest.

I didn't enjoy everybody making plans about my well-being without my consent, but I understood why they were doing it. "If we sense danger," I said, "I'll get myself out, or I'll fight." I refrained from adding, *like a big girl*. "Ray, I want you to take *Kayla* out if anything happens. She's the most vulnerable. We regroup at Julian's, like Tyler said."

Ray grumbled, but nodded. He knew I was right.

"If I may ask, what exactly are we searching for?" Lucas asked. "You mentioned a note, but is it written on parchment paper? Will it be sealed in an envelope? A Post-it Note? I'm pretty good at finding things, and I'd like to help."

"Of course," I said. "We are grateful for your help and

everything you've done so far. Kayla, please show Lucas the previous note." Kayla complied, pulling it out of her pocket. "I'm assuming the next one will be similar, but we don't know for sure."

Kayla held out the small piece of paper. The Kitsune was quiet for a moment, looking thoughtful. "I take it these are the friends of yours who are missing," he said. "The ones Enid wants to swap for your life."

"They are more than friends, they are family, but yes."

"Then it's imperative we get them back," Lucas said. The fox understood completely. I was really beginning to like this guy. "I will do my best to aid you."

"Thank you," I said. "And the first step in retrieving them is to actually set foot on the bridge. Let's move out."

"Marcy and I will stay back and cover the rear," James said.

"I'll cover the rear with you any time, babe," Marcy quipped, giving him a kiss on the cheek.

"Must you?" I joked.

"I must." Marcy linked arms with James, smiling.

Ray and Lucas went first, followed by Nick. Rourke and I went next, Tyler and Kayla close behind.

The moment my foot hit the cobblestones, I felt something was off.

Rourke picked up on it immediately. *What is it?* he asked. *What's wrong?*

Someone's here, I said. My hackles were up, my wolf on all fours. *But it's not a foe.* The message was confusing. *Enid is muting something. Or trying to mute something.* To everyone, I asked, "Does anyone feel that? I'm getting a strange vibe. It's a low hum. I think someone is here, but it's not an enemy."

"I'm not getting any strange vibes," Ray answered.

Lucas and Nick both shook their heads. "I'm not picking up on anything specific either," Nick said.

Tyler passed us, his nose up in the air.
He stopped midstride, his irises flashing.
"What?" I asked. "Can you scent something?"
"Danny."

11

"*Danny*? Are you sure?" My heart gave a quick, irrational beat. Could he really be here? "Tell me he's alive." I grabbed on to Tyler's arm. "I don't smell death or decay," I added hastily, hope filling my voice. "That means he's alive, right?"

Danny and I had an Alpha-to-wolf connection, but we'd never been able to speak internally unless we were both in our wolf forms. I sent my power out, racing to find that bond.

A faint quiver pinged back, a tiny, tenuous tug on a line.

It was enough for me.

"He's here!" I exclaimed excitedly. "Enid is trying to mute the connection, but I felt him!" He had to be okay. Anything else was unacceptable.

"Damn straight he's here," Tyler said. "She tried to mask his scent, too, but I can smell it. She underestimated my abilities."

Tyler began to walk purposefully through the crowd, and we all followed. He came to a stop in front of one of the many shops lining the street. The name on the door, and the awning above, read: E. FANTONI.

It was a small, unassuming jewelry store.

"I think I'm picking up on the same trail," Lucas commented. "I've never scented who you're tracking before, but there is an unmistakable wolf signature here."

Marcy and James came up behind us. "Marcy," I said, "check for any spell signatures you can find, especially anything that would incapacitate or mask a supe."

"Will do," she said.

"And," I added, "you're going to have to spell this area so we can investigate in-depth without causing a scene."

"Double on it," she said as she closed her eyes.

Tyler tried the handle of the shop, but it was locked. A small note was posted on the door, scrawled hastily in Italian. "What does this say, Lucas?" Tyler asked.

"It says they have taken a *riposo* and will be back later. It's the equivalent of an Italian siesta. It's a little early to do such a thing, as it's only midmorning, but not overly unusual. Many business owners take a *riposo* if they have to run an errand. Things are a little less structured here in Italy."

"It doesn't matter if the shop owner is on a siesta, we can get in there if we have to," I said. "Marcy is spelling this area, nobody will notice."

Tyler abruptly lifted his nose and walked around the side of the building. This particular shop had a side that was exposed to the road, without another shop crowded next to it, which was a rarity on this bridge.

We followed him around to find a large metal door full of rivets set in the stone of the building. It had a long deadbolt securing it.

Rourke said, "I can smell him now. He definitely went through this opening." He walked up to the door, which Tyler was currently investigating, and rested his palm against the black steel. "He's behind here"—he gave me a pointed look—"and that's exactly where Enid wants you to go."

I reached forward to set my hand against the cold metal and closed my eyes.

It didn't matter if this was a trap to lure me, we had to help Danny. We weren't going to leave him behind, which Enid well knew. If he was in pain—or, worse, dying—somewhere below us, it would be awful. I filtered my power out and pushed it through the door and beyond, my wolf generating as much energy as she could to fuel us. It finally pinged back with something. "He's down there," I said. "We're going to have to go get him."

From behind me, Ray said, "I hate to break it to you, but look up and to your right. There's the note we've been waiting for. I'm not looking forward to what that Hag has to say. I have a feeling she's going to make this as painful as possible."

I glanced where Ray indicated, and sure enough, there was a tiny folded square of white poking out between two old, crumbly stones. Rourke reached over my head and yanked it out. It was small, folded only once. He opened it so we could read it:

> YOU ARE RIGHT. THE WOLF IS HERE.
> FIND HIM, IF YOU CAN, AND AWAIT YOUR NEXT INSTRUCTIONS.
> JESSICA GOES ALONE OR THE FEMALE VAMPIRE DIES.

I glanced around the group as we processed the message. "Well, on the bright side, she wants us to find Danny. She's just made it harder than it had to be, because she gets off on that kind of thing. However, I think she will hurt Naomi if we don't listen to her. We have little choice but to follow her instructions."

Rourke shook his head. "Jeb specifically told us not to. I have to believe this is what he meant." He shook the note.

"Why else would Enid want you alone? Her prime motive is to kidnap or kill you. There is no easier way to do that than if you go down there alone."

"I agree, she wants me isolated," I said. "But I also truly believe she wants me to come willingly. Without my submission, her retribution won't be nearly as sweet."

"But you can't know that for sure," Tyler pointed out. "If she's a seer, and this is her only opportunity to get you, she won't hesitate. I agree with Rourke, we have to come up with something other than you just going down there blindly."

"That may be easier said than done," I argued. "We don't have a lot of options."

Kayla cleared her throat. "I might be able to help." We turned toward her, waiting. She exhaled a shallow breath. "I...I sense many dead beings below. They are very old, but can be reanimated. There must be a catacomb somewhere inside these pilings where they stored their dead long ago. I can call them up, and they will help protect you." She fidgeted with her hands. "They are not real people any longer, and they are already down there, so you aren't technically bringing them with you, so it shouldn't count against us. At least, that's what I think."

Her suggestion surprised me, but it shouldn't have.

Her talent was necromancy. She reanimated dead bodies and controlled them with her mind. "Okay...that sounds like an interesting solution," I managed. It *was* interesting, but also creepy as hell. "What does everybody think?"

"Just exactly how strong are these bodies you reanimate?" Marcy asked. "Enid is powerful. I don't think a few dead bodies are going to be much of an obstacle for her if she decides to attack."

Kayla stuck her chin out. "I am the strongest of my kind, and there are not just a few dead bodies down there. I sense hundreds. I could raise an army if I had to. But the most important part is that I will be able to see everything Jessica does, so if she's in trouble, we will know instantly."

Marcy nodded, tapping her index finger against her chin. "That's a pretty tricky plan. I'm on board, but only if I spell Jessica ahead of time with a few protection spells. Enid didn't say anything about fortifying her in that little note of hers. I can even put a tracer on you"—she head-bobbed in my direction—"in case she decides to get grabby."

I nodded. "I like it. The plan has merit." Being accompanied by a bunch of reanimated dead bodies wasn't at the top of my list of things I'd love to experience, but freeing Danny was. I turned to my mate. "What do you think? Kayla has a great point. The piling is directly beneath us, and she will technically be with me, so you'll know what's going on. If there's danger, you can react. Enid didn't specify anything against that." He didn't look convinced. I lay my hand on his arm. "I don't think Enid's plan is to snatch me right now. I believe she left Danny for a reason. Whatever he has to say is going to change the course of what we do, so we have to find him. If Enid still has Naomi, Danny's not going to stop until he gets her back." Naomi was Danny's mate, and they were a perfect match.

"I don't know." Rourke ran one hand through his hair, settling the other on my waist. "Letting you walk into known danger is not going to get any easier, but this is the life we're signing up for." Although he was trying to be stoic, I heard the pain behind his words. "There's no turning back now, is there?" His face took on a comical look, a combination of hope and resignation.

"No," I said. "We are committed. But you're right. Walking into the path of danger is never going to get any easier. We're going to be walking into a lot of dangerous scenarios for the rest of our lives. But if we stay strong together as a team"—I nodded around the group—"and make solid, thoughtful plans, I think we can minimize the chances of anything going south. I value that. And what Kayla and Marcy have offered is exactly that. I'm not interested in walking blindly into harm's way, but I *am* interested in getting the job done." My voice was firm, yet gentle. Rourke already knew that I would do anything to get my team back and save Jax.

He just needed to hear me say it out loud.

His expression was reserved. "Okay, I'm in," he finally said. "The plan is for Kayla to have no less than twenty bodies waiting for you down there, and Marcy spells you before you open that door. Any danger arises, and we storm the castle."

"Good." I addressed Kayla. "I want to make sure you're up for this. Twenty is a lot. At the cemetery, you passed out and were near death."

Kayla gave me a look that indicated I had no idea what I was talking about. "When you found me, I'd just reanimated several thousand against my will, and I was hyper-stressed about my brother. I am in a calm state of mind. This will be no problem. I'm happy to help. Anything to get us closer to finding Jax."

Marcy declared, "It's settled, then. Turn and face me so I can spell the crap out of you."

I did as I was told. "Go easy on me, ye ol' powerful witch. I don't want to break out in hives or have hiccups for a month."

She clucked. "Hey, aftereffects happen. Just so you know, I'm spelling you with three things. A protection-from-death spell, dialed to Enid specifically. It's a tricky one, but I've been practicing it since we found out she was on your trail. The second one is a simple protection charm, an oldie but goodie. It basically works like invisible armor. It will protect you from anything physical down there, like a blow to the head with an ax or a dull knife to the heart."

"Jesus," I said. "Okay."

"Relax, that's not happening. But just in case it does, I'm

stopping it before it spills your insides out. Third is a tracking spell. I don't think even Enid can break it—it's *that* good. That way, if you're snatched, we can find you." She began muttering under her breath.

"I'm glad you're so sure of yourself," I said. That hadn't always been the case. Marcy had struggled with her confidence in crafting spells for a long time. "Nothing like a wishy-washy witch to make you second-guess their abilities." A tingly sensation flooded over my body, followed by warmth and, surprisingly, the smell of popcorn. I wrinkled my nose. "Am I supposed to reek like I work behind the counter at a movie theater?"

"Quiet, you," she shushed. "Can't you see I'm working here?" She muttered a few more things. "And, yes"—she opened one eye—"the smell of butter is standard. It's the buttery goodness that allows us to track you."

I laughed out loud. "The *buttery goodness*? Somehow I don't think so."

Both eyes popped open. "Okay, fine, so I threw in a drama charm by accident," she said. "These spells are tricky. One wrong word inflection and it's an entirely different recipe. If you feel like quoting Shakespeare, don't blame me." I arched an eyebrow. "Well, I guess you can blame me, but don't be mad." After a few more moments, she announced, "I'm done. How do you feel?"

"Fine?" I posed it as a question. "Am I supposed to feel any different?"

"No," she said. "But I felt like I should ask anyway. Any obsessive urges to quote Shakespeare?"

"Get thee to a nunnery," I intoned in my best English accent, joking. *Hamlet* was all I had—and maybe a little *Romeo and Juliet*. "What light through yonder window breaks—"

"Okay, enough, funny girl." Marcy couldn't help but laugh. "It must not have been that powerful of a charm, if that's all you got. That, and I put a Band-Aid over it, so your sonnet-oration urges should be in check."

"Happy fun time is over," Ray grumbled from my right. "Time to get to work. I'm going to position myself outside the piling below. I saw some strange windows set in the stone. I wonder what the hell they used this place for. Strangest bridge I've ever seen." He shook his head. "If I need to get in, I'll break a window. Somebody yell if there's an issue, but I'll likely hear her first."

Rourke nodded. "Good. I'm staying by the door, along with Kayla and Marcy. Tyler and Irish, I want you to continue scanning the bridge. I want to know if there's anybody here who's not supposed to be. Nick and Lucas, you stand outside the shop and make sure nobody interferes. If the owner comes back, keep them occupied."

Everyone agreed.

"I'll put a 'there's nothing to look at here' spell ten feet around this spot," Marcy said, indicating where we stood. "If I make it any larger, people will start to arc in a circle around us and it will look funny."

I turned to Kayla. "Whenever you're ready," I said. "Do you need to sit down?"

She barely refrained from giving me the stink eye. "No. I'm fine right here."

I nodded. I had no idea what I was going to find down there, but Danny had better be in one piece. Rourke took my hand, and I leaned over to give him a kiss. "I'm going to be okay," I murmured into his lips. "My wolf is on high alert, and she's not antsy at all. That's a good sign. She's in charge of supernatural threats. If Enid was down there, we'd feel it."

He nodded, but said nothing. His tension radiated outward. He was poised to strike someone or something.

"Okay, I'm ready," Kayla announced.

"That was quick." I glanced over Rourke's shoulder.

"They weren't buried," she said. "So that made it easier.

Oh, and expect there to be some ghosts down there. Many of these people died a harsh death, some from starvation, but many from murder. Souls tend to linger when death is violent. Just a fair warning." She smiled and winked. I found myself enjoying this side of Kayla. It was one we hadn't seen before. "If you're sensitive to otherworldly beings, you will likely perceive them."

Great. I totally was.

Ghosts were not my favorite by a long shot, but they'd been an asset to me in the past. "Unfortunately, I am sensitive. I found that out the hard way crawling around in Eudoxia's backyard. But none of those ghosts were malicious," I said. "Should I expect different today?"

She shook her head. "No, on the whole, ghosts are very passive beings. They are simply stuck in limbo, most of them not even realizing they're dead. If I inhabit a body with a soul attached, I can help them cross over. But other ghosts won't pay any attention to me."

"Got it," I said. "So any ghosts who talk to me are not coming from the bodies you're reanimating."

"Yep, that's it exactly," she answered cheerily. A happy necromancer. Who knew? "It makes it less macabre that way."

I set my hand on the deadbolt. "I'm going to have to disagree with you there, but I catch your drift." I slid the long latch out of the holes, and the door popped open without any impediment. "Okay, I'm going in."

Rourke growled, "If you're down there any longer than necessary, I'm coming in after you."

"Define longer than necessary," I said as I placed a foot over the threshold.

"Fifteen minutes," he deadpanned.

"How about forty-five?" I negotiated.

"Fine," he said. "But not a minute over."

I leaned over, grabbing his shoulders, planting a kiss on his lips. "I'll be back in forty-three."

12

It took my eyes a moment to adjust to the darkness. The transition from bright daylight to black was doable, but it took time, even for a supernatural with enhanced vision.

Once I could see, I noticed the steep staircase in front of me. It went straight down into what I could only assume was the abyss. The steps themselves were shallow, chipped and falling apart, made of old stone, the mortar that originally kept them together long gone.

On my left stood two trash barrels. It was clear the only thing that this space was used for was to store garbage between weekly trash pickups. I couldn't imagine the shop owner descending these stairs for any reason.

Here goes nothing, I told my wolf as I descended the first few steps. She gave me a *you can do it* bark. She still wasn't ruffled, which put me at ease—at ease as I could be knowing we were descending into the arms of almost two dozen waiting dead bodies.

I had to keep my mind on the prize—Danny. He was the reason I was doing this.

As I went lower, my eyes adjusted even more. Wolves had excellent eyesight, and mine was no exception. My retinas were grabbing light from every conceivable place they could find it. It worked to give me a hazy outline of the shapes around me, which wasn't much. Just lots and lots of crumbling stone.

How's it going? Rourke asked in my mind. I wasn't sure how long we were going to be able to be tethered if Enid had any say.

It's going fine, I replied. *I've encountered nothing but steps and crumbling rock. These puppies go straight down.* I began to hear movement below, not so much moaning, but more like sticks clicking together. *I'm hearing some bone-on-bone action,* I told him. *I must be getting close to the bottom.*

You're probably about two stories down, Rourke said. *How are the smells down there?*

My wolf had been parceling them away. *So far it just smells wet, moldy, and old.* There was a little whiff of Danny, but not much. *I'm not getting enough of Danny's signature to let me know where he is. Enid is still playing games.* I wish she'd stop. It was a waste of time. There was a clatter about ten feet below me. It sounded like bodies running into each other. *Ask Kayla if she can see down here. It sounds like the bodies are crashing into each other. I should've brought a flashlight.*

Do you have a Pack phone on you? Rourke asked. *These days they come with a built-in flashlight. Kayla says she's having trouble seeing, as dead bodies don't have the best eyesight. That was a joke, in case you're wondering, since skeletons don't have eyes.*

I got it. Very funny. I do have a Pack phone. I reached into my back pocket and pulled it out. *Ah, technology. We forget in our supernatural-ness that innovation can be our friends.* Rourke was saying something, but he was breaking up. Enid had had enough of our communication. Either that, or these walls were just too thick, because who knew how this mind-action worked anyway? *I'm sorry, babe. I can't hear you any longer. I'll be back before you know it.*

I reached the end of the staircase and swiped on the phone light. I stifled a scream once I got a good look at my compatriots. "Holy gods." It came out as a low moan. The scene in front of me was straight out of some crazy-bad horror movie, one in which lifeless bodies were sent to terrorize the innocent heroine.

A mass of skeletons stood facing me.

All seemingly eager to tear their sharp metacarpals into my flesh and cackle while they did it.

This was so unnatural.

"Kayla," I called. "I know you can see me, but I don't know if you can hear me. We didn't talk about it. You have to back the suckers up so I have some room to move."

All at once, the freaky zombie bones took two steps back and parted so I could get through.

She could hear me. That was a relief. It made it a little less spooky. And at least I had someone to talk to down here. "I've got a flashlight as long as my phone battery has a charge," I said. "Let's get this over with. I'll lead, you and the horde follow."

There was only one direction to go.

A long, narrow hallway snaked out in front of me. It was too dark to see how far it went, but it couldn't be that long. The piling only had so much space. I had no idea what Ray had been talking about, because I couldn't detect any windows.

Can you scent anything? I asked my wolf as we began to walk. *I'm not getting much, but you're way better at it than me.* My wolf infused us with more energy as I drew the damp, stale air over my tongue. I was only getting a little of Danny's signature. Frustrated, I yelled, "You brought me here to get him, and here I am! If you haven't forgotten, you *want* me to find him. So I'd appreciate it if you'd stop playing games and show me where he is." And then I muttered, "What, are we in first grade?"

Something ice cold brushed by my face.

A second later, a moan sounded in my ear.

Oh, goody. A ghost. "Kayla, ghost encounter number one is happening right now." I glanced behind at the stick figures shuffling in my wake. I didn't know if I should address them directly, or if she just heard everything. These would've been good questions to ask before I descended into this pit.

Too late now.

You come...onto my lair. A breathy voice hit my ear. *Seeking...something.*

"That's correct, I do seek something," I told it. "Any chance you could show me where the other living, breathing person is down here?" The hallway took a sharp turn to the left, and I followed. If it got any tighter, my bone army was going to have to go single file. That would make backing me up more difficult.

What price are you willing to pay? the ghost asked on the barest of breath.

I swatted by my ear. It was really cold, which made me wonder why ghosts were always cold. They had to mess with the air molecules. "Kayla," I called. "This ghost wants me to pay it for help. I have no idea what to do. How do you pay a ghost?"

You set me free, the ghost answered.

"That's fine," I said. "I have no idea how to do such a thing, but I have somebody who can help you. In fact, I have two people. There's a necromancer upstairs and a reaper outside this piling. Both of them could help you, if you decide to accept that as your form of payment."

You will set me free now, the ghost insisted.

"We're not getting anywhere with this, buddy," I told it. The hallway abruptly ended. There weren't any doors, just a solid rock wall on all sides. I flashed my phone around, looking for an opening somewhere. I turned around and stifled a gasp. Using a flashlight in a dark hallway and then turning to see a bunch of skeletons bunched up behind you was a heart attack waiting to happen. It didn't matter that I'd known they were there. It was still unsettling. "Kayla, I need you to back these guys up. We ran into a dead end." As they started to shuffle backward, I glanced around for any opening or doorway I'd missed. Ray had said he'd seen windows, so I was certain there was more to this place than I could see right now.

You will set me free, the ghost said once again, brushing by my ear with a little more thrust.

"Ghostman, you're a broken record. If you tell me how to set you free, I'll do it. But I have no idea how to do it on my own. On the other hand, if you show me where the other living person is down here, I can get somebody to help you."

There is one...

I stopped, the ghost snagging my attention. "There is one *what*? A person? Are you talking about another living, breathing soul down here?"

This way...

I chuckled. "I can't see where you are—"

A small orb of light flashed in front of me, taking me by surprise. It began to move, floating into the wall straight ahead.

I walked forward and placed my hand on the stone and pushed. It was solid. "I can't follow you!" I called. "You're going to have to show me a real, honest-to-goodness corporeal way in." I waited. The ghost didn't emerge.

This could be Enid, toying with me again.

Kayla had backed the bodies down the hallway so I had room to move. I ran my hand over the wall, searching for a way through, while still holding my flashlight. "Danny!" I shouted. It couldn't hurt to try. "It's Jessica! If you can make some noise, I can find you." I sent out my energy, searching for our Alpha-wolf connection.

It hit something. I stopped moving. It had been a bigger tug than last time.

Did you feel that? I asked my wolf. *We just have to find out which direction it's coming from.* "Danny, do it again! I felt it, but I need more!"

This time it was a double tug.

He was conscious, and he could hear me!

I frantically drummed my fist on the wall, standing on my tiptoes, and then going down on my knees. Nothing gave way. I should have been able to hear him or scent him if he was this close.

"Enid!" I called angrily. "You're masking a doorway, aren't you? Why? I'm here alone, just as you asked. I know Danny has information you want me to have. It's time to be done with this! Show me the damn door." I refrained from cursing more, which was what I wanted to do.

All of a sudden, I was shoved backward, my spine smashing into the wall, followed by my head.

My phone clattered to the ground, the flashlight instantly blinking off. I couldn't move. My teeth gnashed together. "What…do…you want, Enid?" I grated. "Are you going to kill me now?"

Cold air brushed by my neck, and a different ghostly voice whispered, *I want you to pay for what you did.*

I had no idea if the ghost was Enid or if Enid was channeling the ghost. It was a little beside the point at the moment. "I'm trying to make it right," I told her through a clenched jaw. "Your sister believes there's a way to fix this. I'm sorry about Bianca. I really am. Search my heart and you'll know I speak the truth. I had no idea that ending Ardat Lili's life would have such a dire consequence. But I'm willing to make a sacrifice to get us back on track." The pressure on my chest increased, instead of decreased. Any more and I would lose all ability to breathe. She could easily kill me right here, but she was holding back. I grasped on to that. I sputtered, "If you kill me now, that glimmer of hope dies along with me and you know it. Along with a whole lot of innocent people. I don't know if you're a sadist, but if you're not, give me a chance and I will do everything in my power to make it right. I swear!"

All the pressure let up at once, and I collapsed to my knees.

I rubbed my neck, gasping for air.

Fists began to pound on the stone wall across from me. "Jessica, is that you?" Danny's voice was frantic. "Bloody hell, get me out of this tomb!"

I jumped up, searching for my phone in the dirt, my fingers finally brushing it. Luckily, it was still working. I flipped the flashlight on and scanned the wall. "Danny! I'm here!" There was no door to be found. "How did you get in there? Is there a door on your side?"

"I don't know how she stuffed me in here," he replied. "I was knocked out, which is her favorite pastime. It's as dark as the devil's arse in here, but I'm working my way around the room now."

I was so relieved to hear his voice. He was okay! And he still had his sense of humor. I hoped that meant things hadn't been too dire for him and Naomi during their capture. "I'm going to walk around out here," I called to him. "There has to be a way in."

The orb of light popped through the wall in front of me, startling me. A moment later, coldness touched my cheek. *Look...down,* the breathy voice told me.

This was definitely not Enid.

The ground below me was caked with dirt and old, moldy straw. I got down on my knees and began to dig with my hands, elongating my claws to help with the job. Less than a foot down, my nails scraped metal. It was a grate of some kind. "Danny!" I called. "Check the floor. I just found a grate, and I can hear water below. This must have been a place to smuggle goods in and out of the city back in the day."

A moment later, Danny replied, "I found one! It's going to take me a minute to dig it out." I could hear him cursing and complaining, and smiled.

I propped my flashlight against the wall so Kayla could see while I used both hands to uncover the rest of the grate. This must've been a main way to get goods to the bridge, because it was large. Four feet long by three feet wide. As the dirt and straw were cleared away, a little light filtered in from below. I could see black water lapping ten feet down.

I straddled the steel, curling my fingers around the slats. *We're going to need all our strength here,* I told my wolf. Energy raced through me as I hefted upward.

The thing wouldn't budge.

I got back on my knees, tracing the outline with my hands. I found the problem. The ends were bolted deeply into the stone walls.

I heard metal clang in the next room. A moment later, Danny yelled, "I ripped the bloody thing out of the floor! I'm going to jump into the water. When I come up, call for me, and I'll follow your voice."

Before I had a chance to tell him that I hadn't gotten my end up yet, I heard a splash. He was in the water. I grabbed on to the metal bars near a large bolt and tugged with all my strength. "Danny!" I called. "I'm trying to get this thing up, but it's secured tightly to the stone." A face emerged in the water below, and I couldn't contain my shout of joy. "Danny! It's so great to see you."

"I'm happy to see you, too, but I need out of this water. My most sensitive parts are turning blue already." He was too far down to help me by pushing upward.

"Kayla," I called over my shoulder, "are any of your guys strong enough to help me? I need to get this metal barrier up.

I've got it loosened on one side, but if I had more hands, it would go quicker." Four skeletons stepped forward. They each maneuvered to a different part of the grate. I couldn't believe bare bones would be much help, but it was worth a try. "Okay, on the count of two. One…two." I pulled hard, channeling my Lycan side, shifting just enough until I heard a satisfying crack as the barrier gave way on all sides.

The dead guys had actually been stronger than I'd imagined. One of them had loosened the other side enough to give me the leverage I needed.

"Step back," I told the skeletons. They obeyed immediately. I called down to Danny, "Almost there. Just let me set this thing down." I placed the heavy grate along the stone wall.

"That's all well and good," he answered, shock in his voice. "But who the feck are they?"

13

"They are a bunch of reanimated bodies," I said. "Kayla's helping me out. She's a necromancer we bumped into on our way home from the swamp. There's a lot to fill you in on, but in a nutshell, the reason I'm down here with a bunch of skeletons is that Enid wouldn't let me bring another living person down here, so this was our solution."

Danny had no trouble climbing the ten feet out of the hole. He was dripping wet as he emerged. I hugged him fiercely, stinky water and all, trying not to get overly emotional.

It wasn't working.

"It's good to see you, too, Jessica." He patted my shoulder. "There, there. No need to get worked up. I'm fine. Alive and well. See? No worse for wear."

I pulled back, scrutinizing his appearance, looking for any ill treatment, but finding none. "It's wonderful to see that you're fine, but how are Naomi and Jax? I hope they were treated just as well." My voice was a little disbelieving. "I don't see a single scratch on you. I thought Enid would be rougher on her prisoners."

Danny paled visibly. "What do you mean, how is Naomi? And who is Jax?" His voice was agitated. "I was snatched by the Hag on my own. Naomi and I had just finished—" He cleared his throat. "Well, then, that's none of your business, then, is it?" He combed his dark hair off his face with his fingers, and water trickled down over his shoulders. "I'd gotten up to go to the washroom after the single best night of my life and—that witch had no decency whatsoever. She snatched me right off the bloody toilet!" His voice was indignant. "Honestly, I don't remember much else. I awoke in some sort of supernatural-proof bunker. It was boring as hell, but all in all, I was fine. Then I awoke here." He glanced around. "By the way, where is here?"

"We're currently standing inside a piling of the Ponte Vecchio in Florence, Italy." His eyebrows shot up. "And there's no easy way to tell you this," I started, not wanting to tell him but knowing I had to, "but Enid took Naomi that same night. She also snatched a teenager named Ajax, who's an ice troll and the younger brother of Kayla, who is currently helping us out with these dead guys." I thumbed behind me. "I'll tell you more, but we need to get out of here right now. Everyone is waiting for us up top." The skeletons turned in unison and started to march back the way we'd come. The clacking bones sounded so strange. Not a melody I wanted to remember.

Before I could turn to follow them, Danny placed both his hands on my shoulders, his face imploring. "Where are they, then? Where is she keeping Naomi and the boy? I have to find her." His face was a mask of anger mixed with pain. "We must leave right now."

I knew how he felt.

"We don't know where they are, but we're working on it," I told him. "We will get them back. I promise you. Enid is playing with us. We're assuming you have information to share and that's why she let you go."

He shook his head. "I have nothing to contribute. I was down in that blasted bunker the entire time, alone. Had I known she'd taken Naomi, I would've gone crazy to get out of there! Instead, I just lay there counting the ways I wanted to tear her head off when we met face-to-face."

I grabbed him and began to haul him after the skeletons. "Danny, I know this is a lot to take in, but we have to get out of here. Naomi isn't on the bridge, so the best thing we can do to help your mate is find the others." I tugged him along. "Rourke's up top, not so patiently waiting for me to return. Ray is outside this piling. But I swear to you, we will find her and Jax and get them back. I'll fill you in on everything once we get out. Just trust me."

"I trust you implicitly."

It didn't take long to find the steps. In front of us, the skeletons spread out to either side, pressing themselves against the walls. And then, as one, they fell to the ground, bones clattering, sounding like a giant box of matchsticks being upended.

Danny slapped a palm over his heart. "Well, that was quite horrifying." He arched a look at me. "A necromancer, you say? I suppose it's a handy skill, but it's too morbid for my tastes. I'll take a blood-sucking vampire any day."

We took the steps two at a time, trying not to lose our footing. At the top, the steel door was firmly sealed. I reached for the deadbolt and wrenched it open.

Bright sunshine bathed us as we stepped out. We both blinked.

Rourke pulled me into his arms immediately. "Thank goodness," he murmured into my hair. "When we lost internal contact I was worried. Then Kayla saw you being hurt. Once the flashlight you were holding went out, I tried in vain to get the door open, but it wouldn't budge. I was just about to go over the side of the bridge to try to find you." His relief washed over me.

I pressed my lips to his neck. "I'll make it up to you later," I whispered as I drew back. "But it was a success. Look who I found down there."

Tyler and Danny had just finished reuniting with a big hug. "How'd you get wet?" Tyler asked. "Decided to go for a swim in the Arno, huh?"

"Something like that," Danny replied, his voice distracted. "Listen, do you have any information on where my mate is? Do you know where the Hag has taken her?"

Tyler looked stricken. "We thought she was with you." He darted a look my way.

"Apparently, Enid took them separately," I said. Ray landed by my side a second later. "Danny didn't know she was missing until a few moments ago."

"Damn right I didn't know she was missing," Danny swore. We all stood in the small space next to the jewelry store, looking like a group of tourists regrouping. If Danny had had more room, he would've begun to pace. "We have to find her immediately. Enid is powerful. That Hag could end her life if she wanted to! There's no time to waste."

"Finding her is our top priority," I assured him. I couldn't tell Danny about what had happened earlier. I struggled to keep the encounter completely out of my mind. My wolf picked up on it and began to help, throwing energy at me. *Thanks,* I told her. "Danny, I promise we'll have more information soon. But right now, we have to head back to the Compound. There's a reason why Enid let you go, and we're going to have to figure out what it is."

Tyler placed his arm around Kayla's shoulders. She didn't look any worse for wear after reanimating twenty dead bodies. "I'd like to introduce you to Kayla," he told Danny. "She helped Jessica down there with the bodies." He glanced at me, his grin wide enough to show a dimple. "How was it, anyway? As cool as I imagined?"

"*Cool* wouldn't be the exact word I'd use to describe it," I replied wryly. "It was fine—as far as hanging out with a bunch of skeletons goes." I shrugged. "Now that I think about it, it was actually less creepy than I thought." I addressed Kayla. "There's a ghost down there who ended up helping me. It begged me to free it in return. I feel like I owe it a favor, but I have no idea what to do."

Ray surprised me by replying first. "I'll take care of it." Without another word, he hauled open the door and walked inside.

Kayla nodded. "He's the better man for the job. I would have to search for its body, which would take a while."

Danny held his hand out to Kayla. "It's a pleasure to meet you. Necromancy is quite…impressive." They shook hands. "We appreciate your assistance, of course."

Kayla's face was hopeful. "Do you have any news about my brother? His name is Ajax, Jax for short. I realize you weren't with the others, but did Enid happen to mention anything?"

"No, I'm sorry. I have no news," he said. "I never had words with the Hag."

Kayla looked crestfallen, so I asked, "If you never spoke to her, how did you know it was Enid who took you?"

"Well…" Danny scratched his head, and errant drops of water flicked to the ground. "I'm not sure…I just knew." He glanced up to the sky and then back at me, his face confused. "To tell you the truth, it's all a bit hazy. I do remember the loo, then bits of the bunker, then here. But, honestly, when I heard your voice, it was like I'd just awoken from a deep trance."

I patted his shoulder. "Don't worry about it," I said. "I have a feeling it's going to come back to you bit by bit. Enid wouldn't want to show her cards all at once. We should head out."

"Good idea," James agreed. "Callum will be landing in a few hours, and we need to figure out our plan before then."

Lucas pulled out a phone. "I'll call the driver. He can pick us up a few blocks from here. Unless, that is, you'd like to go check out another museum? There are many statues we can still look for." His voice was insinuating, and I appreciated Lucas trying to keep us on track.

"No," I replied. "I think we've done enough for today. There are more pressing matters to attend to. The first of them being to figure out why Enid let Danny go."

Nick quickly introduced Lucas to Danny, and Danny stuck out his hand. "Nice to meet you, mate. Are you from around here?"

Lucas nodded. "Yes, I was born in Southern Italy. I am part of the Mediterranean Pack. Julian is my Alpha."

Danny bunched his nose, cocking his head. "You don't smell like a wolf. Well, a little bit like a wolf, but not entirely. What are you?" We were smooth when it came to sleuthing out supernaturals. It seemed we could all use an etiquette lesson…or two or three.

"I'm half Kitsune," Lucas replied, holding up his finger as he spoke into the phone, directing the driver where to go.

"Kit-*what*?" Danny asked, looking confused.

I grabbed Danny's wet sleeve and began to lead him off the bridge. "Kitsune. He's part Japanese fox," I told him. "Like I said, we have a lot to fill you in on. You're going to have to be patient."

Danny met my gaze, and I registered the pain and loss in his eyes. "Patience is not my strongest virtue, Jessica."

I tightened my grip on him. "I know. You're worried about your mate, which is totally understandable. But we're going to find her. My guess is she's staying strong for Jax. I can only assume Enid put them together for a reason. The Hag must not have wanted Jax to be alone. Either he's too innocent or too strong. Either way, they're together." Maybe Enid had some redeeming qualities after all. I hadn't had a chance to tell the group about our encounter in the piling, but I was hopeful she let me go because she wanted to give me a chance. "And, just so you know, I'm prepared to swap my life for theirs, if that's what it takes."

Danny looked both horrified and relieved. He shook his head. "It won't come to that, I'm certain."

"How can you be so sure?" I asked.

"Because after Naomi and I…consummated our bond," he said, trying hard to not be his normal, Danny self and reveal too much, which I appreciated, "our internal connection sprang to life. I've been calling to her since you told me she was gone." He grinned. "I'm finally getting something back."

14

"Just try relaxing," I coaxed. "It could take some time to establish a connection." We were walking along the Arno, moving toward the meeting point with the driver. Danny had just lost the tenuous connection he'd established with Naomi.

"I'm telling you she's gone," Danny said, fear and anger ringing in his voice. "It was there one moment, gone the next. Like a plug had been pulled from the socket. Enid has to be controlling this. And she's taunting me. That blasted Hag!"

I rubbed his shoulder. "It's been five minutes," I consoled. "Enid might be moving her. We don't know what's going on. Take a break and try again in a little while."

Before he could respond, Marcy let out a shriek from behind.

My head whipped around, my fists automatically going up. "What? What is it?"

Marcy gestured wildly toward a crowd to her right. "I just saw that witch from Tally's coven! The haughty one. Oh, dang it, what's her name? Exotic-looking and a total nastypants. Ceres, the Goddess of Fertility, is her sister. I think she was the one who made you get on that joke of a scooter and ride into the lake."

"Angie?" I asked, darting a glance at Rourke. "If it's her, we need to find her." This was big. I addressed the group. "Rourke and I will go after her. Tell Ray to take the sky when he gets here."

"I'm going with you," Marcy insisted. "She's a powerful witch. If we try to capture her, we're going to need my spells. There's no way you're taking her otherwise."

"If Marcy goes, I go," James said.

"Okay, fine." I couldn't argue with sound logic. "The rest of you head back to the Compound. We'll find our way back when we're done." Tyler looked like he was getting ready to argue, and I held up my hand. "You're wasting time debating this. There's no way we can all go, we'll attract too much attention. Head back to the Compound, get Danny some fresh clothes, keep an eye on Julian, and wait for Dad. We won't be long. We'll either find her quickly, or we won't."

Tyler nodded once. "We'll see you back there."

Rourke was already halfway down the street, and I hurried to catch up, careful not to run too quickly. We had to blend in with the humans around us. Marcy and James had gone down to the next block over. We were tracking the witch's scent and would meet in the middle. Once I was shoulder to shoulder with my mate, I asked, "Sense anything?"

I received a growl in response. "I never forget a signature. And hers is all over here. There's so much of it, my guess is she is staying somewhere close by. When I find her, she's going to be sorry she ever met me."

"Easy there, big fella," I told him, grabbing his hand. "You're not going to be able to tear her head from her shoulders today. Plus, we're going to need her for questioning. If she's here, alive and well, it has to have something to do with Ceres, which, in turn, has something to do with Tally. It's a lucky break Marcy spotted her."

When we'd first met Angie, she'd tricked us into going out under heavy sorcerer fire on a moped that wasn't spelled, putting both our lives in danger. And, in general, she was a royal pain in the ass. We'd almost died. Rourke had vowed that if he ever set eyes on her again, he'd kill her.

"Her being here doesn't surprise me in the least," Rourke said, his emerald irises flashing, his predator side at the forefront. "If she's dumb enough to stay in this city, we'll find her. I can't guarantee I'm going to be magnanimous when I do, but I'll allow you to question her before I end her life." As much as I disliked Angie—and I did wholeheartedly—I was from a different era than Rourke. Settling our differences with death wasn't my first choice. But I was going to reserve judgment until we found out what Angie had to say.

Rourke wouldn't kill her unless we agreed, no matter how angry he was.

We followed her scent trail for a few more blocks, turning right, coming face-to-face with Marcy and James. "Pick up on anything new?" I asked Marcy.

"No," she groused. "Nothing concrete. My nose is not as good as yours, but she's left a magic signature around this neighborhood. When a witch casts spells, they leave a residue, especially if the witch who is casting doesn't give a crap who finds her trail. As a child, you learn to clean up after yourself. But I guess I'm thankful she's a sloppy amateur. Her signature is particular, too, which is why I remembered it. It tastes like onions and Pop-Tarts." I made a face. "Yup, it's as unappealing as it sounds."

Rourke stalked across the next street, his nose in the air. "Her scent ends here." We all looked up, scanning the buildings.

In the next instant, Ray was beside me. "Errant witch on the loose, I heard?"

"That's correct," I answered, proud of myself for not startling. "A particularly scheming one too. She's the one who led Rourke and me astray when we were trying to escape the Coven when the sorcerers attacked. She is Ceres's little sister."

"The goddess?" Ray said, and when I nodded, he whistled.

"The very same," I answered. "My guess is Ceres has Tally. When I killed Ardat Lili, a shockwave blasted through the supernatural community. Ceres must've been in tune to the message and knew the Coalition needed a witch. Tally is the most powerful witch around, and the likely choice. From the little I know about Ceres, she's self-centered and spoiled. I'm sure she felt like she should've been given the mantle of Coven leader when the former witch leader died years ago, but the power passed over her and went to Tally." That had made for one pissed-off goddess.

But you can't argue with power.

It chooses its own master.

Who knew how the process worked, but the power of a Sect always found its true leader. And once it did, it infused that person with superior strength, allowing the chosen one to lead the group. It was how it had been for millennia.

Marcy nodded. "Now that I've seen Angie here with my own eyes, I'm confident Ceres has Tally. The witches who I've been in contact with since her disappearance must be hedging their bets. If Ceres wins, she'll be the new leader of the Coven, and these witches will owe her fealty, so they are hesitant to cross her. It's totally slimy, but understandable. Ceres has enough power to render them infertile, which is her specialty. That's a big threat for a witch. We're only fertile every few years as it is. I just hope my old, crotchety aunt holds on. If Tally comes out on top, the witches who have kept quiet have lost nothing."

I nodded. "It looks like we're going to have to find a witch in this town who will trust us, and who is ultimately on Tally's side. It's not Angie, that's for sure."

We crossed over the next street to where Rourke was standing. Marcy's fingers were up. "Angie cast a spell here a few moments ago." Marcy muttered something under her breath. "She's masking herself, but I can't tell as what. I don't know what Angie's special talents are. I wish I did. She could have excellent glamour skills and now looks like an Italian bag lady who smells like olives."

I angled my nose in the air and took in a breath. *Are you picking up on anything?* I asked my wolf. She responded with a frustrated bark as she tossed our energy outward in every direction. After a moment, it came back empty. "I'm getting nothing," I said. "In fact, there's not an unknown supernatural within a mile radius around us at the moment. Unless she can cloak herself like a master spell crafter, she's not here."

"I say we keep looking," Rourke said, beginning to pace. "She's not that smart. We witnessed that firsthand. That leaves room for mistakes. Who knows how long she can hold on to a complicated spell?"

"Fine," I agreed. "Let's scour a few blocks in every direction and see what we come up with. If we don't pick up on anything, we'll have time to look again tomorrow. She has to know we're on to her, or she wouldn't have taken the time to spell herself so well."

"My guess is she was sent to spy on us," James said, arching his head around to glance up at the buildings. "If I was Ceres and knew we were in town, which she must, I would have someone tail us. It would have to be someone she trusts, and who better than her sister who has a grudge against you?"

Rourke nodded. "That sounds about right. If we can't track her here, another way we can get to her is pretend we're not looking for her and let her find us."

"Yeah," Ray said. "And let's not forget she won't be expecting an attack from above. I'm just the guy for the job."

We searched in vain for another few hours, but came up short. There hadn't been a whiff of anything, not even a single sweat molecule. Angie was nowhere to be found. We'd finally hailed a cab and had it drop us off a mile from the Compound.

Ray had gone ahead.

"It's going to be hard to get my father away from Julian tonight," I said as we walked along the picturesque road leading to the villa. It was late afternoon. The sun would set in an hour or two. "We can't discuss any of this with Julian or his wolves." That put us at a distinct disadvantage. How were we going to come up with a plan before dawn? We didn't even know where we were supposed to be heading, as Danny couldn't remember anything yet. Enid had to have more up her sleeve. She wouldn't let a valuable captive go without a good reason.

"I've been in contact with Callum on and off today," James said. "He's aware of most of what's been going on. He trusts our read on Julian. We will be discreet until we can find time to talk amongst ourselves."

"If it doesn't happen tonight," Rourke stated, "we'll head into town before dawn and talk about it then. We'll find a way."

"If Julian leaves at any time during the night, I can put a containment spell around you guys while you discuss things," Marcy said. "In fact, the first thing I'm going to do when I get back to the villa is scour the house for spells and whatnot. There might be a chance Julian and Ceres are working together. I wouldn't rule it out. Powerful supernaturals often align, especially at a time of upheaval."

With everything that was going on in our world, *upheaval* was a kind word.

"Did anybody remember to ask Lucas if he knows who Julian's sleeping with?" I asked. "What if the two of them *are* together? That would thicken this plot considerably."

"A witch and a wolf?" James joked as he slung his arm around Marcy's shoulders. "I highly doubt it." He pulled her close, running his stubble over the top of her head. "You have to be made of sterner stuff than Julian is to put up with a witch."

Marcy elbowed her mate, giggling. "Ceres did start out as a witch, but she's been a goddess for several centuries. And a powerful one at that. I don't think they're a mated pair, but like I said, power attracts power, especially from two people who desire it above anything else in the world."

"Is Ceres beautiful?" I asked curiously. "Julian seems to indulge in vanity."

"Do ducks float?" Marcy chuckled. "Do gerbils love to run around in clear balls?" Um, maybe? "She's stunningly beautiful. We're talking flawless beauty. Most gods and goddesses are. Back in the day, they had to get people to believe in them and pray for them. Nobody is going to put faith in a toothless bag lady. They'd just run screaming. So, yes, she's a looker."

I chuckled. "Only you could put ducks, gerbils, and flawless beauty into one sentence. You're talented, my friend."

"I don't think Nick had a chance to talk to Lucas while we were out," Rourke said. "But I hope he did on the way back. If Ceres and Julian are together, it's going to complicate things tenfold."

We were getting close to the villa, so we had to wrap up our discussion. "We say nothing more until we get to a place where we can talk freely."

Everyone nodded in agreement.

As we neared, Julian opened the front door and walked onto the veranda. "Sounds like you had quite an adventure today," he called. "Sorry to have missed it. I had business that couldn't wait. I hope you'll forgive me."

"We had a good day," I answered. "And of course we forgive you. We were happy to find our friend Danny, so it was a productive day." I knew no one had divulged any details to Julian about what had transpired with Danny's rescue.

"It seems he took a little dip in the Arno River," Julian replied. "I can't wait to hear the details." Even from this distance, I could see the hard look in Julian's eyes. He didn't appreciate being left out when things were happening on his turf.

We're going to have to give him some details, I said to Rourke. *He's an Alpha, he can scent a lie. He won't be content with half a story.*

Let me take the lead, Rourke replied. *He doesn't respect you, or your power. Hostile energy radiates from him. If I give him the story and tell him that's that, it will be done.*

Fine with me, I answered. *But with Julian, I don't think it will* ever *be done.*

15

We were all seated around the big kitchen table once again. We'd just finished a late afternoon meal of pasta and fresh vegetables prepared by Lucas. It'd been utterly delicious. My father's plane was about to land in less than an hour, and we were heading out to the landing strip soon.

Ray was prowling the grounds somewhere, and Eudoxia was gone. Otherwise, we were all accounted for. During the meal, we'd stayed away from any big topics, keeping the conversation light. Julian hadn't pressed us yet for Danny's rescue story, which was fine by me.

Marcy's chair scraped over the tile floor as she stood. "If you'll all excuse me, I'm going to head upstairs and change before we go." She inclined her head at me. "Julian was kind enough to get us all some toiletries and some new clothes when he noticed we hadn't brought much luggage."

Some days, I wished I had an internal connection with Marcy. Other days, I was as happy as a clam that we didn't. Having her in my head would've driven me slowly insane, but it would've been completely useful right about now.

Her voice had come out even, but there was something she wanted me to see. I nodded along with her. "Changing might be a good idea," I agreed as I stood. "I've been in these clothes for days." I addressed Julian, who sat at the head of the table. "It was incredibly nice of you to think of us. Buying supplies hadn't even entered my mind today." My gaze settled on Kayla, who was the only other woman in the room. "Would you like to join us?"

"Sure," she said, pushing her chair back.

"If you'll excuse us, we'll go freshen up," I told the assembled group. "We'll meet you guys on the terrace in a few minutes, then we can head over to meet my father's plane."

Julian rose, walking around the table. "Take your time," he said. "The plane won't land for another forty minutes. The wolves and I"—he glanced over his shoulder at my team—"will have a cigar on the veranda while we wait. I am still eager to hear how you ran into your friend today." His voice held an unmistakable order.

He was done waiting.

"No problem," I said. "We'll only be a few minutes. The guys can fill you in on some of it while you wait." As I turned and walked away, I said to Rourke, *I'll let you know what happens. Marcy's either found something, or she has something to tell me. We won't be long.*

I knew Rourke would handle it, but alerting Julian to exactly what was going on would open a lot of questions. Ones we weren't able to answer. It would piss him off to be kept in the dark, but there was nothing that could be done.

Kayla and I followed Marcy up the right side of the massive curved stairway. It was crafted of white marble, totally ornate and gorgeous, with a wrought-iron banister. Marcy made a beeline toward a room near the end of the right wing. Eudoxia's room had been on the left.

I was about to say something, but she turned, bringing a single finger up to her lips. She shook her head as she slowly opened the door, motioning for us to follow her into the room. I wasn't moving fast enough, so she hooked her hand under my elbow and, with surprising strength, yanked me the rest of the way in, shutting the door firmly behind us. I gave an unladylike, "*Ooof*," as I stumbled. "You don't have to be so—"

She glared at me, effectively silencing me.

Then she smiled sweetly at Kayla, who hadn't said a word. She began to walk around the room, arms animated, making small talk. "Isn't it gorgeous here? This is my room with James. You and Rourke are next door on the end, and Kayla and Tyler are across the hall." My eyes darted to Kayla, who blushed and bowed her head, but didn't deny she was sharing a room with my brother. Marcy picked up a pair of jeans and a white blouse that had been neatly folded on a massive king-size bed and began to disrobe. "There are so many new smells here in Italy." She arched an eyebrow at me. "The scents are only a little like home." She donned the pants quickly. "Don't you think?"

My wolf was already processing the air as I began to pace. It wasn't until I reached the closet that I picked up on something. My head shot to Marcy.

She grinned and nodded, tapping her finger to her temple.

Angie had been here.

I opened the closet door, announcing in a singsong voice, "Oh, good, they have robes here." It was an asinine thing to say, but I had to fill the void. Small talk had never been my specialty.

It seemed Angie had spelled the room to get rid of her scent, but had forgotten the closet and that smells tended to permeate spaces. Her signature lingered in the corners as I moved the hangers around to inspect it further.

This meant only one thing.

Ceres and Julian *were* together in some aspect, and Ceres had likely sent her sister here to keep tabs on us, like James had thought originally, with Julian's permission.

I closed the closet door and turned to see Marcy holding a pad of paper and a pencil. She turned the tablet to me so I could read it.

> DON'T SAY ANYTHING IMPORTANT. ENTIRE VILLA IS SPELLED.

I walked over and took the pad from her and began to scribble.

> CAN YOU COUNTERSPELL IT?

She arched a perfectly manicured eyebrow at me like I was a moron and plucked the pencil out of my hand like she had better places to be.

> OF COURSE. BUT IF I DO, IT WILL ALERT MS. NASTY WE'RE ON TO HER.

I nodded as I tore the paper from the pad and folded it up, sticking it in my back pocket. Angie was incompetent in so many ways, but we didn't want her to know we were on to her just yet. Her haughty expression and sneering gaze were forever etched into my mind. It made me wonder why Ceres would trust her with such an important task.

Who knew? Maybe the goddess had only her to depend on, which was kind of sad in a way. But not sad enough to keep me from kicking her ass seven ways from Friday.

Kayla had been quietly processing everything, not saying a word.

"I'm going to go to my room and change," I told them. "I hope we have robes in our closets too."

"I'm sure you do. This place doesn't skimp on a single

thing," Marcy called. "Knock on my door on your way down. I'm just going to brush my teeth. They're a little ratty." She made a show of running her tongue around the inside of her mouth and grimacing. "New toothbrushes were the best surprise ever."

I chuckled as Kayla and I made our way out. "What isn't a little ratty about us these days?" I said.

"True," Kayla replied. "I'm looking forward to changing as well. I grabbed a few of my own things before we left. I'll meet you down there when I'm done." She nodded at me in the hallway and inclined her head. She was a smart girl, and I was happy she was coming around. She would make a good partner for Tyler.

"Sounds good," I said. "I'll see you in a few." I opened the door next to Marcy's. My room was almost the mirror image of hers, but since it was on the corner, it had a fairly large balcony with two big French doors that swung inward. I walked over and opened them, enjoying the fresh breeze and the majestic view of rolling hills and vineyards as far as the eye could see.

Next, I went to my closet and opened the door. Sure enough, Angie's scent was all over. What a moron. I smiled, thinking about Rourke scaring the living daylights out of her once we found her. The thought made me insanely happy.

There was an outfit like Marcy's folded on my bed, and I chuckled, imagining Angie being ordered to buy clothes for me. It must've burned like the flames of Hades. I held up a pair of jeans that were exactly my size. No wolf here would know my size. I had a similar top to Marcy's, but mine was dark blue.

I would bet my life that, if she could have, Angie would have bought me something ridiculously awful. She was likely vetoed. Julian had very upscale taste. It would've been a glaring mistake on his part to buy me something tacky. It would've been a dead giveaway that someone else was involved.

The adjoining bathroom was decked out in expensive marble, just like everything else around here. It was light and airy, even in its massiveness, with a double sink and a huge walk-in shower with a huge glass door. My mind immediately sped to Rourke and what we could accomplish in this space. I licked my lips and started to undress. As I was changing, I decided to see what was happening with him and Julian.

How's it going? I asked my mate. *Have you told him anything about Danny?*

No, haven't had a chance. He's making a big show of offering us his boxful of Cuban cigars. What's taking so long?

Angie's been here, I said. *It's not exactly a surprise. But now we know, beyond a shadow of a doubt, that Julian and Ceres are connected. This place is bugged with spells. We need to tell everybody to make sure they say nothing of importance out loud.*

Rourke growled, *I don't like that we have to stay here. We should get a place in town.*

We'll consult with my dad when he gets here. Who knows how long we're going to be in Florence? It might be wise to have a place of our own, but it would be rude to leave abruptly. We can't afford to have the Alpha of the Mediterranean Pack angry with us. He could retaliate, and we don't need that right now.

He's asking me a question, Rourke said. *I'll keep you posted.*

In my mind, I switched gears and called out to Tyler. *Ty, this place is spelled,* I told him. *Careful what you say and pass it on to the rest of the group discreetly. I'll tell Dad as soon as we have a connection.*

Got it, he said. *Spelled by that witch you were chasing today?*

Most likely. That means Ceres is working with Julian. It complicates things.

Boy, did it ever.

Great, Tyler said.

I couldn't tell if he was being sarcastic or not. Mind communication wasn't that subtle. *What do you mean by great?* I asked. *I'm thinking this is not wonderful news. I'm thinking this is going to turn into a shit show very soon.*

Jess, finding Tally and the others could've been way more complicated than this. Instead, it's all here for the taking. What if Tally had been taken by someone we didn't know, couldn't find, and had no idea how to get to? Yes, this will most likely turn into a shit show, but it's a show happening right at our feet. We should count ourselves lucky.

He had a point.

I catch your drift. I'm changing. I'll be down soon. You'll be happy to know your cute roommate is changing too. I couldn't resist. *You know, she's the first roommate you've had in quite some time.*

I'm not going there with you, he stated evenly.

Why not?

Because I'm scared enough about it as it is. I don't need you to add anything to stir the pot.

What are you scared about? I asked.

Everything. What if she doesn't accept me as her own? he asked. *A million things could go wrong.*

Why wouldn't she accept you? It's clear that you two are mated. I knew the first moment I saw you together. It just takes time. Go slow. Think about Danny and Naomi. It took them a long time to accept the facts, but everyone comes around at some point.

I hope so. I have to go, he said. *Julian is insisting each of us take a cigar. Man, these things are stinky. How can other supernaturals stand the concentrated smell? The stench will linger in my nostrils for a year.*

You have an overly sensitive nose, both a curse and a blessing, I told him. *I'm on my way down now.*

I came out of the bathroom, and as I passed the French doors, a whooshing noise sounded. A nanosecond later, Ray stood in front of me with his hands on his hips.

I pressed my index finger to my lips.

Ray got the hint, but instead of nodding and flying away so we could talk later, he stepped forward and grabbed my waist. We were in the air before I knew what was happening.

16

"Jesus, Ray!" I exclaimed once we'd landed. "You could've given me fair warning!"

"There's no way to give you fair warning when this place is crawling with spells. Plus, I found something you're going to be mighty interested in, so I had no choice but to take you."

"Where are we?" I looked around. We appeared to be standing in the middle of the vineyard. The villa wasn't visible from here. "Are we still on Julian's property?"

"Yep," Ray answered. "I've been out here these last few hours scoping it out. He keeps his wolves in bunkhouses a couple miles away, which is strange. None seem to be hanging around the main house except for Lucas and a few drivers. There are two buildings, and they look to hold fifty to sixty wolves, twenty-five to thirty in each. But that's not the most interesting news. I found what appears to be an underground bunker, or at least the entrance to one. I scented that witch we were tracking around the area, so I didn't get too close. I didn't want to leave my signature for them to find."

"Where is this bunker? Is it nearby?" I asked, turning in a circle, trying to get a better view of the area.

He nodded. "It's down the road about three miles. There were other smells lurking as well. One that smelled like jasmine and mint. Definitely female. I couldn't pick up on what kind of supe it was for sure, but it had a familiar ring to it, close to someone's I know."

"Whose?" I asked.

"Selene," he said.

My eyebrows went up. "That must be Ceres. They're both goddesses."

"That's what I was thinking," he agreed.

"What about Tally? Did you pick up on any witch smell?" I asked. "It's risky for Julian to keep them on the property."

"I didn't scent her, but she's been gone awhile. If she hasn't been outside, her scent signature could be covered up. Plus, I didn't get that close. If we want to investigate, we're going to have to bring Marcy here, so she can clean up after us."

"Okay, all this is good information. Now take me back to the villa. They're expecting us, and we have to meet my father's plane."

"There's one more thing," he said.

"What?"

"I spotted a strange power signature, but it wasn't on Julian's land. It was right outside of it."

"What do you think it was?" I asked.

He shrugged. "I have no idea. I flew over, but as I got closer, it disappeared. Then when I was flying away, it popped back up in the same spot."

"Was it like when you found Jeb?"

"Sort of," he said. "But this one was bigger and more muted. Jeb's was more like a spotlight."

"I don't think it was Enid, but we can't know for sure."

Ray shook his head. "I don't think it was either. It didn't

feel heavy. That Hag would give off a lot of hate. It was just weird, kinda like it was messing with me."

Jessica, can you hear me? It was my father. He wasn't always able to get through, and we didn't know why.

Yes! I answered, excited to hear his voice. *Have you touched down yet?*

No, we're being diverted.

What do you meaning you're being diverted?

The pilot just announced that we couldn't land as planned. They're taking us to a runway approximately two hours south of where you're located.

I glanced at Ray. "My father just told me that their plane is being diverted to a different location. We have to head back so I can figure out what's going on."

Ray grunted. "I'm not surprised. That guy doesn't want to be outnumbered on his own turf, nor does he want any surprises. Especially if he's in up to his neck in all this shit." He waved his arm, gesturing up and down the valley.

"What do you think all the shit is? He's working with Ceres, but to what end? What does he stand to gain from of all this?"

"How do I know? But it's clear she wooed him with something. Her scent is all over this place. And if they're sleeping together, that makes things more complicated. My guess is power. It's always about power."

He was right.

Jessica, what's going on? my father asked.

Sorry, just talking to Ray. My best guess is Julian has decided it would be a threat to let you land here. We've been keeping information from him and poking around on his Compound. He's not happy. We just found out he may be working with Ceres.

The goddess?

Yes, which may have something to do with Tally being missing.

He's a shrewd Alpha who has to look out for his Pack, my father answered very rationally, not mirroring the way I felt at all. *I may have done the same thing in his situation. Let him know we will stay just outside the city limits of Florence. I'll wait to hear from you or Tyler. If anything changes, and there's significant danger, we can be there quickly.*

How many wolves did you bring? I asked.

Enough.

I had to hand it to my father, always calm in a crisis. To Ray, I said, "Take me back. Let's make an entrance on the veranda. I want Julian to know this news is not welcome. We have to show some power. I have a feeling that things are going to get messy around here soon."

Ray snorted. "They were ugly before we got here. If you want power, we've got it in spades." He wrapped his arm tightly around my waist and whipped me upward.

I kept my wits about me, but just barely. Flying through the air felt so wrong.

Luckily, we weren't up there for long.

On the way down, we were moving fast, but I saw Rourke glance up a second before we landed on the terrace. It was hard to look all put together with my hair flying in my face, but I managed.

Before I could address the mostly stunned group, Tyler, sensing my mood and tension, asked internally, *What's going on? Why'd you come in with Ray?*

Julian's not allowing Dad's plane to land here, I told him. *It's time to get to the bottom of everything.*

"Sorry to come in with the surprise landing," I told everyone, not sorry at all. "But I just found out that Julian's not allowing my father's plane to land." I gave the Alpha a hard look.

"That's correct," Julian said, unfazed. "But it wasn't my choice. I just got word from the air traffic controllers. His plane is too large for the runway."

Bullshit, Rourke said. *He doesn't want to risk more wolves on his land.*

Agreed, I said. *Ray just took me out to the vineyard so we could have a chat. He found a strange supernatural power signature outside the borders of Julian's land. And scented Angie, and possibly Ceres, at the entrance to what he thought was an underground bunker. There's a lot going on here, and Julian is in the thick of it.*

They all held the ridiculous cigars, the air full of burning tobacco. I swiped my hand in front of my face. Tyler was arguing with Julian about allowing the plane to land.

"I wish I could help you." Julian shrugged. "But this is out of my hands. Large planes cannot land on my small runway. He will be diverted to the city two hours south of here."

"The city run by nymphs?" I asked.

"Yes," he said. "He will enjoy his stay there, and you will be reunited with him tomorrow, no one the worse for wear." He took a puff of his cigar like he didn't have a care in the world.

There was nothing we could do. The Mediterranean Alpha's word was final.

A moment later, Marcy banged out the front door, followed by Kayla. "Oh, this is heaven. I could get used to this," Marcy chirped happily. "I brought the wine." She held a bottle in her hand. Lucas followed behind them with a platter full of glasses. "Would you like some?" she asked me, her eyebrow arching up into a *where in the heck did you go* question. "We can bring it with us to the landing strip."

"Sure, I'll take a glass," I said. "But bringing it with us won't be necessary. We're not going anywhere."

Marcy didn't miss a beat. "Well, all the better to stay here and enjoy the sunset. I think it's just about to set now."

"Yes," Julian said. "The view of the sunset from atop this bluff is remarkable. Let's move around to the south side." He strode down the veranda.

I hung back to get my wine from Lucas. Marcy pulled me close. "What's going on?" she whisper-yelled. "When you didn't knock on my door, I searched this entire villa for you! I thought Enid snatched you out from under us. Then, all of a sudden, I heard your voice on the porch. What gives?"

I murmured softly into her ear, "Julian is not letting my father's plane land, and I was gone because Ray took me on a short, but interesting, flight."

She pulled back, looking horrified. "Sorry to hear that, but I can't wait to hear more about the interesting part."

I sipped my wine as we followed the guys. "There's more than one robe in the closet," I said cagily.

The sun was just hitting the horizon, and Julian was right, it was more than beautiful, it was breathtaking. The sky turned orange, pink, and then red, reflecting in the billowy clouds as it disappeared beneath the rolling green waves of the distant vineyards.

Once it had set completely, Julian strolled to an area that held couches and chairs a short distance away. He lifted his hand and invited us to sit. "Please," he insisted. "Be my guests and have a seat." He directed his gaze at Danny, who had been unnaturally quiet throughout our meal. I knew, without a doubt, that he was focused on trying to make his internal connection with Naomi work. By the look on his face, he hadn't been successful. "So, were you someone's prisoner, then?" Julian asked very casually, even though we all knew his intention was anything but casual. "I'd love to hear how you ended up in the Arno."

Before any of us could speak, Lucas interjected, "Oh, that was my fault. It was entirely by accident, of course."

I struggled to keep my face impassive. Danny was my second, and power radiated off of him. There was no way Lucas would've won a challenge between the two. Danny rose to the occasion. "Yes, that's right. Your fox here managed to catch me by surprise."

What are they doing? I asked Rourke. *This could get Lucas into a lot of trouble. If Julian finds out he's lying to him, beating him will be the easy way out.*

I have no idea, Rourke answered. *But Lucas is no dummy. Let's wait and see. If he can keep Enid out of the discussion, it's worth it.*

Lucas nodded. "I had no idea he was a friend of theirs. I thought he was a rogue. So when he approached Jessica from behind, I shouldered him into the river, fearing he was after her."

Julian took a glass of wine from the tray, bland skepticism all over his face. "And why would you think this wolf would be a danger to Jessica?"

"Jessica is your guest," Lucas said. "She is in this city under your protection. And unless I'm mistaken, there are many factions after her. I perceived this wolf as a threat and will uphold the integrity of the Mediterranean Pack above all else." Oh, Lucas was good. "So I reacted first and asked questions later."

"On the way into Florence," I said to Julian, "Lucas and I discussed a variety of things, including the fact that the supernatural world is currently in upheaval. He was right to be cautious. There are many who are praying I won't make it through the night. It's a shame, but out of my control."

"I was only in the water for mere moments." Danny shrugged. "Normally, I would've fought him, rightly so. But when I found out he was only trying to protect my Alpha, I thought better of it. I would harm no one who seeks to shield her." Danny emphasized the word *shield*, making it clear we all knew that Julian wasn't that wolf.

Julian leaned forward in his chair, his expression changing. "Your *Alpha*? What do you mean by that? Callum is your Alpha."

Danny was relaxed as he could be, leaning against the thick stone railing, his body loose, belying what I knew roiled just underneath. He would not sleep until we found his mate. "I have sworn fealty to Jessica, with Callum's blessing. Yes, it's unusual. But then again, a female wolf in and of itself is unusual," Danny said. "Have you not felt her power, mate? It deserves reverence. So I gave it." He ended on a shrug. Like all wolves would kneel to the female.

"I'm not a *Pack* Alpha," I added. "This was a special circumstance, as was my birth. With all the danger chasing me, we agreed it was imperative that I have wolves around me for protection. They decided to swear their fealty on their own. There was no pressure from my father. Tyler is next in line for Pack Alpha of the U.S. Territories. That doesn't change."

Nice save, Tyler told me. *But he is not going to buy it for a minute. Your power is greater than mine. He'll put two and two together soon enough.*

But it's true, I answered stubbornly. *I can't be a Pack Alpha* and *sit on the Coalition. My job is Enforcer, whether I like it or not.* Before I could insist to Julian that I was telling the truth, my mate cut in.

"Jessica's place is on the Coalition," Rourke stated calmly. "You must've heard that news by now." His words were a challenge. If Julian said no, he would be lying. If he said yes, he would admit to having information.

And just like that, everything was out in the open.

Julian opened his mouth to answer, but was interrupted. "This must be where all the ingrates hang out," Eudoxia stated in a bored tone as she strolled around the corner. "So we've decided to discuss the Coalition out in the open, have we? Well, don't be droll, please go on."

17

Eudoxia had a knack for popping in at the exact wrong time. But I was happy for the interruption at this particular wrong time. Now I could sit back and watch Julian deal with the hurricane that was Eudoxia.

Vampire Queen was dressed in a new gown, this one sky blue. She swept it in front of her as she sat down, her spine stick-straight, her small feet elegantly covered in shoes more expensive than my car. Julian had yet to respond, but Eudoxia had no problem filling the gap. "So, Julian," she said, her voice full of pretentious humor, "what is the word here in Florence amongst the supernaturals about the Coalition? I spent the day outside of town in a small, yet regal, vampire Coterie, and they are atwitter about the news the Coalition is forming. Surely you have something? This is your city after all."

Julian cleared his throat. "Yes, there has been some news, but I just took it for idle gossip." He darted a glance at me and then back to Eudoxia.

Bullshit.

Lucas had already told us that my dealings were somewhat public knowledge, eagerly shared between wolves. I crossed my arms. "The new Coalition forming is pretty heady gossip to ignore," I said. "It must've been swirling around for a while. I'm curious about what supernaturals are saying too. I'm also wondering why Florence, in particular, happens to be the chosen place. What's special about this city?"

"Florence has always been a draw for supernaturals all over the world." Julian struggled to keep his voice relaxed. If he gripped his wineglass any tighter, it would explode. "We are a city of magic, and proud of it. Many different Sects call this place home. It's a natural converging place."

"We did run into a witch today," I agreed. "But we figured we'd encounter many more supes. But, to our surprise, the city was empty. This runs contradictory to what you were just saying. If Florence is a hub, it should be filled with supernatural activity. Is there a ban within the city limits we don't know about?"

Julian looked even more uncomfortable. "Florence is my city, under my jurisdiction. All supernaturals know that. Seeing that you were set to arrive today, I had the city cleared for your safety."

All except for one lone witch.

That was a big mistake, Julian.

I cocked my head, affecting a confused look. "We never informed you that I was in any danger, so what gave you the idea you needed to clear the entire city and not tell us about it? That must have put a lot of supes out. Being forced to leave your home is inconvenient."

When he didn't readily respond, Eudoxia once again filled in, glee infusing her voice. She wasn't picky about whose discomfort she enjoyed. "The vampires had lots to say." She shot a glance in my direction. "Shall I tell you about it?"

"Of course," I answered. "After all, in a very short while we will be sharing *all* of our information"—and power—"as we take our positions on the Coalition together." That was for Julian's benefit. He had to know Eudoxia was slated for a seat, though he likely didn't know it was the fae seat.

I wasn't going to mention that part.

Eudoxia gave me a steely glare. "You need not remind me of my duties, ignorant wolf." Well, so much for any civility we'd just cultivated. "The vampires have detected the presence of a few extremely powerful and extremely secretive supernaturals in the area." I glanced at Ray. He gave me a short nod. The magic signature he'd detected across the border of Julian's land must've belonged to one of them. "It's rumored that these supernaturals only come into our realm when there's a big shift in power. They are the ones in charge of passing the baton, so to speak. It seems the swearing in of the Coalition will be soon, and everyone is aflutter."

"These powerful supernaturals, do you know what kind of supes they are?" I asked. Since one was basically camped in our backyard, it would be nice to know.

"They've only heard rumors, of course. The last swearing was too long ago for most to remember," she answered. "But I believe them both to be celestial. Two birds of a different feather—one dark and one light."

When Eudoxia mentioned the word *celestial*, I had to work hard to scour my brain, which was more difficult than you'd think. Steering the conversation away from anything that had to do with angels, I asked, "Did the vampires mention a specific time frame when everything might come together?"

Eudoxia waved her hand, barely refraining from rolling her eyes. "No one would know that exactly, but the agreement is soon." She glanced casually at Julian. "Very soon. I would assume when all Coalition members have gathered."

"We're missing a few key players," I said. "It can't start until everyone's together."

The Vampire Queen settled back in her chair. It was hard for her to achieve a casual demeanor, but she was trying. "The rumors are that two of the missing supernaturals are already here in Florence." She raised a single eyebrow like a champ in Julian's direction. "Have you taken note of that, Julian?" She swished her hand out in front of her before he had a chance to answer. "But of course you have. Or you wouldn't be an all-powerful Alpha who's in control of this city and every supernatural in it. Isn't that correct?" Eudoxia challenged.

If he said no, he'd look weak.

If he said yes, he'd be caught with information we needed.

We all awaited Julian's response.

Instead of looking meek, he looked furious. He stood abruptly, his wine sloshing out of his glass. "Of course I know what goes on in my city! But as I just stated, I've had Florence cleared. There are no supernaturals in it. So the ones you seek are not there."

"Well," I started, "you had it cleared, except for my friend here"—I gestured to Danny—"and that one witch we saw." I turned to Rourke. "What was her name again?"

"Angie," Rourke growled.

"Ah, yes, Angie," I repeated as I stood, meeting Julian's stare brazenly. "Can you explain to us what one of Tally's witches was not only doing in Florence, since you had it cleared, but also snooping around in my *bedroom*?"

Julian's glare didn't waver. "If there was a witch in the city, she was defying my orders and will be punished. As for having her in this house, I know nothing about that. I will have it investigated thoroughly."

"Um." Marcy cleared her throat. "I hate to break it to you, Julian, but there are witch spells crawling all over this villa, like termites snacking on a rotten log. It's hard to believe you wouldn't be aware, but it's possible. After all, as far as I know, wolves cannot detect spells very easily. But some can if they have a good sniffer." Marcy just gave us the reason why Julian didn't have his wolves living in the villa. And she was giving him an out, which was likely the best course to take at the moment. If we pushed him any harder, we'd have a war on our hands. With my father so far away, that wasn't advisable. "But I can help you get rid of them, if you'd like."

The Mediterranean Alpha managed to keep his composure. As we were finding, he was a gifted actor. If he had hoodwinked his wolves by consorting with witches, he must be really good. "If my home is spelled, I will have it taken care of." His voice was harsh. "It is not as surprising as you'd think to find spells here, as I am an influential leader with a long reach. Not everyone is happy with the way I've decided to conduct my business across the city."

No, Julian, we're certain they aren't.

Marcy rose to the challenge. "Honestly, it's no big deal. I can wipe this villa clean faster than a maid on steroids, and it won't cost you a dime." That was saying a lot. If Julian hired it out, it would cost him a small fortune. Witches were expensive. "I'll put it all toward my room and board."

There was a collective intake of breath.

If Julian refused, he would confirm that he knew they'd been here all along, that he'd possibly even ordered the witch to cast them. He took a sip of his wine, ignoring the wetness on his hand from the recent spill, still trying to appear like he was in control of the situation. "That would be wonderful," he finally stated. "It will save me the trouble of hiring someone else to do it." He abruptly set his wineglass down on the table and nodded at each of us. "Now if you'll excuse me, I'm going to call a meeting with my council so we can get to the bottom of this. I will not abide by unwanted supernaturals invading my private sanctum. Enjoy the rest of your evening." He turned without further ado and hastened back into the house like he was late for a meeting.

He couldn't get out of here fast enough, I told my mate.

He had no choice but to scurry away or face our wrath, Rourke replied. *He was caught red-handed. If his Pack knew of his deceit, they could rise against him.*

Before anyone could move or say anything, Marcy raised her hands in the air and began to chant something as she turned in a circle. We waited for her to finish, as we didn't want anything we said reaching any snooping ears.

When she was done, she lowered her arms. "Okay, there are still more spells to dissolve," she said. "But in the meantime, I'm going to cast a containment charm around this area so we can talk freely. Then I'll head into the house and finish the rest. I've never met a sloppier witch." She placed her hands on her hips. "The spells crumble under my words, disintegrating like dried leaves on the wind. She didn't take the time to cement them in place, which is such a newbie move. If you secure them, that doesn't make them unbreakable, but it makes them harder to crack. I could've been here all night, and instead, it'll take me no more than ten minutes to wipe this place clean." She waved her hands around the seating area, and there was an audible pop. "Okeydokey, talk away. Nothing is getting out of this bubble until I say so."

Danny went first. "That is the strangest Alpha I've ever met. He was openly lying like he thought we wouldn't pick up on it. His wolves are either stupid, or completely in the dark." He shook his head, settling his fingers over his temples and rubbing.

I got up and went to sit by him on the railing. I placed my hand on his back to give him some comfort. "Are you picking up anything from Naomi? I'm confident that's the reason Enid led us to you. You have a direct connection to Naomi, which will take away the necessity of her having to plant notes for us."

"No," Danny said, his voice miserable. "I keep trying, but nothing is going through."

"Don't worry about it," I said, knowing he would no matter what I said. I glanced around at the rest of the group. "I have a plan for tomorrow morning. Rourke, Danny, and I will head into Florence before dusk. I want the rest of you to fan out." I hadn't had a chance to discuss the plan with Rourke, but I knew he'd agree. Trying to keep certain details out of my brain made it hard to formulate things, but I was trying. "Marcy, James, and Ray, I want you to stay here. Ray, first thing in the morning, take them both to the bunker. You guys are officially on the hunt for Tally. Julian has to be in cahoots with Ceres, since Angie's scent is all over this place. They have to be holding Tally someplace close, so she can be under Julian's protection. The bunker's a good place to start. Ray also picked up on a scent that could be Ceres. Marcy, maybe you'll recognize it when you smell it."

"What were the flavors?" Marcy asked Ray.

"Jasmine and mint," he replied.

Marcy nodded. "Jasmine sounds about right. I'm not sure about mint. It's been a long time since I've seen Ceres, but if it's her, I'll know. That cheating, snatching, good-for-nothing goddess. I can't wait to get my fingertips near her."

"I don't want you to approach any of them," I warned. "Don't forget that Ceres has the ability to render you infertile. Once we find her, I'll deal with her myself."

"Whatever you say, boss," Marcy said. "I'd prefer not to battle that hateful goddess alone. But once I get the chance, I'm going to spell her up good." She cracked her knuckles.

"Noted," I said, turning to Nick. "I want you and Lucas to stay in the villa and be our eyes and ears." I addressed my brother. "You and Kayla are going to rendezvous with Dad first thing in the morning. I want you to fill him in on everything. He won't be welcome here, especially after what went down tonight. I'm not sure if we will be either. Dad and his wolves will have to find a new place to stay. Once you get settled, let me know. I'm hoping we can meet you there at the end of the day." I had no idea how my day was going to go, so there were no promises. "I'll keep you posted."

Rourke stood. "Jessica's plan is sound. We can't rehash

more specifics right now, so I say we all turn in early and get a good night's sleep. We regroup tomorrow night."

Danny fiddled with the stem of his wineglass. "I have to find her."

"We will," I assured him. "You're coming with Rourke and me in the morning. We'll fill you in tomorrow. When Enid wants us to locate Naomi, you will be the conduit, I'm sure of it. And we will be ready."

More than ready, I hoped.

18

Rourke and I were allowed to enter our bedroom only after Marcy had gone over everything with a fine-toothed spell, opening all the drawers, all the doors, including going out on the terrace, and hitting under the bed. "This is as clean as this room has ever been," she declared twenty minutes later. "But just to be safe, I'm putting you in a private bubble and adding a few alarms. If anybody comes within ten feet of this room, we'll all know it. The shrieks will be loud enough to wake the dead."

I chuckled. "It's nice to have you around in a pinch. Your witchy skills can save lives."

She snorted. "Please, anyone stupid enough to approach you unannounced will be thankful for a quick death. I'm just making any interlopers known a bit sooner. That, and so I can sleep without worrying about your big, beautiful head being split open."

"That's very kind of you," I told her. "I wouldn't want anything to happen to my big head either."

She chortled as she walked out the door. "I can't help it if you're beefier than I am. It's purely genetics. I just call it like I see it."

I was exhausted.

Once Marcy shut the door, I sat on the edge of the bed and glanced over at my mate. "Do we really get to sleep through the night? I feel like that hasn't happened in such a long time."

He sat next to me, tugging me close. I rested my head on his shoulder. "Yes, but it's only eight p.m." He chuckled. "I plan to have you well rested, but not before we have some quality time together." He said the last bit on a rough whisper that sent shivers racing down my spine.

I craved him, my body desperate with need to have him.

The adrenaline of the day was still coiled tightly inside me, ready for some kind of release. I tilted my face up toward his lips, the heat of them searing me before contact.

His mouth was hot, his lips firm.

My hand dove into his hair, holding on. Needing to feel him, forcing him closer, wanting as much as I could get.

He would give everything, like he always did. It was mine for the taking.

I took greedily.

Fire roiled under the surface.

"Mine," he groaned as he stripped us down and pulled the covers back, each of us mindless, our tongues intertwining. "I need you."

"Need you more." I moaned into his mouth as he thrust himself into me in one sure motion. I took him deeply.

The pace was frantic, both of us holding on, never wanting to let go.

This wasn't about the act.

It was about our love, our passion, and the fear of the unknown.

It was about the two of us and no one else.

My hands gripped his shoulders as he rocked faster. His fullness filling me with each thrust. I wondered if there had ever been another time when I felt so safe and free. My thoughts ran to his cabin in the woods. The place where we had mated and discovered our bond. I yearned to go back, to have a normal life.

"Jessica..." Rourke arched up, his hands racing to my hips, seating me firmly to him.

"I'm there," I said.

One last thrust, and I broke.

Rourke followed, holding me tightly, his head angled toward the ceiling as he called my name.

Afterward, his lips found mine in a sweet kiss, his hands stroking the sides of my face. "I love you," he whispered. "Now and forever."

I pressed my forehead against his, loving his scent. "Now and forever."

It was four-thirty in the morning. We had approximately an hour and a half until the sun crested the horizon, but we weren't taking any chances. There was a distinct possibility Enid knew of our plan this morning, even if she didn't know who the supernatural we sought was, because no amount of brain scrubbing would deter a powerful seer.

Danny and I were in the backseat, Rourke sat in the front, and Lucas drove. "Feeling anything now?" I asked Danny. I was certain Enid had released Danny because of his connection to Naomi. Nothing else made sense. She needed a direct line to us, and this was her way to get it. It was hard to be patient.

"No." His voice miserable. "I tried all night—" His expression suddenly changed, and his hands flew to the sides of his head.

"What? Are you picking something up?" I asked excitedly.

He held up a single finger as his face broke out into a

wide grin. I took that as a good sign. I squirmed in my seat.

Finally, he darted a glance in my direction. "I can hear her," he said. "But it's faint. She's warning me not to come, of course. But there's no chance I'll listen to that nonsense."

"Is she with Jax?" I could hardly contain my joy. I knew Enid would keep her word and swap their lives for mine.

"She says she is with the boy."

Relief swept through me. "Are they okay? Have they been hurt?"

Danny's face looked hopeful. "The signal is getting stronger. She says they are not hurt, and the boy is strong. She says Enid has left them alone for the most part."

Immediately, I called out to my brother, who was likely still asleep. *Tyler! We just got word Jax is okay. Danny got through to Naomi. We're either breaking them out or making a swap. Let Kayla know. I'll keep you posted.*

Wait, what? His voice was sleepy, but changed to alert instantly. *You're not making a swap. That wasn't the plan. If you can't break them out, come back here and we'll figure out the next step.*

The plan is to do whatever it takes, I said firmly. *Enid isn't playing. We either have the advantage, or we don't. We'll know soon enough.*

But, Jess, that's... He trailed off.

The way it's going to be, I finished for him. *Listen, I didn't have time to tell everybody yesterday what happened when I rescued Danny. But Enid had a chance to harm me, and she backed off. There was a reason for that, and I'm going to find out what it is. She wants her sister back above all else, we can't forget that. If there's a way I can do that, I'm going to make it happen. Naomi's and Jax's lives are important. Tell Kayla immediately. She deserves to know.*

Of course I will, he answered. *Stay safe, Jess. I mean it.*

I plan to. That's why we're heading into Florence. It has to work, Tyler. There's no other choice.

I hear you, he said. I could picture him running a hand through his blond hair. *Keep me posted. We leave here at six and rendezvous with Dad by eight.*

If something happens with my internal connection, I'll have Rourke call Nick. I've got to go. We're almost inside the city limits.

Kick her ass, Jess.

I laughed. *That might be a possibility.*

Lucas turned down a narrow street. "We'll get a ticket for driving into a restricted zone, but that's fine. We try to stay off human radar as much as possible, but this is an exception worth breaking the rules for."

I nodded. "Lucas, once we get out, I want you to head back home. I've instructed Nick to stay at the villa. You guys are going to be our eyes and ears. If you can, try and get as much information as you can from Julian's wolves."

"Got it. I'll head back as soon as I drop you off," he said.

"We appreciate that," Rourke said. "By the way, has anybody asked you who your Alpha is sleeping with?"

"Nicolas asked me, and I will tell you the same thing I told him," he replied. "I don't know for sure. I have not seen her in the flesh, but by her scent alone I believe she is either a witch or a goddess. In the past year, Julian has kept his wolves far from the villa. His second and fifteen to twenty other wolves who had once lived inside the house were suddenly instructed to move out. Everything changed in one day."

I moved forward in my seat. "Are his wolves angry with him? What about his second? Do they all suspect he's sleeping with a witch?" The area Ray had showed me that held the underground bunker was not far from where the wolf bunkhouses were. They had to have scented Angie and Ceres on their land.

"I would assume so," he answered. "But they do not share their thoughts with me. Julian has kept me at the house only because he believes I am inferior—less than a real wolf.

That I am inept at understanding what's going on around me."

Rourke grunted. "He's the one who's inept. He couldn't find his finger if it was inserted straight into his ass. He was guilty as hell last night and acted like everything was fine."

"Even though he seems inept, you must be wary of him," Lucas cautioned. "He will protect what he perceives is his right at all costs. The only reason he would pair up with a goddess over his own wolves is because he believes doing so will bring him greater power and status."

I nodded. That's what Jeb had already confirmed. "We realize he's powerful," I said as Rourke snorted. "But this is not going to end well for him. We believe he might be hiding our kidnapped friend on the Compound under our noses. We will be forced to fight him to free Tally." I paused. "We believe she is the witch who will sit on the Coalition."

"I understand," Lucas said. "I don't concern myself with what happens to Julian. My loyalty is to you. I will help you in any way I can."

"My friends are going to be investigating the area today," I said. "Do you know anything about the underground bunker?"

"Yes," he answered as he turned down a narrow street. "It was built eighty years ago when there was a threat of invasion in Italy. It's meant to withstand bomb blasts. It's spelled and set deeply into the ground. No one is allowed to go near it without Julian's explicit approval. We don't know what he does down there, but we know he visits often."

"Well, I know what he does," I muttered. "He kidnaps witches and canoodles with goddesses." I thought about Maggie, Tally's tiny daughter. If Julian was keeping the toddler down there, there would be trouble. "Have you ever been inside? How big is it?" Not only was Tally missing, but the entire Coven was too. I couldn't believe he had room to stash them all down there, but who knew how big that space was.

"I was in there once many years ago," he said. "I was

tasked to clean out some of the rooms. It's fairly big, set up like a two-bedroom apartment. There are artificial lights to mimic the sun. Julian spent a lot on furnishings, and there is power. Someone could live comfortably down there for a while."

"Is it large enough to hold, say, twenty to thirty witches?" I asked.

Lucas pulled over to the curb and turned around to face me, his arm slung across the back of the seat. "No, there's no way there are that many witches down there. Not only is there not enough room, but we would know because there would be gossip. I'm sorry. Your friend could be there, but not the others. We are at the Piazza della Signoria." He gestured in front of him. "It's down the block in front of us. You will find the statue of David in the square. I'll head back to the villa now."

I gave him a quick hug. "Thank you for your help. We owe you."

"You owe me nothing." He smiled. "It's my duty to help you. Every race of supernatural is counting on you. If you're successful, we're all successful."

Danny opened the side door, and I followed him out. "Lucas, you have a place on my team after all this is over, if you want it." There would be no room for him in Julian's Pack after everything shook out. "I value trust and respect over all else, and you've given it freely. I'm proud to call you friend."

"I am honored," he said. "And I accept."

Rourke reached out to shake Lucas's hand. "I'm hoping this will be over soon."

"Me too. Be safe."

The street was dark, only a few streetlights to light the way. It was approximately a quarter after five in the morning. We made it down the short block in less than a minute.

The square was mostly empty, save for a few tourists who

either had serious jet lag, or wanted to avoid the crowds. They wouldn't be a problem, as we were just another set of tourists up early to see the sites.

As we hurried up to the statue of David, movement behind the sculpture caught my eye.

Leo stepped out of the shadows directly in front of us.

We stopped.

He bowed his head, and very slowly, two gigantic wings unfurled.

19

Seeing Leo morph into an angel was one of the most amazing things I'd ever witnessed. His power leaped in front of him, abrading us with its ferocity. This supernatural was strength personified. I honestly didn't think he had an equal in the entire world. I'd never witnessed such raw beauty.

He was bare-chested, his bronze skin radiant in the low light. His clear eyes glittered, his cheekbones casting their own shadows. His wingspan was easily fifteen feet across. His wings were a glorious white, the feathers thick and well defined.

"Bloody hell," Danny murmured. "Is that what I think it is?"

"Yes, it is," I whispered, not knowing why I was keeping my voice down, but feeling the moment deserved reverence. "That's Leonardo—who is actually Michelangelo—the celestial angel who is going to help us get your mate back. He's cloaking us from Enid."

Danny glanced at me with a stunned expression on his face. "You weren't kidding when you said you had a plan."

"No, I wasn't," I replied. "We were just lucky he decided to help us."

"He's one of the only supernaturals who can block Enid from seeing our movements," Rourke added.

"I am," Leo agreed as he came forward. "The moment I unleashed my power, we became invisible to everyone, including these humans in the piazza. Until I decide, we stay cloaked."

I turned to Danny. "Are you still getting messages from Naomi?"

Danny nodded, his gaze darting back to the larger-than-life celestial being who stood in front of us. "Aye, she's still coming through. She was describing her whereabouts, but I'm not sure it will help us much. It seems they are locked in a room with crumbling walls, which describes just about every residence in this city. She never got a glimpse of the outside. It is secure. No power can get in or out. Jax has tried to tear his way through, but he hasn't succeeded."

"Is it like an apartment, or a bunker, or something else? Ask her to be as specific as she can," I instructed him.

"I have been doing so." His voice was strained. "She feels that maybe it's an old monastery or something of the like. She hasn't heard any vehicles or casual human sounds, so she is guessing that they're outside the city limits, somewhat secluded."

"We have to remember that Enid wants us to find her," I said. "That's the only way we can make a swap."

"Wait." He held up a finger while pressing another one against his temple. "She was speaking but abruptly stopped. Something's going on." His voice rose in accord with his panic.

I reached out and touched him, giving him strength, pouring as much calm into him as I could. "Enid is not going to hurt them," I assured. "She wants me and only me."

"This is true," Leo confirmed, his baritone sounding lovely

and melodic. "She will have felt my power, and Jessica has disappeared abruptly off her radar. She will put them together immediately. She will not be happy, but she will find a way to achieve her goals, likely by speaking through your mate."

Danny nodded slowly, trying to keep his composure. "Yes, I think Naomi's speaking with someone else."

"If we don't think she's within the city limits," Rourke said, "we're going to need to figure out how to get to our next destination. We let Lucas take the vehicle back to the villa."

"That won't be a problem," Leo said. "I can get us there merely on a thought."

"Well, that's…handy." I exhaled. It was actually unbelievable. What incredible power. "Danny is worried about Naomi, so the sooner we find out where she is, the better."

"I understand," Leo answered. "But you must not worry overly much." He directed his comment at Danny. "Your mate is strong."

"Do you know who she is?" I asked.

"Yes," Leo said. "I know all who will sit on the Coalition."

I was both shocked and relieved. "So it's true!" I exclaimed. "Naomi *will* take the vampire seat."

"What? What are you saying?" Danny sputtered. "Naomi will sit on the Coalition?"

"I didn't mention it before, because it was only speculation," I told him. "But it does make sense. When she ingested my blood, she became the most powerful vampire after Eudoxia. But Eudoxia can't take two seats, so it's up to the power to find the best vampire suited for the job, and that happens to be your mate."

"My mind just shattered into a million pieces," Danny said. "This is a lot to take in at the moment."

"Of course it is," I told him, patting his back. "It's probably best not to tell Naomi right now. We don't want to shock her. She's got enough going on as it is. It's going to take her some time to process the news, especially since she's so used to taking orders from others." I imagined her denying her place for a while. I was going to have to remind her that she'd learned a long time ago that she was destined for this, when she first spoke to the Hag who spared her life all those years ago, after Selene had sent her on a doomed mission. The Hag had said if she pledged herself to someone, she would live to see the wrongs of the world righted. I wondered if that Hag had been Enid?

That would be a full-circle moment.

"Wait, wait," Danny said, holding up his finger. "Naomi's come back. She says she has a message for us. Enid knows you have enlisted the angel's help. She says this has changed nothing. It's Jessica's life for theirs. If you dare to break them out, she will kill them without hesitation."

I looked to Leo for guidance. "We knew this was her game all along," I said. "She's always wanted me. Do we have a chance to defy her if we're cloaked? A chance to break them out anyway?"

Leo gazed off into the distance for a moment, then turned back. "We are cloaked, so she cannot see our movements. We can achieve many things in this state. But that does not mean she can't harm the innocents while we are doing so. We risk much if we go against her wishes."

I sighed. "Jeb told me that if I followed her missives directly, I would die. That means if we let Enid decide how to proceed, we lose our advantage and the outcome might be dire."

Leo nodded. "I suggest we change the plan without telling Enid. Instead of finding Naomi and the boy, we locate Enid. Once we do, you will have a single chance to state your case, as you did to me. If you can convince her that there is an alternative to ending your life, and a chance to bring her sister back, you will prevail. If not, you will die. I see no other way around it."

"Wait a minute. That's not part of the plan," Rourke said, his voice heavy with emotion. "There has to be another way that doesn't involve Jessica walking straight into danger."

I glanced at my mate, knowing this was incredibly hard for him. "Rourke," I answered calmly, "Leo's right. There is no other way. I have one chance. I can't follow her orders blindly, so we have to use the only advantage we have. Even if we were somehow able to rescue Naomi and Jax, she isn't going away, and my life is still in danger. It's the only way." Juanita had told me to make decisions with my heart, and I knew this was the right choice, wherever it led me. Before Rourke could protest further, I turned to Danny. "Tell Naomi to let Enid know we're ready to make the swap, and we await her direction." I reached out to grab Rourke's hand. "We're cloaked by Leo. Once she gives us the information, we can figure out where she is and try to take her by surprise. I believe this is the only way."

"I don't accept that." We all heard the anguish in Rourke's voice.

I squeezed his hand. "You'll be standing right next to me. I'll state my case, and we'll see what she says. Leo and Danny will be there too. That's a considerable amount of power. It will force Enid to listen. I don't believe she can snatch me right under your noses. It will have to be a compromise in the end." I nodded to Danny, who seemed to be waiting for us to come to a decision. "Go ahead, contact Naomi."

Leo gave me a long contemplating look, and I wondered what was going on in his perfectly symmetrical head. He finally said, "My job over the last thousand years was to stand witness to the formation of the Coalition. I knew your successor." He nodded to me. "You carry her very soul within you. There are similarities, of course. You both have dark hair and similar builds, but you have a softer side—your human side. Something that is missing with most supernaturals. Your capacity for empathy, and for compromise—it rarely exists for us. That makes us harsh and unforgiving creatures, continually out for the betterment of ourselves and not the greater good. I believe this is what sets you apart, and what will make you better than all the rest. This is the reason I agreed to help you."

I was overwhelmed.

What was I supposed to do with that? "Thank you," I settled on. "My father would probably agree with you. He has tried all his life to balance both worlds for me, and I think he did a good job. Sometimes, however, I feel that my human side is a hindrance, but mostly I feel pride that I've managed to retain it. I find it confusing when I meet other supernaturals who do not love and care for others first and foremost. It feels foreign to me, and I hope it always does. I don't know about it making me a better leader, but I will try to be the best one I can be. I plan to bring my team with me. I think it's important to have more than one viewpoint at all times, or it's too easy for one to get lost."

"You will set a new precedent," he said. "I look forward to your reign." He turned toward Rourke. "I believe Enid will look inside your mate and see the same. She will see that Jessica is meant to do this job. All that stands in Enid's way are anger and grief. She will not be expecting a face-to-face meeting, so anything that was written before has now changed. If Jessica is to meet with her, it must be now."

Rourke said nothing.

Danny interrupted hesitantly. "Naomi has given us directions. They are in Tuscany, about two hours south of here. They are in an old deserted abbey called San Galgano."

"I am familiar with this place," Leo replied.

"My father is south as well," I said. "As soon as we arrive, I'll contact my brother." I looked at my mate. "Are you going to be okay with this?"

He sighed as he ran a hand through his hair. "I'm not at all okay with losing you, so we're going to have to make sure that doesn't happen." He addressed Leo. "Do you think Enid resides in the same place she is keeping them?"

"We won't know until we get there," Leo offered. "Her signature is masked to most, but if I'm near enough, I should be able to detect it."

"Then what are we waiting for?" Danny asked excitedly. "Let's get to the rescuing."

"Join hands," Leo ordered as he spread both of his toward us. I grabbed on to his left hand, and Rourke grabbed his right. We both clutched Danny. "The journey will be swift, but you may feel ill afterward. This is one of the drawbacks of spanning time and space, even for a mere moment. But you will recover, do not worry."

I had no idea what to expect, but I was ready for anything.

"Our bodies aren't going to burst apart or anything like that?" Danny asked. "I rather like this form, and it's the only one my mate will recognize." There was levity in his question, but he was voicing what we were all concerned about. Wolves and shifters were very concrete creatures, wary of magic and things they didn't understand. Popping out of time and space qualified as worrisome. If this hadn't been an emergency, and we hadn't been dealing with a powerful Hag, we would've tracked down Lucas and driven the two hours.

Leo laughed. It sounded like harp chords being plucked, melodic and mesmerizing. "You will retain your body, I assure you. We are simply moving faster than light, space, and time. We will arrive at our destination earlier than when we started."

Say what?

"That's a bit of a mind bender," Danny said. "Hopefully one I'll live to tell my children about one day when I bounce them on my knee." He appeared wistful for a moment. "I wonder what a half-vampire, half-wolf child will look like? I hope they take after her and not me. They will be beautiful bloodthirsty little fliers."

Before I could comment on Danny being a father, Leo said, "They will carry traits of you both and be very powerful beings. Now we go. Enid's and Jessica's fates await."

20

"Holy hell." I coughed, wiping my mouth with the back of my sleeve. I was on my knees, retching. Traveling through a time continuum was not at all advisable. My stomach felt like it had a rubber band cinched tightly around it. Rourke was pale, his arm braced on a tree, head bowed, but so far he was faring better than I was.

Danny, on the other hand, was passed out cold.

I staggered to stand. "Are you sure he's going to wake up?" I asked Leo. "It's been about two minutes, and he hasn't moved."

"He'll awake very soon," Leo said. "I don't take many passengers with me, but in the past, some have preserved their minds by shutting them down. It's actually a fairly intelligent way to handle the situation."

"Now you tell us," I said, coughing into my fist but managing to keep what I had left in my stomach where it belonged. "You mean I could've just passed out and all would've been well?"

"No," he answered, humor behind his words. "Supernaturals

with vast power cannot put their minds on hold. It's a coping mechanism your body has developed to keep you alive no matter what." My wolf barked her agreement. Even though I was puking my guts up, she was happy as could be, urging me to get on with the business at hand.

My body was righting itself quickly, which was a relief. "As much as I'm thankful for the experience, I think we'll be taking a car home."

"Agreed," Rourke said, dropping his arm. "I appreciate the ride, but I prefer to stay within *this* time and space."

Leo chuckled. "It's your call, of course."

Danny sputtered as he awoke. "Good gods! The world's gone pear-shaped." He grabbed on to his head. "Is everyone spinning, or is it just me?"

"Don't worry," I said, kneeling beside him. "It'll calm down in a minute or two. You took the smart way out and disengaged your brain."

"I did?" he replied. "Then why does it feel as if I've taken bits out and had them blended and stuffed back in?" He rolled over and got up on all fours. "Have we arrived, then?"

"The abbey is just over the hill," Leo confirmed, his wings fully expanded and glorious. The sun was getting ready to rise, and I knew that once the first rays hit his feathers, it would be like nothing any of us had ever seen. "Enid is cloaking herself well, no doubt trying to keep her location secret. But I'm picking up on something nearby." He walked up the crest of a short hill.

"So she doesn't know we're here at all?" I asked, following him. "She can't even scent us?"

"It is like we do not exist," Leo answered, glancing over his shoulder. "Although, she will infer that we are already somewhere nearby, as she's given us directions. She knows my method of travel."

Rourke came up behind us. *I'm not handing you over to Enid without a fight,* he told me. *It can't come to that.*

I don't think it will, I replied. *But there's a good chance we won't have a choice in the matter. Whatever happens today, Naomi and Jax go free. We won't get another opportunity. If we try to run away or fight, she will kill them. And then eventually she'll catch up to me. There's no use running. It's time to face her.*

We could have brought an army of wolves with us, Rourke growled. *We could have at least given a show of power.*

It wouldn't have mattered. I knew this to be true. *Enid is not your typical supernatural, much like Leo is not anything close to something we can fight. If Leo decided that he wanted to incinerate us, he would. And that would be the end of it. My only chance right now is to convince Enid that there is a way to bring her sister back.*

And what way is that? Rourke asked. *We haven't been given any clues about how to go about doing that.*

I know, I said. *But I have to trust Juanita. She said I had to sacrifice something, and if I did, things would right themselves. I'm ready to do whatever it takes.*

What if that sacrifice is yourself? Rourke asked. *What then?*

I shook my head. *It can't be,* I told him. *With my death comes chaos, remember? I've already thought of that. It has to be something else. I'm hoping Juanita will give me some guidance once I confront Enid. Or at least a hint of what I'm supposed to tell her. We'll have to wait and see.*

Rourke grunted. *Let your brother know where we are. Have him leave the Compound immediately, if he hasn't already. If we need backup, at least they can be here quickly.*

Tyler, I called in my mind. *Are you up?*

Yep, we're ready to go. Julian is nowhere to be found, but we discovered a van with keys in the garage.

It wasn't surprising that Julian had bailed. He was probably out trying to cover up his deceitful tracks or cook up something with Ceres. *Talk to Ray, Marcy, and James before you leave and let them know Julian's gone and to be careful when they snoop around. We're approximately two hours south of you. I don't know where Dad ended up staying last night, but when you meet up with him, let him know. I'm not going to give you our specific coordinates right now, because Enid can't see us. I don't want anybody else to have that information.*

What's the plan? Tyler asked. *Are you going to break Naomi and Jax out?*

No, I answered. *We have another strategy, but again, I can't tell you what it is. Just know that when we're all done with today, I will have done my very best to try to ensure a positive outcome.*

Be careful, Jess. Tyler's voice became serious. *I don't like not being there, but I'm glad you are protected. We'll be rendezvousing with Dad as soon as we can. If I have to, I can shift and make it to you in record time.* My brother was known for his speed.

My goal is to come out of this alive, I reassured him. *Tell Dad there was no way to avoid this. I love you both.*

Stay safe, he said. *Kayla wants me to thank you. She's happy Jax is coming home.*

I smiled. *Tell her all will be well and that she'll be reunited with her brother shortly.*

Leo stood on the top of a knoll. We had to make our way around his wings so we could see the valley below us. "I'm getting a very faint signal from that church. It's about a half a mile from the abbey where your friends are located." He gestured to a dilapidated stone building in the distance. "Try as she might, Enid can't keep herself fully cloaked. It's because she's still practicing magic by keeping her prisoners in a cell they can't escape from and scrying for you. If she ceased all magic, I would have a hard time locating her."

"How angry is she going to be when we show up on her

doorstep?" I asked. "Will I have time to negotiate, or will she strike me down the moment she sees me?"

"You will not approach her alone," Leo said. "That would be folly. When we get close enough, I will drop my cloak and call out to her."

"Can you protect Jessica from Enid's magic?" Rourke asked. "I need to know before we reach her."

Leo appraised my mate. "You are a mighty warrior from the days of old," Leo said. "You are from the fiercest clan of the fiercest cats. That is why you—and you alone—have endured. Between us, we could hold Enid back. But she will not negotiate with us. Her terms will be with Jessica alone. It is unknown if she will allow us to accompany Jessica inside. We must wait and see."

Rourke tensed. "Are you telling me there's no real way to back her up if Enid wants to talk to her alone?"

"I'm not saying that exactly," Leo answered carefully. "Jessica is a warrior in her own right, with great power. Her wolf will help fortify her, and she will be able to fend for herself until we can arrive to back her up. I would not allow a lamb to walk willingly into slaughter. That said, there are no guarantees. Enid is a powerful being. But there is no other way around this."

I agreed. "I can't keep running. This meeting has to come eventually, and I'm glad I get to have it on my terms."

"You are very brave," Leo said, appraising me. "I have no way to tell which way Enid will lean, but she would have to outright ignore your strength and power to harm you, which I don't believe she will do. She is passionate, and angry, and fearful, but she has never been stupid. She is one of the oldest supernaturals ever to be created. We have to hope that she will see what her sister does. Now, would you like to walk there, or shall I take us?" He grinned.

"Walk!" Danny shouted, answering for all of us.

We made our way down the hill toward the church.

I contemplated my next moves. First and foremost, I had to reason with Enid and implore her to listen to me. Rourke was right. I had no idea how to bring her dead sister back. Instead, I would have to convince her of my willingness to make a sacrifice. If she didn't believe me, or take my words to heart, she wouldn't keep me around, and that would be the end of it.

My heart felt heavy with the risk we were walking into, but I knew I was headed in the right direction. "Juanita," I muttered under my breath, "I could use your help about now. I know you said you wouldn't interfere, but if Enid doesn't listen, what am I supposed to do?" Immediately, one of Rourke's back pockets buzzed, and I arched an eyebrow at him. "Do you have a Pack phone on you?"

"I do," he answered as he reached around. "Unlike you, I can't talk internally with anyone but you."

I held my hand out. "I think Juanita is trying to get a hold of me." She was using the same tricks she'd used before.

The screen flashed: YOU ARE HEADED IN THE RIGHT DIRECTION.

Then the words disappeared and new ones popped up.
GO WITH YOUR HEART.

I glanced up at the sky as dawn broke over the rolling hills of Tuscany. "I'm glad you're with me," I said, "even if you can't be here in person. I hope your sister hears me out." Then I looked at Leo. "How come Juanita knows where I am, but Enid can't see me?"

"You and Juanita have a very special bond," he answered. Then he shrugged. "And I may have left a little doorway open for her to get through. She's crafty, that one. I only knew her in another form when she went by the name Pandora. She chose to go through a rebirth so she could watch over you. It's very rare for a supernatural to do that, but the process has strengthened her. She has been immersed in human culture for a long while now. It has made her more amenable to change, as she knew it would."

I almost tripped, launching myself down the hill. "Pandora?

As in Pandora's box?"

Leo chuckled softly. "That is an old myth, indeed. But, technically, yes, she is *that* Pandora. Pandora was the first woman created by the gods, but there wasn't just one woman. Three sisters were tasked with keeping a watchful eye over Fate for both the humans and the supernaturals. Pandora's box was said to contain plagues and diseases and all the evils of the world and that Pandora unleashed them by opening the box. But that is far from the truth. The sisters were forced to watch as the diseases came, sometimes wiping out entire civilizations, along with wars, death and destruction, famine, all of which led to civilization as we know it. And they could do nothing to stop it. Pandora's box, as I know the origin of the myth, actually contained her tears and sorrow. Of course, it's not a physical box, but a metaphor for her emotions. But the tellings of tales get twisted through the ages, as to be expected."

That was incredible news.

Juanita was Pandora.

It was hard to believe that she had been reborn to protect me and keep me from harm so this day could come. It felt momentous. "I don't know what to say," I answered truthfully. "It seems the supernatural world is much larger in scope than I'd ever imagined. Growing up, I heard myths and tales about angels and demons, gods and goddesses, from all walks of life. But even for a supernatural, it's hard to grasp that those myths are actually truths."

"Indeed, it is," Leo agreed. "As a leader on the Coalition, you will be privy to every detail of this world and every realm contained within it. There will be a lot to learn. There are a lot of creatures and beings that have thought to have been extinct, but who still exist. Your job will not be an easy one."

Rourke said, "She won't be alone. Her family will stay by her side."

Leo nodded, his face contemplative. "The Coalition has

been made up of five females for as long as it's existed. They interact and share power, but each has her own job to do. Jessica will bring new dimension by opening up the Coalition to others. I believe this is the right thing to do, as it's been stagnant for far too long. I believe this will be the most successful Coalition ever created. Supernaturals will be forced to obey the laws, not just by five, but by many."

"Why has there been such a long time between the last Coalition and this one?" I asked. "I was told my birth was late, but that I killed Ardat Lili too early. I don't understand how it works."

"Fate is incredibly complicated," Leo said. "I don't think anybody is really meant to understand it. Not only were you born late, but so was the vampire you seek today. But it had to happen that way, for she met with Enid long ago. And when Enid took her this time, Enid remembered her from those long years ago, and what she had said to the vampire. It's all part of the fabric."

We were almost to the church. "Do you feel Enid inside?"

"I do," Leo replied. "In fact, she has let me know she is expecting us. She has deduced that we would come here, even though she had no prior knowledge."

When we got within fifty yards, the church door swung open.

A lone figure stood in the doorway of crumbling bricks, the sun just poking its rays over the treetops.

She was dressed in a simple white gown. Her hair was also white, flowing freely down over her shoulders. Her face was aged, but not overly so. She looked to be roughly sixty human years. She glanced at us and swung her arm toward the interior of the church. "Won't you come in?"

21

I was unsure what to do. I was relieved Enid was here and willing to talk, but I looked to Leo for guidance. He didn't hesitate as he moved forward with grace, tucking his vibrant wings tightly to his back. I'd been right—as the first rays of sunlight glinted off them, they shone the purest white. In contrast to his olive skin, it made him look ethereal.

"I trust you have been well," Leo said as he approached Enid. "It has been many years since we last encountered each other. You have not changed overly much."

"Nor have you, Angel of Light," Enid agreed. Her voice was softer than I'd imagined. I'd expected the wicked witch and instead got a grandmother. She turned her gaze on me, her irises contracting. Her power was tightly coiled, but I knew if she unleashed it, all would be lost. "I had not expected such a blatant play on your part." She inclined her head. "I would've kept my word and would have exchanged you for my prisoners."

"That's still the deal," I said. "But instead of a complicated runaround, I decided to show up at your doorstep." I placed a hand on Danny's shoulder. "If you set them free now, my second will retrieve them and move away from this area."

Her eyes landed squarely on Rourke. "But this one stays," she stated. "I can see that he will not be moved from this place."

"He stays. I hope you can see that I will continue to cooperate," I said. "And I'm willing to discuss matters civilly."

She closed her eyes no longer than two seconds. When she opened them, she said, "They are free. You may go retrieve them." She abruptly turned and walked back into the church.

"Go see them to safety," I told Danny. "Leo said the abbey is a half a mile from here. Tyler's on his way to this area. Get a hold of him, and hopefully, we'll be able to follow shortly."

Danny looked unsure. "It will go against my wolf to leave you here," he argued. "A second does not leave their Alpha in danger for any reason, including for a mate. Well, that is, a mate who's not in danger. Naomi says they are already out of their cell, and she awaits our arrival. They are both in good health. She says that she and Jax can also come here and help."

"No." I shook my head. "I want you all away from here. I have no idea what's going to happen in there. Enid may look unassuming, but if she wants me dead, there is no stopping her, whether you, Naomi, or Jax are here. I am ordering you to go retrieve them and take them to safety. That's the highest priority." I was relieved to know they were okay. My body felt more relaxed than it had in a long time. "No arguments, Daniel Walker. Do as I say. We will meet up with you later."

Danny surprised me by embracing me. "Please stay safe," he murmured. "I can't thank you enough for finding my mate. We will get through this. There's no other way around it."

I pulled back and kissed his cheek. "I believe that too." I had to. The possibility of my life ending right here in this church seemed unreal, even though I knew it could happen. "Now, go. Make sure Jax is comfortable and get him to Kayla as soon as you can." Without looking back, I turned and walked into the church, Rourke right behind me.

Once I stepped over the threshold, cold air abraded my skin.

We had to pick our way over fallen stone and debris. Enid hadn't bothered trying to make it homey in here. We had entered the main chapel of the church. Most of the roof was gone, but some pews were still in place, as was the altar. The large structure looked to be made of marble or some sort of granite.

Enid stood on the top step, facing us as we moved toward her.

I hadn't anticipated her allowing Leo and Rourke in here with me, but I was glad she had. I rubbed my arms.

"I had thought to kill you on sight," Enid said, cutting to the chase. "But I've changed my mind. We will talk for a moment instead."

I hoped it would be more than a moment. "I'm happy to discuss whatever you'd like."

"You killed Ardat Lili." She stated it as fact.

"Yes."

"You regretted this decision." Again, she phrased it as a statement, not a question.

"In a way, yes," I answered honestly. "Ending another life is something I will never take lightly, but when I saw all the hatefulness she had perpetuated, I knew I had no choice." I didn't regret removing such evil from this world.

Enid began to pace back and forth in front of the altar as we stood in the aisle. "You took away the rebirth of my sister," she chastised. "A rebirth I've been anxiously awaiting for over five hundred years."

"I did, and I'm sincerely sorry," I said, bowing my head. "I had no idea at the time that killing Ardat Lili would have such consequences. But I'm prepared to make it right. I'll do whatever it takes."

She paused with her back to us. "When our sister was killed by Lilith, I had never really known what pain was. I had never grieved another personally, in all my years. At first, I thought Fate had played a cruel trick on us. That it was testing us. Pandora and I scried and scried, but to no avail. We could not find our sister. For many years, we thought all was lost." She turned to us, sadness etched in her features. "Until one day, we were given the gift of sight that she would be reborn. We felt such joy. But it was to be short-lived. We saw that Ardat Lili would be killed before she gave birth to the child. We saw *you*." Her expression was accusing, like I'd somehow known that my prophecy was to harm her, and I'd been determined to carry it out no matter the cost. I tried to speak, to tell her otherwise, but she cut me off, continuing, "We saw you end Bianca's life before it had a chance to grow. For days, we scried, Pandora certain that our beloved Bianca would be born again. We did not see it. Instead, things became jumbled as they never were before. One day we would see one path, the next day another." She began to pace again, her hands clasped in front of her. "Pandora saw something and insisted it was the correct vision. But I, on the other hand, saw something quite different. Both results would bring our sister back, but which one was true?" She paused as she turned, her face contemplative.

Leo cleared his throat. "Pandora believed in her visions enough to be reborn. To entrust that her sister would live again."

"She did." Enid's voice was bitter. "She left me over fifty years ago to see this done."

"And you haven't forgiven her," I said. The words tumbled out of my mouth before I could take them back. I'd been caught up in the story, feeling Enid's pain and anger like they'd been my own. She'd already lost one sister, only to lose another because of me. The pain must've been excruciating. "I'm sorry," I said. "I spoke out of turn. I don't presume to understand how you feel. I was only projecting how I would've felt in the same situation. If I lost Tyler, the grief would be overwhelming. He's my twin, and he's been with me every moment of my life—if not physically, mentally. I wouldn't know how to be myself without him. I can't imagine losing two siblings. It must've been hard. I'm sorry."

She stared at me for so long, I began to fidget. "Yes, it continues to be hard." She turned her back on us once again. "Pandora and I separated on bad terms. I was angry with her for not siding with me, with my vision. I'm still angry with her. But more than that, I want her back by my side where she belongs."

"Killing me won't achieve that," I said, feeling the need to explain. "Juanita…I mean, Pandora will not forgive you if you make that choice. Not after the sacrifice she's made to keep me alive."

"Don't you think I know that, child?" Enid snarled, whipping around to face me. "But I will not risk Bianca's chance at life one more time! I have been without her for far too long."

"Jessica stands before you, the vision that Pandora foresaw," Leo said evenly. "Do you not see the same as she now?"

"I do." It sounded final. I didn't understand Leo's statement, but before I could ask him to elaborate, Enid continued, "But so many things could still go wrong. If I end her life, I will be certain. I will have my sister back. If I don't, things could change."

"If you end Jessica's life, there will be needless death and destruction for far too many, and Pandora will not stand by your side," Leo stated. "Letting Jessica live is preferable to all, and in the end, you will get both sisters back."

"Perhaps," Enid said as she stepped off the altar and strode up to me. My mate growled, but she paid him no attention. It was like he wasn't even there. If she hadn't been pursuing me, kidnapping my friends, and in general trying to kill me, I would've considered her fairly reasonable. She was hardly the cruel and conniving Hag I'd envisioned. "My hunting you happened for a reason, don't doubt it for a moment. It is because of my actions that we stand here today, and nothing else. You are as you are, because of me."

Huh? That was more than a little confusing.

"I don't doubt it," I said, deciding to roll with it. "I am well aware that everything happens for a reason. But, ultimately, my purpose here is to get back on track." Our eyes locked, and I saw compassion there, which I hadn't expected. But I also saw anger and resentment. "Am I close to achieving that?"

"You might be," she answered, turning and striding back up toward the altar. "But I'm not entirely certain you will be able to make the sacrifice that is needed to complete Pandora's vision."

I took a breath in. "I don't know if I am either," I replied, the words once again tumbling out before I was ready to speak. She spun around, her face registering something close to surprise. I kept going. "I can't stand here and tell you, in all honesty, that I'm willing to do absolutely anything, which is what you expect me to say. If I don't know what it is I must give up, how can I tell you I will?" Enid picked up a small chalice and focused on it, not me. I took that as a sign that she was listening and kept going. "In this moment, if you asked me to take my mate's life, I wouldn't do it. No matter the benefit. Even if it would ensure the greater good for the entire supernatural race. I'm not wired that way. I love too deeply and care too much. I would never be able to kill someone I love. So if you asked, I would say no. But that doesn't mean I will fail all tasks. If you want assurances that I will make a sacrifice, tell me what it is, so I can give you an honest answer."

"That's the quandary, then, isn't it," she stated. "I must wait a long time—possibly too long—for you to fulfill this sacrifice. And in the end, if you do not, time will have passed and your death might not set things to right. I will no longer have a guarantee, and I will be stuck."

"Stuck is perhaps not the correct word," Leo said gently. "Your sister will be alive, and maybe that will have to suffice. Is that not the end goal?"

"No." Enid's voice was sharp. "The end goal is for me and my sisters to be *reunited*. For us to stand by each other's side until the end of time. It is *not* to have her alive but unreachable, for her to love others more than she loves us. She was taken from me, and I will have her back *as she was*."

I wasn't getting the whole gist of the story, but I did understand what Enid was worried about. I cleared my throat. "Um, if your sister is reborn, I don't think it's possible for her to be exactly as she once was. She will be reborn, just as Pandora was, but with a different set of experiences. As we grow, we're shaped by our environment, by what we experience. Things are vastly different today than they were five hundred years ago. It's not possible for her to be the same, but," I pointed out helpfully, "she will *still* be your sister."

"You don't know that," Enid said, tossing the chalice aside. It skittered across the floor, making hollow clinking sounds. "You have no idea what she will be like! Or how she will think, or what she will remember. We are powerful supernaturals! The most powerful. Bianca is strong and courageous. She will weep when she finds out how long she has been away from us. When we reunite, we will be as we once were."

"That's a fairy tale," I said as Rourke tensed beside me. I had to speak up, no matter the cost. "Something you've conjured in your mind after all these years. And I don't blame you for it. If Tyler was gone, and then I found out he was coming back, I would fantasize about picking up right where we left off too. But if Tyler was reborn to a new family and grew up with a different set of experiences, there's no way he would be *exactly* the same as the brother I once knew." I met her gaze. "But I would love him just the same, and I'm certain we would forge a new relationship, one that was just as fulfilling."

"Your opinions mean nothing to me," Enid replied snidely. "You don't know our ways, who we are, or where we come from. I will not allow you to influence my decision. I will have my sister back the way I want her, nothing less!"

Before I could respond, the church door flung open with a loud bang.

Leo, Rourke, and I turned, surprised by the intrusion.

"If her opinion means nothing to you, maybe mine will."

22

"Juanita!" I raced up the aisle and embraced my friend. She laughed in her good-natured way. "I guess I should call you Pandora now, since that's your real name. It's so good to see you. I wasn't sure if you would come."

"I wasn't sure either, Chica," she answered in her same Spanish accent. "If it had not been for Leonardo, this wouldn't be possible." She beamed at the angel who had also come to greet her. "I thank you from the bottom of my heart for making this happen." She settled a small, perfectly manicured hand over his. This time, her nails were colored a bright fuchsia. "I know the life you have chosen, as a mortal, has given you much peace. And now that peace has been interrupted. But you have provided a great service to us—one that neither myself nor my sister foresaw. Fate has always been tricky, and it has proven to us once again that it is the one who is powerful, not us." She bowed her head to Leo.

"Even though I play the mortal, which I do enjoy," he said, "I am not one, or am I without my wits. When Jessica entered my sanctuary yesterday, I knew what had to be done. She is special. Her aura is bright, unlike any other I have ever seen. You were right to protect her. I only hope that your sister sees the same thing before it's too late."

Pandora nodded as she made her way past us, walking slowly toward Enid, her heels clacking against the stone floor. "I know you have seen the same thing as I, dear sister. And I am here to assure you that even though Bianca will be reborn, as I have been, she will retain the same memories, feel the same love, and be connected to us as she once was. But Jessica is correct." She turned and flashed me a brilliant smile. "I am not exactly the same as when I left you, as you can see. This life has given me many new experiences and has made me the richer for it. There is value, where before it had been waning. There is love, were none was before. I am stronger, the weakness that lingered all but flushed out. I would not trade it for anything." She spread her arms wide. "I stand before you, remembering our life together, yearning for your love and companionship once again, and it will be the same for Bianca. You must believe it."

Enid's face was hard to read. Then she frowned. "It has been a long while since you sought me out. Why is that? If you are the same sister I remember, and you have retained your whole soul, why not come to me before this? It's been over fifty years. Make me understand."

"I could not see you without interfering in Fate's plan." Pandora shook her head. "You and I were given different visions on that day for a reason, as well as each day afterward. What I see is not always what you see. Fate has not tested us, it has *changed* us. If I had come, it would have interfered with getting Jessica to this very moment, right where she needs to be. Maybe you would've understood, maybe not. Or maybe you would've killed her before you saw the proof standing right in front of your very eyes. It was not my place to make you understand, until today."

What proof was she talking about?

"I come to you in love," Pandora went on, "and implore you to let her live. Allow her to make the sacrifice she needs to make things right again. Save the world from the chaos you know will descend upon us with her death." As I watched, Pandora's visage wavered, changing into something else. Her hair became thicker and longer. She grew a foot taller, and her short skirt and blouse morphed into a long white dress, much like what her sister wore.

Enid's expression changed from angry to satisfied. "Now you look as I remember you. It seems your human bonds are not that strong after all."

"Do not let the human guise fool you. I glamoured myself by choice at a young age," Pandora said. "I wanted to mirror the family and the culture I grew to love. It allowed me to live as Leo does"—she gestured to him—"to fully immerse myself in the human world. I will be sad to see it go. But my place is here with you and our beloved Bianca."

"Bianca will not be with us for some time," Enid stated, turning to pace.

"That's true," Pandora replied, heading up to the altar by her sister. "But if you allow Jessica to live, it will save us one thousand years of heartbreak and even more waiting. Why do that when we have already waited for five hundred years? In the scope of things, what's another twenty?"

"This is not a guaranteed path," Enid insisted. "The wolf could still die. I will not play Russian roulette with Bianca's life!"

"What are your terms, then?" Pandora asked.

Enid looked surprised. "What are you talking about? What terms?"

"I believe Jessica's sacrifice is guaranteed, you don't. In order to make it a success, what are your terms?" Pandora turned to give me an encouraging smile. I returned her smile with a sharp intake of breath. She was beautiful, with long, flowing dark hair, wide eyes, full lips, all her makeup gone. I missed the old Juanita, but the person in her place was elegant and regal—a powerful supernatural in her own right. I couldn't believe she'd given up so much to be my guardian.

When Enid didn't respond, Pandora turned back to her. "Surely there is something that will make this a certainty for you."

Leo spoke, surprising me by getting down on one knee, facing Enid. "Let me help you with this decision. I vow to be your sister Bianca's protector, beginning now until she returns to you. She will have no greater guardian angel than I. Those who seek to harm her will not succeed. You have my solemn oath."

I cleared my throat. I was getting worried. "I don't understand what's happening," I said. "Does anyone care to explain?"

Pandora came down the step and grasped my hand. "I realize this is confusing for you," she said, her voice low and melodic. "But the timing to tell all is not right just yet. There are still things in motion that must happen without our interference. But you will find out soon enough."

Rourke stood shoulder to shoulder with me.

His tension rolled off of him in waves. He pinned his gaze on Enid. "What are your terms?" he said. "I will see my mate safely from this place."

Enid appraised him thoughtfully. "On second thought, I do have terms, and if they are not met, I will kill your mate. She is in a precarious position. I will not sacrifice my sister's life for anyone, no matter how much you try to convince me." She turned her eyes to me. "You are missing a member of the Coalition, and she will not be given up easily. There will be fighting, and there will be bloodshed." Her gaze was piercing. "My conditions are as follows: When all is revealed, you will come to me. Alone. I will be the judge and jury of your sacrifice. If I deem your answers satisfactory, you will live. If not, you will die. Do you accept?"

Rourke began to growl.

I answered, "I accept."

There was no other way.

Enid had just heard her sister and Leo plead their cases and offer their help. This was what it had come down to.

It would be her and me in the end.

She crossed her arms. "The moon will rise twice before your coronation is set to take place. You will meet me here, alone"—she glared at Pandora and Leo—"at midnight the evening you are to take your sacred vows. You will answer my questions to my satisfaction, or die."

I nodded once. "I vow it."

Enid seemed satisfied. She turned her back on us and walked off the altar and out of sight. Pandora came to embrace me, giving me a bear hug like the ones I remembered. "You did well!" she said enthusiastically. "You have so much intelligence and will make a great leader. My sister is headstrong, and her heart is in need of mending, but I am confident she will see things our way. And you are just the person to make her understand."

"I'm not going to lie," I confided. "I don't understand everything that was said here today, and I know you have faith in me—and I hope to uphold that—but I'm scared. I'm worried the sacrifice will be too great and I won't be able to answer the questions to Enid's satisfaction." I didn't want to think about what would happen if I didn't.

Pandora placed her hands on either side of my face, stroking my cheeks. "The sacrifice will not be too great, I promise you. I know you well, Chica," she whispered. "I would never ask you for something that you would not be able to deliver. Now stop worrying and go with your mate. Reunite with your family. There will be much to do tomorrow. Love each other and be happy. You are moments away from being fully back on your true path. And once you are there, we will celebrate."

Leo gave Pandora a small bow. "It was nice to see you again," he said. "Your rebirth has done you well."

"It has," she agreed. "The world has much to offer still."

He glanced at me. "If you are choosing to take another route back to Florence, I will take my leave," Leo said. "Now that my presence has been revealed to the masses, I must make some provisions for my new life." He took my hand, his power unsettling in its strength as it raced up my arm. "I look forward to seeing you again, Jessica. You are a brave warrior." He bowed his head and then turned and walked out of the church.

"Are you coming with us?" I asked Pandora.

She shook her head, her shining locks swaying. "No, I will stay and talk with my sister awhile. We have much to catch up on. I've been gone for over fifty years. That's a long time for wounds to fester, but it's time for them to heal. All will be well. Trust me." She leaned over and kissed the top of my head.

"Will I see you again soon?" I asked.

"Yes."

I hugged her. "Thank you for always being there for me. I was lucky to have you, even if I didn't realize it at the time."

"It was my pleasure," she said.

Rourke took my hand and led me down the aisle. The sun was bright, the morning alive. We'd been in there longer than I'd thought. At least an hour, maybe more.

"It's hard to believe Enid is just letting us walk out of there," I said. "I thought in the end we would have to fight her."

"I did too," Rourke said, his voice reserved. "The only reason she let us go is because you vowed to return to her alone. She will get her chance to end your life if she wants to."

I gazed at my mate as we walked along the path away from the church, toward the abbey. "I know you're angry," I told him. "But I'd already weighed all the options in my mind, and there was no getting around making a deal with Enid. I believe Pandora and Leo are correct and I will survive. If I didn't believe that, I wouldn't have brokered the deal. I don't want to be on the run from Enid for the rest of our lives." I stopped walking, pulling him close. Our lips met, and all of our fear and adrenaline flowed outward. The kiss was hungry. I broke away, leaning back, my arms still folded around him. "Our lives are going to change dramatically in the next few days. We can't stop it from happening, we can only try to steer the ship. But knowing you will be by my side every step of the way makes everything bearable. We can do this. Together."

Rourke rested his forehead against mine, his arms crushing me to his chest, his voice barely audible as he murmured, "I will never leave your side."

23

"I'm so happy you're here," I said, embracing my father. It was good to see him. He and his people had managed to secure a house outside Siena, which wasn't too far from where we'd been.

Tyler and Kayla had gone to pick up Danny, Naomi, and Jax. Apparently, Danny had managed to hail a cab in a small nearby town, but it had taken them in the complete opposite direction due to their cabbie not understanding a lick of English.

"So tell me about the meeting," my father said as we sat at a large table. "Then I need to know about Julian."

I told him everything that had happened, including our initial meet-up with Leo and what I'd just promised Enid. "Juanita, now Pandora, previously told me to make decisions with my heart. And I felt promising Enid that I'd show up tomorrow night was my only choice, given the circumstances. We can't outrun Enid. She sees the future. But I have faith that with Pandora's and Leo's backing, things will work out as they are supposed to."

"I don't like that you've promised something blindly, but I understand your reasoning." My father appeared tired, the sleeves of his standard work shirt bunched up at his elbows. "We are currently situated between a rock and a very hard place. We may not be able to go inside the church with you when you meet Enid, but we will stand our ground outside. I've brought fifteen wolves, and we will gather Julian and his wolves as well. She will not harm you without severe retaliation."

"I'm not sure that is going to work," Rourke said, leaning back in his seat. "Julian has disappeared for the time being. We think he's in league with Ceres, the Goddess of Fertility."

My father said, "That's what Tyler told me, but I'm having a hard time believing it. The picture he painted was that Julian had shut out his wolves in favor of this goddess." He rubbed his chin. "That doesn't sound like the Alpha I'm familiar with, but I admit things have changed in our world. If Julian is on a quest for greater power, it has led him astray—far from the road he should be on."

"I think it's safe to say he's veered completely off the path," I said. "All of our information leads to Ceres having kidnapped Tally for her place on the Coalition. I'm assuming it's been tougher than the goddess intended to kill the leader of the witches, which is why Tally is still alive. I'm certain Julian is furious that things haven't gone quicker. Our arrival has likely put a crimp in their plans to dispose of Tally, hoping the power would choose Ceres. It's unclear what the goddess would've promised Julian in return. What can she give the Alpha of the Mediterranean Pack? Julian already has supreme power over Florence, being the strongest supernatural in the area." Other than Leo, who kept his presence quiet.

"Maybe she promised to make him a god." Rourke shrugged. "Either that, or she promised him once she took her place on the Coalition she would put him in a prominent position of power. Either way, he's turned against his wolves and us. We haven't checked in with Ray, James, or Marcy yet, but if Julian has turned up and offered to help them, I would be stunned."

"I've been in contact with my second," my father said. "But not since early this morning. James said they were on the scent of this goddess, which had led them to some sort of bunker. Let me try to get a hold of him and see what their progress is." My father stood up and walked away from the table.

There was commotion outside, and Rourke and I went to investigate.

"Naomi!" I exclaimed as I rushed down the steps to embrace my friend. "You look no worse for wear, and I'm relieved."

"Indeed, *Ma Reine*, it wasn't so bad," she answered. "But then, I was in good company." She gestured to the back of the SUV as a large figure emerged. I stepped forward to get a good look.

Jax was, by far, the biggest fifteen-year-old I'd ever laid eyes on.

He had to be at least six-five and still growing. He resembled his sister, with olive skin, bright amber eyes, and dark tousled hair. Even though he was tall, he still looked boyish. He was darling. I was happy to note his skin didn't even hint at any shade of blue. It must change only when he shifted into an ice troll.

Kayla climbed out of the car after him, beaming with happiness and pride. She grabbed his arm and dragged him over to Rourke and me. "I'd like to introduce you to my kid brother, Ajax." She nodded at us. "Jax, these are the people who were instrumental in freeing you, Jessica and Rourke. We owe them big-time."

Jax stuck his hand out, giving us both a lopsided grin.

Rourke clasped it first. Their hands were almost the same size. When he was done growing, he might clock in as one of the strongest supernaturals around. "Nice to meet you," he said, his voice pleasant and boyish. He gave an exaggerated sniff before smiling. "Cat shifter, huh? I've never met one before. But that's not saying much, since I haven't met that many other supernaturals."

"I'm the only cat shifter you're likely to meet," Rourke said. He turned to me. "This is Jessica McClain. You owe your rescue to her."

"I don't know about that," I replied, grasping Jax's outstretched hand, mine disappearing inside his. "It was a team effort. But I'm so thankful you're back safe and sound. We were happy to help."

Jax shifted his eyes downward. "My sister said you guys are going to keep us protected from now on. Is that true?"

"It is," I told him. Jax and his sister had been on the run for a long time, and it had worn them down. "You're welcome to stay with us as long as you like." He nodded once, satisfied. "Are you hungry? If the answer is yes, there's food in the kitchen. Go help yourself."

He mumbled, "Thanks," as he made his way inside. Other than being huge and extremely strong, he was a typical teenager.

Tyler came up next and gave me a hug. "Glad to see you're in one piece, sis. I was worried Enid was going to tear you limb from limb."

"It seems she's had a change of heart, for at least the next day or so," I said.

Danny chuckled, coming up behind Tyler. "She would've been hard-pressed to do any damage with that angel around. I've never seen the likes of him in my entire life. Glad it was a success." He gave me a quick hug.

"I am too."

"I'm sorry we got lost. The cabbie didn't speak any bloody

English," he groused. "And I might've misheard the name of the city when Tyler told me on the phone, as I was distracted." He beamed at Naomi. "But we're here, alive and well, albeit late."

"No problem. Come on in," I said. "Dad's trying to get a hold of James right now so we can see where they're at. We're going to need to head back to the Compound soon."

Before I could follow the group back into the house, Kayla grabbed my elbow. "I just wanted to say thank you," she said as happiness radiated from her. "Jax is all I have left in this world, and if something had happened to him, I don't know what I would've done. You stayed true to your word, and you have my loyalty for it."

"I appreciate that, Kayla," I told her, settling my arm around her shoulders as we walked inside. "We are happy to have you guys as part of this team. I meant what I said to Jax. You are welcome to stay with us as long as you like. There will always be a place for you here. And we will continue to do everything in our power to protect Jax from the gargoyles who want to force him to be a part of their pack. I'll be able to facilitate that better once I take my seat on the Coalition. From that position, I will instruct them to back off permanently."

"That would be outstanding," she said. "I hope they listen. From what I understand they stick to themselves and don't follow any conventional rules. But I'm confident that, between all of us, we will be able to keep my brother safe."

My father paced in from another room, looking distressed.

"What is it?" I asked, concerned, pulling out a chair and taking a seat at the table.

"James isn't answering," he said.

"Are you sure?" I asked. "Maybe he's tied up with something." There were only two reasons James wouldn't answer my father—he was either incapacitated, or Marcy was injured and he was trying to help her.

Either scenario didn't bode well for us.

"I'm sure," he answered. "I commanded he answer me, and all I got in response was silence."

I glanced at Rourke, who had taken a seat beside me. "Have you tried the Pack phone? Nick and Lucas should be at the Compound keeping an eye out."

He nodded, setting the phone on the table in front of him. "I just tried, and no one picked up."

As we stared at the phone, it rang.

Rourke grabbed it and handed it to me to answer.

"Nick?"

"It's me," he said, sounding out of breath. "Jessica, where are you? Things are falling apart here. Ray went missing first. Now we can't find James or Marcy."

His voice held a strange echo. "Where are you?"

"Lucas and I are in an abandoned shed near the edge of the Compound, trying to stay out of sight. Ray took James and Marcy to the bunker this morning. There was a small explosion of some kind a few miles away, so Ray went to investigate. He never came back. James wanted to go search for him alone, but Marcy wouldn't hear of it. They went together and didn't come back. Lucas and I have been trying to figure out what's going on. For a supernatural to have that much strength—to take all three of them—makes me think that maybe Ceres and Julian aren't working entirely alone. Ray mentioned a strange power signature nearby. Not sure if we should go and check it out or not. We've been waiting to hear from you."

"We can leave here in five minutes. Don't go near the bunker for now," I told him. "If you can, have Lucas reach out to any of Julian's wolves who he thinks are willing to defect. When the Alphas come face-to-face, there will be a challenge. If Julian has an ounce of respect left inside him, he will fight. My father will win, and Julian's wolves will be accountable to him."

I heard Lucas in the background say, "Will do. There will be more than a few who are willing to defect."

"Is Eudoxia around? Does she know what's going on?" I asked Nick.

"We haven't seen her, so I'm assuming she's not here. There was quite a bit of commotion. I would think she would've come out to investigate if she'd heard."

"Leave it to her to be a no-show when we need her most," I muttered. "We'll be there soon. Hang tight." I punched off the phone and stood, addressing my father. "There's no doubt Julian and Ceres are in this together. They've kidnapped Ray, James, and Marcy. My guess is that since Julian and Ceres's plans have fallen through, and they haven't been able to kill Tally and grab the power, they will try to ransom them to us for immunity."

"That's not going to happen," my father said as he pushed up from his chair, his voice tight. "If you act aggressively toward me or mine, you're going to pay the price. This is not a time for us to show weakness. I want the supernatural community to know how strong you are—*we* are—together. Once you take your vows, I want any and all uprisings to be halted in their tracks. Supernaturals around the world need to understand who's in charge."

I nodded as we moved toward the door. "I agree. If we're easy on them now, the supernatural community will take notice. We go in with force, rescue our friends, and move forward in strength."

"If Julian forces your hand," Rourke said to my father, "we will have to figure out the logistics of what you being the Alpha of the Mediterranean Pack means."

"I've thought about that," my father admitted as he ran a hand through his hair. "I won't be able to linger in Europe past the coronation. It will be too confusing for the wolves, and I have too much to deal with back home as it is." He looked directly at me. "But I think you need to stay in Italy. At least for a while. I'll name Tyler temporary Alpha of the

Mediterranean Pack in my stead, and he can run things here. Having an Italian wolf as a second, if there is one strong enough, should quell things for a while. Once things quiet down, we can reassess."

"You think I should stay in Italy?" I asked, stopping in my tracks. I hadn't even thought where we would reside after we swore our vows.

"Europe is the heart of the supernatural community," he replied. "It's much older and steeped in tradition, with at least ten times as many supes as we have in the States. It makes sense for you to run things from here, at least for a while. If we defeat Julian, you can stay in the villa. There should be enough room for your entire team to live comfortably." It was true that there was more than enough room.

"*If* we defeat him?" Tyler said. "There is no question you will bring him down. And I'm happy to be the temporary Alpha for as long as it takes. Staying in Italy for a while doesn't sound so bad. I like it here."

I glanced at my mate. He didn't need me to voice the question. "I'm fine with staying here," Rourke said. "Home is wherever you are, and your father has a valid point. While you establish power and dominance on the Coalition, which will take time, it makes sense to be nearest to those who will help you, as well as those who will do you harm. That way we can hear about it that much sooner and tamp it out before it becomes a problem."

I was getting used to the idea. "Okay," I answered, continuing to head toward the door. "We don't have to decide anything at the moment. Before I make a commitment, I want to see how things shake out. For now, what we need to do is get going. If there's going to be a fight today, we need all the strength we can amass. I hope Lucas is able to rally some of Julian's wolves and Eudoxia finds her way back."

Jax walked out of the kitchen, a sandwich in one hand, a Coke in the other. "Did somebody say strength? If so, I'm in."

24

"I don't want you fighting with us." Kayla argued with her brother in the backseat as we sped toward Florence. "You're not ready yet. Your powers are...unpredictable."

"Not anymore," Jax answered proudly. "Naomi and I practiced a bunch. She was a great coach. I can shift and hold my control now, no problem."

Naomi smiled and turned in her seat to face Jax. "*Oui*, he did very well. He was very brave and tried to break us out many times. After the first few times he shifted, his control was impeccable."

"I was always worried before," Jax explained, "that somebody would see me, or I would hurt someone. So when I shifted, I freaked. But not anymore." Jax was clearly proud of his newfound control over his skill.

Any supernatural in their teens went through a rocky transformation when they came into their magic, especially wolves. It was all about hormones and power swirling around at the same time.

Danny chuckled. "When I shifted for the first time as a

young lad, I was a wild animal. It was a horrid experience. It took me months to figure out how to shift without pain, much less control myself once I got there."

"You're still a wild animal when you shift." Tyler shook his head from the backseat next to Kayla. "When you shift, it's like you lose your damn mind."

"What can I say?" Danny shrugged. "I love to feel the wind running through my fur, and I don't give a damn what anybody else thinks. Indulging my wild side makes me feel whole again. Shedding this skin feels glorious." He patted his arm. "It's completely liberating."

Tyler leaned forward to address Jax. "It takes time to master the art of shifting and reining in your animal side, who is always fighting for control. I'm not familiar with what you are, but it sounds like you are figuring it out, no problem. I'd be proud to have you fight alongside us."

Kayla seemed to soften. "Okay, Jax, you can join us. But if I feel like it's getting too dangerous, you have to leave, no questions asked."

Jax was about to protest, but I cut in. "Your sister is right. If you want to be part of this team, you agree to take orders without argument. We can't be efficient in defeating a threat if we're worried about you. Do you understand? If your sister is distracted, or if I feel like I need to intervene on your behalf, or Rourke does, it could make or break a fight. In time, when you come fully into your powers, you will be an incredible asset to us—possibly one of the strongest players we have. But at fifteen, and as a new shifter, you have to agree to listen to all of us, either that or you're not invited to the fight." My tone was final. "If not, you're welcome to wait in the villa."

Jax glanced around the group for a few seconds, seeing that all of our faces mirrored the same expression. This wasn't playtime, this was real life. "Got it," he replied. "If anyone tells me to leave, I'm out of there. But I promise I can help.

When I shift, my skin is like stone. Nothing can pierce it, not even wolf jaws." His chest puffed up a little. He was beyond cute.

"What about magic? Are you resistant to spells?" I asked.

He looked uncertain, glancing at his sister. "We think he is," Kayla answered. "But he's never encountered a witch before, so we don't know for sure."

I nodded. From what I understood, gargoyles could resist magic because their skin was so dense that spells couldn't penetrate. Sounded like Jax might be the same. "I certainly don't want this fight to be your first exposure to magic," I said. "You can deflect the wolves and help us get into the bunker, but stay away from the witches and the goddess. She used to be a witch and can cast spells."

Rourke drove the SUV. There were two other vehicles behind us carrying my father and his wolves. "Almost there," Rourke said. "We park outside the Compound and walk in."

"Yes," I said. "Nick and Lucas, and whatever wolves he's been able to amass, should be waiting for us at the end of the driveway." I'd talked to Nick halfway through our drive back to Florence. They were having luck talking to the wolves, although a few had gone to join their Alpha already.

It seemed Julian knew he had a fight in front of him.

Ten minutes later, we pulled over and parked on the dirt road that ran parallel to the villa and piled out of the car. Nick and Lucas, and what looked to be twenty to thirty wolves, had gathered up the road. That was a significantly higher amount than I'd thought would show. Julian must've been ineffective for a long time to cause this kind of defection.

My father took the lead.

The wolves would respond to his power, instinctively wanting to follow the most powerful Alpha they could find. He didn't waste any time. "My name is Callum McClain," he announced in a voice ringing with strength. He immediately commanded an audience. I watched as the faces of the wolves changed from trepidation to interest, which would quickly morph into loyalty. "I am Alpha of the U.S. Territories. It has come to my attention that your Alpha here has broken sacred Pack rules. He chose to pursue personal endeavors for his own gain, rather than for the wealth of Pack. He has put my daughter, Jessica, in jeopardy and has kidnapped my allies, including my second. He will pay for this with his life." His voice held certainty, and we all believed it. "You are not required to fight alongside me, but if you wish to join my Pack when this is all over, I suggest you do."

They didn't need any more convincing.

As my father stood with his arms folded, his feet spread apart, the wolves came up one by one and placed a knee to the ground in front of my father, bowing their heads. They freely gave him their fealty. It would take more to officially become part of his Pack, but this was what wolves did in a time of change or stress.

Once it was over, my father asked, "Who among you is at the top? Come forward. You will serve as my advisor. Anyone who has specific details about where Julian is and who is with him speak now."

Two of the bigger wolves stepped forward.

One appeared to be Scandinavian, judging by his height, build, and honey-colored hair. The other seemed to have Greek heritage, with jet-black hair, dark features, and light skin. But it was hard to be certain. The Scandinavian bowed his head as he addressed my father. "I am Carl, the highest-ranking wolf in attendance. There are two above me, including Julian's second, Stephen, and one other. Both have gone to fight alongside our former Alpha's side. This is Alastair." He nodded toward the Greek wolf. "He heads our communications and is privy to information you will need. Julian has been careless. When he brought the goddess and the witches here, he had no regard for how we would feel about it. He has forced us to accept his new ways, or face death. We no longer fear him."

"My son tells me you are all installed in bunkhouses nearby. Is that correct?" my father asked.

"It is," Carl confirmed. "But that was not always the way of things. The top ten ranking wolves lived at the villa until approximately eight months ago."

"I see," my father said. Wolves enjoyed Pack mentality and living close to their Alpha. The higher-ranking wolves would feel the bite of separation the greatest and likely be the most bitter. That Julian's second, and the next in line, had gone to fight with their Alpha now was likely nothing more than a reflex of wanting to be in his good graces again. Wolves craved attention and command, much like a toddler tugging on a mother's skirt. It didn't diminish their physical strength, just explained how Pack functioned in the minds of wolves. "The underground bunker where they've been holed up, tell me about it."

"It is heavily fortified, made to withstand bomb blasts," Carl stated.

"Julian also paid a lot of money to have it spelled," Alastair added. "If he doesn't want you in, you'd have a hard time breaching it."

"When a wolf is challenged, he fights," my father answered vehemently. "That is our way. That has always been our way. He will come out and face me and own up to his wrongdoings."

"He might come out and face the challenge," I said from my position just behind my father. "But he might choose to have Ceres fight his battles for him. If he knows he could lose to you, which he should, it would be to his benefit to have her take you out, rather than come and fight you and lose his Pack."

Judging by my father's expression, I could tell such thoughts hadn't occurred to him. He was old-school to the bone. Honor and respect were revered in his world, as they should be. Julian hadn't been playing by the same rules lately, which made me doubt if he would actually stick to the old ways when a grab for power was on the line.

"Jessica's right," Rourke said. "We prepare for a battle against a goddess and her witches, and after we beat them, we fight the wolves."

"We just have to figure out how to breach the bunker," Tyler added. "They've got the advantage. And who knows how many are down there against us?"

"We can't forget we have allies in the bunker," I pointed out. We assumed that was where Ray, James, and Marcy were being held, but we could be wrong. "Including a pissed-off reaper vampire who's going to be mad as a hornet that he got snatched. If we can free them once we break in, that would be ideal. Then they can fight alongside us." I was about to say something more when there was a noise to my left.

We all turned our heads and watched as Eudoxia emerged from the brush beside the road. Apparently, she didn't take joy in landing right next to us and scaring the crap out of us like Ray did.

Today's outfit was foam green, her skirts dragging over the ground as she moved. She looked a little ragged. I squinted. Was that a piece of straw in her hair? Before I could inquire as to what had happened, Danny quipped, "Did you fancy a roll in the hay before coming back, then?" He chortled at his own joke.

She reached up and plucked the errant hay out of her coif and flicked it away angrily. "They thought to take me unawares," she fumed. "It was the last mistake they ever made!"

"*Who* tried to take you?" I balked. Eudoxia's reputation preceded her. I didn't know many—*if any*—supernaturals who would dare to try such a thing so blatantly.

She stalked forward. "A school of witches. Obviously a

kindergarten group. They thought to spell me, but did not realize that I can spell right back," she huffed. "I left them stunned, if not dead. They will think twice before approaching me again. Fae magic is of a different breed, one that they have not prepared themselves against in far too long. They were easy prey. They were squirming in pain."

"But why would they want to kidnap you?" I asked, stunned. "That doesn't make any sense. They have Tally." I glanced at Rourke and my father. "Ceres can't take the fae position on the Coalition. She can only hope for the witch seat. Why would they want Eudoxia?"

Rourke shrugged. "Leverage? Things must have gone badly down there, and now they're trying to clean up their mess. If they had the Vampire Queen as their prisoner, she could swear a vow to exonerate them in exchange for her release."

"That would never happen," Eudoxia scoffed. "If anyone dared keep me captive, they would die. There would be no vows or exchanges."

I addressed her. "They have Tally, Ray, James, and Marcy. We're about to go and break them out and fight the wolves. This is now a personal fight for you. I can't believe I have to ask this question, but are you in?"

"Of course I'm in," she answered in a condescending tone. "Anyone who dares give the order to harm me will pay the price with their lives. Those witches didn't act on their own. They were following orders from their superior."

"And they have our friends," I suggested helpfully. "That's reason enough to go after them." Eudoxia gave me what amounted to a snort as a reply. My friends were clearly not an issue for her. "One of them is Tally, who will claim the witch's seat on the Coalition. You at least have to care about that." She rolled her eyes. "I know your heart is several sizes too small—that is, if you have one at all—but I have to believe there's a little bit of love or some speck of emotion in there someplace. If anything, you can tell yourself it's a necessity to join us, because without Tally, we can't take our vows. And let's just be thankful she's still alive, or Ceres wouldn't have gone to such great lengths to nab you. If Tally were to die, there's a good chance that Ceres would take her place."

Eudoxia placed her hands on her hips. "She might've." She raised one perfectly sculpted eyebrow. "But once Ceres was dead, the power would be forced to choose another."

Okay, then.

25

We formulated a quick plan as we moved forward. It basically consisted of: We're stronger and tougher than you are, so we will prevail.

It wasn't heavy on the logistics.

My father addressed the wolves, ordering them to fan out around the bunker. If Julian had left his wolves to guard the door, defeating them would be our first priority.

Once we got within a few yards of the bunker, we could see there were no guards stationed. "Don't you think it's a little strange he hasn't positioned any of his wolves here to be the first line of defense?" I asked. I lifted my nose and scented the air. My wolf growled low.

Something was wrong.

Before I could voice my concern, my brother said, "I smell something strange. Like smoke mixed with ash. I've never smelled anything like it before in my life."

"I smell it too," I said. "Ray spotted a strange signature out here before, one that he couldn't identify."

Eudoxia stood next to me. She didn't have the same nose

as a wolf, but she was old and had been around the block a time or to. "The vampires were right," she stated flatly. "A celestial being is nearby. I've smelled that scent twice before in my life. Neither time was particularly pleasant." She didn't bother to elaborate.

"Why would a celestial being be helping Julian?" I asked. "I thought they were here to facilitate formation of the new Coalition. We've already met Leo. I can't imagine him helping the opposition. And he didn't smell like sulfur. In fact, he smelled good." Like a sweet, musky earth coupled with fresh air.

"I am not here to do anything other than observe." The voice filtered through the wind, and my head snapped toward it. I couldn't tell if it was male or female.

We all glanced around, but saw no one.

Danny walked up to me. "A voice with no body is a bit peculiar, isn't it? I don't like this one bit. Getting into another battle with an opponent we can't see is not high on my to-do list."

"I will not battle you," the voice said.

"If you are no threat to us," I said, "show yourself."

Approximately twenty feet in front of us, the air wavered, and a female figure solidified.

She was dressed in black leather, with long, flowing blonde hair. She looked as angelic as Leo, but feminine, her eyes bright and clear. I knew she had wings underneath her glamour. She looked badass as she walked purposely toward us, like a biker chick with a serious Harley parked somewhere nearby.

My wolf howled in my mind, her hackles up. *Is she a threat?* I asked. My wolf clicked her jaws together decisively. I took that as a yes. *What do we do? Her power is crazy strong, just like Leo's.* It lashed against us, its tendrils stinging our skin. My wolf only continued to growl, which was not exactly helpful.

"What's your name?" I asked as she stopped before us, openly assessing our group, her eyes landing on Rourke and staying there.

If she didn't let up, *I* was going to start growling.

"Romeial," she said. "But you may call me Romy."

"You're the Angel of Fertility," Kayla said softly. It was a statement, not a question.

"I am, among other things," the angel replied.

It seemed Ceres had some things in common with this angel. I would doubt it was a coincidence an angel with the same powers as the goddess was standing here in front of us.

"Do you protect those inside?" my father demanded.

Romy casually glanced over her shoulder toward the bunker. "Yes and no. I'm ultimately here for another reason. Normally, another dark angel would preside over this, but orders are orders."

My eyebrows reached my hairline. She sounded like Jeb. This was just another day at work for her.

"You're going to have to explain," I said. "None of us is familiar with how the Coalition works, or who you are, or why you're here. So if you could be a little more specific, that would help. Our friends are inside, and we're anxious to free them."

"I know," she replied. "I helped put them there."

"*What?*" I had trouble keeping my voice at a normal volume. "If you're not helping Ceres, why would you do that?"

She rested her hands against her hips and tapped a foot. "Well, I figured you'd want this to be over with sooner rather than later, and this was the best way to handle it. They are all in one place, no need to search for them. One confrontation and it's over."

"I'm extremely confused," I said. "If you helped Ceres, she thinks you're on her side, which is likely why no wolves are present to fight us. She thinks you're going to do her dirty work for her."

"If I gave her that impression"—the dark angel shrugged—"that's on her. She didn't ask for specifics, and I didn't give them."

"But you're the Angel of Fertility, and she's the Goddess of Fertility," I said, still frantically trying to piece this story together. *Aren't you on the same side?*"

They might even have the same gene pool. Who knew?

"Nope. It doesn't work that way," Romy answered. "I was born into my position, she was voted in. Much different. If humans had prayed to her in another capacity—say, as Goddess of Anthills—she would've gladly taken that route, presiding over the ants of your world. It's hardly the same thing."

I was completely stymied. "But…you helped her kidnap our friends."

"I did," she replied. "But I just told you it was out of necessity. And, of course, to make sure what comes next doesn't get out of hand."

"Okay." I hesitated. "The only choice we have is to take your word for it that you won't fight against us. If they're down there, how do we get them out?"

"I tell them to come out." She intoned it like I should be following along closer than I was. *Pretty angel lady, I'm trying, I swear.*

"We're having a hard time following what you're telling us, and it's not because we're not intelligent, it's because we need more information," Rourke said. "You helped our opponents by kidnapping our friends, and now you're just going to tell them to come out and everything's going to be fine?" I'm glad he spoke up. "That sounds too easy."

"I never said fine. You will fight," she said. "It's not going to be overly easy. I will tell them to come out, and if they do not listen to my wishes, I will force them out. When they come up, you will do what you will with the confrontation. Once it's over, we will have an outcome." She still had her hands comfortably settled on her hips like we were just having a nice little chat.

"Do you know in advance what that outcome will be?" Danny asked. His facial expression—a cross between shock, confusion, and awe—represented most of ours. This angel was clearly powerful, and rare. Even though her countenance was bright, she was dressed in all black. Everything about her seemed dark—much darker than Leo.

As Eudoxia had said before, two celestial beings from very different origins.

That couldn't be truer.

"I am no seer," Romy said. "I am here to protect and facilitate, nothing more."

"Then let me get this straight," Danny said, spreading his hands apart like a game-show host. "You tell them to come out, and they have no choice but to oblige. Then we fight. I understand those rules. But what if they gain the upper hand? Are you going to step in for our side or leave us to flounder? If you don't mind explaining a wee bit more, as we lot"—he moved his arms in a circle to indicate all of us—"are confused as to what your actual errand here is today."

"I will not interfere with either side"—she tossed her hair over her shoulder carelessly—"unless the outcome reaches a specific point."

"You've already interfered on their side," I pointed out. "And, if I can ask, what specific point are you referring to?"

Rourke placed his hand on my waist and leaned down. "I believe this angel can't share all the details," he murmured. He straightened. "Isn't that right?" He gave her a pointed look. "You have coordinated these events so the outcome happens right now, which I understand. You can't fight our battles for us, which I understand. But you're staying here in case something happens"—he paused—"to Jessica."

Why would she need to do that? I gave Rourke a look. "Why would she need to protect me specifically?"

"I believe we will find out shortly," he answered, a little cryptically.

Do you know something you're not telling me? I asked. *Because if you do, now's the time to spill it.*

Nothing for sure, he said. *I'm just putting all the pieces together, including what we got from Enid today. I'm happy Romy is here. I believe it means that Fate is invested in this outcome. And that end result is tied to what Pandora wants, which is good for us.*

I'm glad you're able to reason all this out, I replied somewhat sarcastically. *All I am is extremely confused and worried about our friends. It's time to tell her to call them up.*

Agreed.

I cleared my throat, glancing at my father. "Are you ready for Romy to bring them out?"

"Yes," my father answered. Internally, he said, *I'm not sure I trust this being, so be wary. She has a strange signature, and this all seems a little too easy, just as your mate suggested.*

I'm with you on that one, I answered. *I consider myself fairly intelligent, but I'm not picking up on all the subtleties here. Rourke believes that she's interested in achieving Pandora's outcome. If that's true, we have nothing to worry about.*

Let's hope for our sakes that's what she wants.

"We're ready whenever you are," I told Romy.

She stared at me intently for a few seconds, which made me uncomfortable.

It didn't seem fair that all these beings knew about me, yet I knew nothing about them. Hopefully, that would all change when I took my seat on the Coalition. I'd no longer be in the dark. I looked forward to that day. It couldn't come fast enough.

Tyler shouted some directions to the wolves. My father and Rourke stood by my side. Kayla, Jax, Lucas, and Nick stood just behind us. Eudoxia was off to the side, looking bored, as usual.

Without comment, Romy turned, her long hair swaying as she paced back toward the bunker, her high black boots crushing everything in their way.

I addressed Kayla. "Do you sense any dead bodies nearby? I don't know if we'll need them, but it would be nice to be prepared."

"I do sense a few," she said. "But they are supernaturals, likely wolves who died. It is risky to call them up. Not all bodies behave the same way, especially supes."

"Okay, we'll keep them in reserve," I said.

"What is she going to do?" Tyler asked, coming to stand next to my father. "Knock on the door and tell them it's time to come out and play?"

"I have no idea," I replied.

The question was answered in the next moment.

A sizable chunk of the bunker blew up, debris and concrete flying everywhere. It looked as though Romy had tossed a stick of dynamite through the front door.

"I guess that'll do it." Rourke chuckled. "They must not have taken her directions seriously."

We waited for the dust to clear.

Julian emerged first, followed by about ten wolves. His face showed his complete surprise. I'm sure he'd spent a small fortune to have the bunker spelled for situations exactly like this. But apparently, regular witch's spells didn't work against celestial beings. Either that, or Romy's dynamite was something from another world.

We might never know.

"Julian de Rossi." My father addressed his peer in a booming voice. "I'm glad you've chosen to come out and fight this challenge like a wolf."

Julian squared off in front of us, his feet apart, his arms crossed. His demeanor was careless, even though he'd been caught red-handed, and we had enough of his wolves lined up behind us to make him uneasy. He had to know his time was near.

"Times are changing, Callum," he answered. "I'm not going to fight you, or lose my Alpha position."

"Is that so?" my father retorted. "And exactly how are you planning to do that? Our laws are very clear, Julian. When you're challenged, you fight. The wolf with the greater strength wins. It's that simple."

Julian didn't have time to answer, because a small commotion erupted behind him. Up from the rubble came another figure. She was tall, with long jet-black hair and pale pink skin. She wore a simple blue silk dress. She reminded me of a real-life Snow White—except Snow White was a gentle creature with good intentions, unlike Ceres.

Behind her trailed three witches, one of whom was Angie. The lesser witch shot me a triumphant smile.

Did she not realize she'd just emerged from a pile of rubble?

Beside me, Rourke emitted a low, menacing growl. The odds for Angie coming out of this unscathed were about as low as they could get.

We patiently waited, some of us not so patiently—for Ceres to take her stand next to Julian.

Once she did, she squared her shoulders and stuck out her chin, her arms rising in the air. "You will all bow to me, and I will spare you a painful death."

Um, what?

26

Ceres repeated her command about us bowing. She had to be out of her ever-loving mind. Or maybe she was high on some sort of hallucinogen? It was hard to know for sure what drove her insanity.

My father was stunned, so I stepped up and addressed her.

"None of us are going to bow down to you," I told her in my deepest voice, injecting as much power as I could into it. "The best thing you can hope for now is to go get our friends, hand them over with gracious apologies, and hope that we decide to jail you instead of kill you."

Angie sneered. "You have no right to talk to us like that, dog—"

Ceres held out a single finger, and her sister shut up. "If you do not acquiesce to my wishes," the goddess said, "your friends are as good as dead. I will not bargain with you."

It took everything I had not to glance at Romy to see if she could give me any indication if Ceres was telling the truth. I chose not to look at her, because I knew Ceres was lying. I had to go with my heart. My wolf backed me up with a small yelp. "I don't think so," I countered. "The way this is going to work is you're going to hand our friends over and hope you don't get killed in the process, and then Julian is going to fight my father. After that's over, we'll decide what to do with you."

Ceres began to speak, but Eudoxia cut her off with a sharp noise that sounded remarkably like a whip. I had to glance over to see if she was actually holding one. "We once knew each other." She addressed Ceres. "Back then, I believed you might be smart, or at least intelligent enough to understand the way things work in our world. You don't win this battle, goddess. We do. We have superior strength and magic, and those are the only equations that matter. Jessica is being far too generous, which is her bumbling, uneducated way, offering you a reprieve for your wrongdoings, including trying to snatch me"—she made an indignant sound—"when I would kill you where you stand and figure things out later. You would be wise to take her offer. It's the most generous thing you will receive in this lifetime." Eudoxia shot me a glare, telling me exactly what she thought of my little plan of amnesty. Relief instantly shot through me that the Vampire Queen wasn't tasked as the Enforcer and wouldn't be making decisions about things like this on a regular basis.

"I will not surrender, and you cannot kill me," Ceres declared. "You do not hold the upper hand, I do. I will take my rightful place on the Coalition, or die trying."

"If Fate wanted you to sit on the Coalition, Tally would be dead already," I challenged. "As long as Tallulah Talbot is alive, you've lost. Why is it, do you think, that you haven't been able to kill her? Can you answer us that?"

Ceres balled her pink hands into fists and huffed. I'd gotten under her skin, which was exactly where I wanted to be. "She will die, don't you worry," she stated. "You are wasting valuable time. Get down on your knees and submit to me." The small amount of wolves Julian had rounded up were restless, most of them pacing in their human forms behind Ceres, appearing agitated.

Dad, I said, *make an appeal to Julian's remaining wolves. See if any are interested in joining our side before this starts. I have no idea what Ceres is talking about, but it's clear she's got something up her sleeve. If we can get a few more of them to defect, it will weaken whatever's coming next.*

My father didn't waste any time. "Julian's wolves, I address you directly. Your Alpha has denied me a fair fight. That is not our way. If you want to follow a strong Alpha"—he emphasized the word *Alpha*—"then come to our side now. There will be no repercussions. This situation is unprecedented. I've never been denied a challenge, but it's clear your leader has steered you wrong. I'm here to make it right." He crossed his arms and met each wolf's eyes with a hard gaze, one by one. "There will not be another chance. If you stay and fight for Julian, you die."

After this announcement, they would surely die, as my father wouldn't be able to trust where their loyalties lay. Wolves who dug in and denied the reality right in front of them tended to be rabble-rousers, and he'd learned that the hard way with Hank. My father had taken him in, and Hank had ultimately betrayed him.

It wouldn't happen again.

Four wolves moved forward, and Julian snarled, "If you desert my cause, you will never be welcomed back!"

My father snarled even louder, "You have chosen the stronger side. With me, you will flourish. With him, you die!"

Two more wolves followed the four, none of whom bothered to look back as they cross to our side.

One of Julian's wolves who'd stayed put spat on the ground. "You were always weaklings! Good riddance. We will fight this battle without you, *and* win." That had come from a tall, lanky wolf with short brown hair. That must be Julian's second.

No more wolves came forward.

"Your team is dwindling by the second," I called. "And there will be no kneeling. We want our friends back and will take them by force if we have to. What's it going to be, Ceres? Are you going to fight or play nice?"

Her pale face was reaching apoplectic. That pleased me to no end. Angie was getting restless as well. She kept glancing at her sister. It was clear Angie was not used to waiting for much. "If you do not submit," Ceres reiterated, "I will kill them all."

"That's a bit of an empty threat, isn't it?" Danny asked, his voice filled with anger. "We're thinking they would be dead already if you could've achieved it. Instead, this gracious angel right here"—Danny gestured toward Romy, who stood off to the side—"was nice enough to blow the roof off your hidey-hole for us. Now you're out here, and we're ready to fight. So let's get on with it, then."

Ceres glanced in Romy's direction. "That's exactly who's going to do the killing," Ceres retorted. "One word from me, and she kills them all."

I began to laugh.

There was no helping it. Too much stress built up from the day. "That's not what she told us," I said. "You're on your own with exactly three pitiful witches, six wolves, and one Alpha who thinks you've promised him some kind of absolute power. He's going to be mighty disappointed when he finds out it was all a lie."

Ceres stalked forward. "You know nothing," she spat between a very clenched jaw. "That angel has been helping us all along. She was instrumental in capturing your *friends*."

"She may have been," I agreed, crossing my arms. "But she was also instrumental in keeping them alive. Haven't you wondered why you haven't been able to kill Tally? By all means, you should've been able to figure it out by now. You've mistakenly thought Romy was here to help, but I'm thinking you should've inquired about her intentions earlier than right this minute. Because she just told us this is our battle, and she isn't here to interfere. Honestly, Ceres, this kind of judgment doesn't show strong leadership skills. And really, that's what we're looking for on the Coalition, haven't you heard?"

"Enough of this banter," Eudoxia huffed, directing her wrath at Ceres once again. "If you refuse to surrender and beg for mercy, we fight, and we do it now." She took a step forward, pulling the sleeves of her dress up to her elbows. "I am the guest of honor at a very lavish dinner tonight. I do not wish to waste another moment dealing with you."

Burn, Eudoxia-style.

Julian whistled, and his wolves dropped to their knees and began to shift.

I heard shuffling behind me as Julian's wolf defectors did the same.

Danny leaned into me. "Do you want me to shift and lead the new wolves into battle?"

"No," I said. "Our opponents are seriously outnumbered. I don't understand why they would risk battling us in the first place. We're missing something."

I had my answer in the next thirty seconds.

One of the witches in the back raised her arms, and a spell slammed into me, tossing me backward.

As I fought to catch my breath, a terrifying noise rent the air. It was a cross between a war cry and the scream of a caged animal.

Magic had entered my body, but my wolf had it well in hand. The spell wasn't particularly strong, but it had a strange smell. Rourke leaned over, reaching his hand out. "Are you okay?" he asked.

I grabbed hold, and he pulled me up. "I'm fine, but what was that noise—"

A huge blue shape lunged in front of me. It was so big it blocked the sun from my body.

I'd only seen the likes of a giant like Jax in the movies.

He was massive—at least nine feet tall—slate blue, and one of the most imposing creatures I'd ever laid eyes on.

I couldn't see Julian or Ceres past the hulking figure who stood protectively in front of me. My heart melted a little. My first thought was that I didn't want him to get hurt. My second was that I didn't think he could be.

It would take a lot to bring this *blár risastór* down.

"Your spells can't hurt me," Jax roared, his voice so low it made the blood in my veins vibrate. "Nor can your dogs' teeth pierce my skin."

"Holy shite, he's massive," Danny exclaimed. "Wait a minute, did he just insult us? We're not dogs, we're werewolves. Mighty big difference there, as our teeth are a bit longer and a tad sharper."

I chuckled. "He's trying to intimidate Julian's wolves, so we're going to let it go." I couldn't see what was happening, so I stepped to the side. I found my father gaping at Jax, his expression confused.

We'd, of course, told him what Jax was, but seeing it was believing it.

"Is what he says true?" my father asked. "I've never met another supernatural with those abilities. I've heard of them, just never encountered one before."

"I think so." I glanced at Kayla. Her face was rightfully concerned, but I saw pride there too. I turned back to the business at hand. I could see Julian and Ceres now, both looking confused. "You're not getting through our secret weapon," I called. "We can still do this peacefully."

"No, we can't," Eudoxia immediately challenged as she lifted her fingers. A spell shot out, hitting Ceres squarely in the chest. The goddess flew back, crashing into the three witches behind her, who tumbled like bowling pins. Eudoxia gave me a cocky glance. "This goddess won't stop until the fight is over. She feels that the Coalition is her rightful place. We must teach her otherwise. There will be nothing peaceful about this."

I nodded. The Vampire Queen was right. It just seemed senseless to fight when they were so outnumbered. I had to tuck my human side away for a moment.

We all watched as Ceres staggered to stand. She hadn't been expecting a fae spell. I wasn't sure what made Eudoxia's spells different than a witch's spell, but it was plain to see that Ceres was not immune to Eudoxia's power.

I reached out to touch the back of Jax's arm so he'd know I was there. One false move and he could bash any of us out of his way, and I didn't want to be at the receiving end of his fist. He stepped to the side to give me more room, but I knew he would lunge in front of me again if any real threat surfaced.

Julian's wolves began to snarl, pacing in front of Jax, not knowing if they should attack or not. My father lifted his hand and made a circle gesture. The wolves behind us began to fan out, forming a semicircle around the battle ground.

By the look on Ceres's face, she was less than amused with the current turn of events. She glanced in Romy's direction for a brief moment. She didn't dare engage the angel, who stood by with arms loosely crossed, a slight look of amusement on her face.

"*Ma Reine*, would you like me to look for the others?" Naomi asked from her position on the other side of Danny. "If you are busy fighting those here, I can fly into the bunker to see if I can locate them."

"In a minute," I said. "There's something going on here that we aren't grasping just yet. Even with our show of force, Ceres isn't acting like she's going to lose. Neither is Julian. It doesn't make any sense. They'd only feel that way if they have an ace in the hole we don't know about."

"*Oui*," Naomi replied. "It would seem that way. Give me the command when you are ready, and I will go."

"It's surprising our friends haven't emerged on their own," Danny said. "That bunker's in shambles, and no one is guarding them. It doesn't make any sense."

"No, it doesn't," I agreed. "Something's going on here." I turned to my mate. "Are you picking up on anything? They are radically outnumbered. They should be fleeing or battling hard."

"Nothing of any significance," Rourke replied. "I don't understand it either."

"I think we're about to find out," Tyler said. "Look, she's coming this way."

Sure enough, Ceres marched toward us.

Eudoxia sniffed, "Don't let her get too close to you."

I looked at her. "Why?"

"Because she'll render you infertile."

27

"Can't she do that from anywhere?" I asked. After all, fertility was her specialty. You'd think it wouldn't matter how close she was.

"From what I understand," the Vampire Queen stated in a bored tone, "she must be touching you. And by the look on her face, she's planning to do something of the sort."

That, she did.

It was amazing that she looked as confident as she did. The three witches trailed in her wake, the wolves moving in behind them. Julian was the only one who stood back. His face showed trepidation, but also satisfaction.

"Okay." I addressed the group. "I want you on high alert. They are outnumbered, but still looking sure of themselves. If anybody catches a glimpse of anything, I want to know about it."

"Do you want me to dispatch her?" Jax rumbled.

I was taken off guard by his question. Did he mean kill her? I didn't want Ceres's death to rest on his shoulders for an eternity. I also hoped a fifteen-year-old, even though he was ensconced in a gigantic, fearsome body, would have a little more hesitation when it came to killing. But Jax had seen his parents killed and had witnessed a lot of bloodshed in his brief years. With gargoyles hunting you, wanting to capture you as their own, it would be enough to put anyone on edge. I cleared my throat. "If she tries to touch me," I told him, "you can bat her away, but don't crush her skull or anything like that."

Eudoxia turned her gaze on me. "This will end in her death. Let the giant dispense with her, and then we can all go home."

I shook my head. "If anyone's going to do the killing, it's Tally. Once we free her, I'll leave it up to the leader of witches, and she can decide what she wants to do. For now, we take control."

"And how do you propose we do that?" Danny asked. "This goddess is seemingly fearless."

I stepped slightly in front of Jax, facing the approaching goddess. I held my hand up in front of me. "Stop," I commanded. "The games end here, Ceres. Name your threat, so we can answer it."

Her lips were pressed in a thin line, but she halted her progress, stopping twenty feet in front of me. "You will kneel before me," she smirked, "or I will rip the children from your womb. You risk their lives by trifling with me. Once you all have submitted, we will kill the witch leader and come to an agreement about power. I am the most powerful witch in this realm, and that Coalition seat is *mine*."

I was so stunned at her words, I stumbled.

Gigantic hands steadied me as my mate let out a low, threatening sound.

What was she talking about?

I wasn't pregnant, was I?

My hands immediately went to my stomach, covering it protectively. I looked inward to my wolf. *Is it true?* My wolf yelped. I concentrated deeply and could sense the presence of two beings, but they were only days old—if that. Nothing more than tiny clusters of cells.

I slowly raised my head.

Rage engulfed me. "You threaten the lives of my unborn children?" Beside me, Rourke dropped to the ground and began to shift. "Not exactly a wise move, Ceres." My voice was hardened.

"It's you who threaten them by not surrendering to me," she scoffed. "I will not be defeated. I have lived a thousand years and will live a thousand more. It is not your place to take over. I deserve that power!"

"It has nothing to do with deserving anything," I said, anger radiating through me. "Power chooses those who are strong and worthy. You are neither." Rourke rose on all fours, a towering big cat with three-inch fangs. "You've gone too far and there is no way back. It has always been my way to seek clemency where I can. But to leave you alive, knowing you would harm my children, is unthinkable."

"There is nothing you can—"

Rourke bounded forward, taking no more than two strides before leaping, hitting the goddess squarely in the shoulders, knocking her to the ground.

"Take out the witches and the wolves," my father bellowed as he stalked forward, his eyes pinned on Julian. The wolves around him whipped into action.

Tyler's voice was frantic in my mind. *Stay here,* he pleaded. *Don't risk the babies. I can't believe I'm going to be an uncle. That's totally awesome.*

"I will not leave your side," Danny stated. "And apparently, neither will this big guy." He jabbed his thumb toward Jax, who had not moved an inch and growled if any of the wolves got too close. They gave him a wide berth, even the ones on our side.

"Naomi," I ordered. "Take Kayla with you and go check

out the bunker. This will be over shortly." I scanned the scene in front of me, eyes locking on Romy. The angel gave me a small nod, then turned and walked away.

Naomi addressed Kayla. "Have you ever been for a ride before?"

"No, but I'm ready," Kayla stated firmly.

I felt pride in my team and in my family.

My hands crept down to my belly. Now that I knew I was carrying twins, there was very little chance my family would allow me to fight, and they were right to be protective.

Now I knew why Enid had spared me.

A long time ago, my wolf had flashed me an image of two children, a boy with dark hair like my own and a girl with blonde hair like her father's. It moved me then, as much as it did now. Piecing together all that had been said today, I understood.

I would be giving birth to a reincarnate, not Ardat Lili.

The female child inside me would have a special soul and memories I would have to help her understand. And once she became old enough, I would have to let her go.

This was my sacrifice.

To give up a child I called my own.

But it wouldn't be only my sacrifice. It would be Rourke's, as well as her unborn brother's, who would both feel her loss acutely. I glanced up at the sky as the battle continued around me, tears forming in the corners of my eyes. "I can only thank you for granting me two," I whispered to anything or anyone who happened to be listening. "I will do my duty and carry out my sacrifice. I can only hope the love we will share between us will see us through."

I lowered my head, and my eyes immediately locked on Rourke.

He was still in his cat form, blood staining his face and neck. *I love you*, was all he said as he began to pace back to me.

My mate had likely figured this was a possibility before

Ceres's announcement, and yet he'd stayed strong for me. He was a fierce warrior, but this would challenge the bounds of his love. Relinquishing his daughter to the unknown would be unbearable.

I love you too, I told him.

We will figure this out. His voice held pain as well as strength.

I know.

"There's Naomi." Danny gestured excitedly. "She's carrying someone. It's a small someone, so it must be the witch leader."

Naomi indeed carried a body out of the bunker. Tally was petite, barely five feet tall. She looked breakable in Naomi's arms and was out cold.

The battle for the most part had ended, and I rushed forward, Danny and Jax by my side. "Set her down over here." I indicated a clear patch of grass.

Naomi complied, laying her down gently. Tally's snow-white hair fanned out beneath her. I knelt next to her, my hand going to her shoulder. "Tally, can you hear me?" I angled my head down over her chest, listening for a heartbeat. It was there. I glanced up. "Where are the others?"

"We're right here," Ray grumbled as he emerged from the bunker, followed by James and then Marcy.

Marcy rushed to my side, dropping beside her aunt. Her eyes were frantic. "Why isn't she waking up? We woke right up when Naomi touched us."

"I don't know," I said. "What happened to you? How were you taken?"

"I can't really remember," Marcy said. "We were all walking around investigating this area, and then I woke up two minutes ago with Naomi looking over me."

"You woke up on your own?" I asked, glancing down at Tally, who was still unconscious. "Or you woke up when Ceres ceased to be alive?"

"I have no idea," she answered. "But it doesn't matter right now, because she's not waking up."

I put a hand on Tally's forehead. "I think your aunt is in Stasis," I said. "Maybe she didn't start out that way, but her body, in trying to protect itself, got there on its own." My body had done the same for me once before. It had formed a protective cocoon, and I hadn't been able to escape it on my own. My brother had had to step in. That much powerful insulation could preserve a supernatural for years on end.

"Okay, that makes some sense," Marcy said.

"Do you know if there's a spell for breaking Stasis?" I asked.

Marcy bit her lip. "Not that I know of. We have many spells to put you to sleep, but not to wake somebody from a self-imposed hibernation state."

"I was like this once, and Tyler got me out by giving me power," I said. "I can do the same for her, but it's risky. She's strong, but my power is magnified and unpredictable. It will be hard to know how much to give her."

"Oh, please. This old biddy will figure it out on her own," Marcy replied confidently. "Give it to her, and I bet she wakes up in less than a minute." There was a growling noise behind us, and we both glanced up. The last of Julian's wolves was defeated. Marcy appeared shocked as she glanced around at the battle scene. "What the heck happened up here while we were out? Is that Ceres lying on the ground without her *head?*" Marcy made a sound in the back of her throat. "Well, I guess that's one way to kill a goddess."

"She threatened to kill my unborn children." My voice was hard, as it would be every time I recalled the incident. "Rourke did what he had to do."

Marcy's mouth fell open, then a big grin encompassed her face. "You mean I'm going to be an auntie times two? That's fantastic!" She leaned over and threw her arms around me. When she pulled back, her expression changed to anger. "If

Ceres threatened to harm them, losing her head was a kind way to go. She deserved a heap of pain for even uttering such a thing."

I nodded once, my focus back on Tally.

"Just hit her with the juice," Ray said over my shoulder. "She's a tough SOB. It won't harm her."

"Yes, by all means," Eudoxia said, strolling up to us, "do it now. I have places to be."

I tilted my head up at Eudoxia. "Does every single thing always have to be about you?"

"Of course," she said. "Now hurry up."

Eudoxia moved almost too quickly for me to track.

Something had come up behind me.

By the time I'd jumped to my feet, the Vampire Queen held someone by the throat. "If you threaten one of us, you threaten us all," Eudoxia seethed into Angie's scared face. At least the witch had the gumption to look afraid. She should be. She'd just pissed off the Fae Queen.

"Let go of me," Angie snarled, recovering her bravado quickly. "She deserves to die, and I'm finally going to be the one to do it! I should've done it the first time we met," she raged, "but I'll make it right." She lifted her hands, her fingers beginning to wiggle.

Jax let out a huge roar and took a step forward.

I stilled him with a look. He obeyed and stayed put.

"I think not, little girl," Eudoxia said. "My spells don't require me to move my fingers." Within moments, Angie was gasping for air. Her eyes widened as she realized her fate. Her body began to shrivel at a rapid pace as we watched, the liquid inside essentially drying up. When the Fae Queen finally let her go a minute later, she was nothing more than a shell as she crumpled to the ground. I gaped, only to incur Eudoxia's ire. "She was going to kill you!" she snarled. "You still have much to learn about the ways of our world. You had better catch up, because there is no room for children on the Coalition."

I smiled. "I'm not freaked out about what you did to Angie," I corrected. "I'm certain Rourke wishes he'd been in your position right then. What I'm freaked out about is what you said a few minutes ago, and I quote, 'If you threaten one of us, you threaten all of us.' Did you *actually* mean that?" I arched an eyebrow at her. "You had my back. Amazing. It's a brand new world."

She scoffed, looking down and adjusting her skirts. "If we do not protect each other, we appear weak. The Coalition is fragile, and it will take time for the world to respect us. We are a united force, whether we like it or not."

"So, in other words, you finally found your itty-bitty heart," I said as I knelt beside Tally again. "It's about time, you know. I was getting tired of waiting." I grinned, knowing she was scowling.

Before Eudoxia could retort, Marcy sighed. "Sorry to interrupt, but I'm anxiously waiting to hear from *this* bag of bones. I need to know where my baby cousin-niece is. Let's get this show on the road."

I closed my eyes. My wolf was already gathering power, which had manifested in a throng of different colors all wrapped into one. *One concentrated burst should do it,* I told her. *I don't want to give Tally too much at first. We can always give her more. I have a feeling Marcy is correct, and once will be enough.*

I settled my hands on Tally's shoulders and inhaled, forcing the magic out of my body through the tips of my fingers. "Here you go," I told her. "If you can hear me, use this power to burst out of the bubble."

The moment my magic entered her body, she gasped for air, her eyes flicking open. She lunged upward, grabbing the front of my shirt in her fists, her voice hoarse as she demanded, "Where's my daughter?"

28

"I don't know," I answered. "But we're going to find her."

Tally scrambled up, looking no worse for wear. She'd been out for weeks, ever since we left the Underworld, but she did not look it. She was back to her badass self in less than one minute, just like Marcy said she would be.

There was no greater witch to sit on the Coalition. This was why the power had chosen her.

"What about my Coven?" she asked, glancing around, spotting Angie, and turning back to me for an explanation.

Marcy said, "I've been trying to get a hold of them, but they haven't answered my calls."

Tally embraced her niece. "It's good to see you." She turned back to me. "Who was with Ceres?"

"There were only three witches with the goddess, including Angie, and I believe they are all dead." Angie's death had been gruesome, but not unjust. "Do you remember what happened? You've been out for a couple of weeks, at least."

She pressed a hand to her temple. "Yes, I recall most of it.

We were keeping the circle open, awaiting your arrival, and there was a big disturbance. Something changed." She dropped her hand and met my gaze. "I'm not talking about the weather changing. I'm talking about a piece of the fabric in all of us changed in an instant." She snapped her fingers.

I nodded. "I believe that's when I killed Ardat Lili. It somehow rerouted the course of Fate for many of us. What happened next?"

"I got a sinking feeling immediately, like a pall of darkness descended over the Coven. I knew something was coming. I ordered all the witches out, except for a scant few to try to keep the circle open. For those who left, I demanded they not show themselves again until I called for them."

"Was your daughter among them?" I asked.

"Of course," she answered, her eyes scanning the horizon. "Protocol is for them to split up in groups of ten, each journeying to a different safe place." She turned to Marcy. "You said you've reached out, but none have tried to get a hold of you?"

"No," Marcy answered, bowing her head, trying to appear unruffled. But I knew the fact the witches hadn't let her know what had happened to her niece had bothered her. "They've been loyal to you, and let me tell you, I've tried everything to wring information out of them. I've called Covens all over the world. Not a peep of anything. I've been worried sick."

Tally patted Marcy's shoulder. "We will remedy how they treat you as soon as I find them. I give you my word. Thank you for trying to locate Maggie. But for now, we must find out where she is."

"How do we do that?" I asked.

Before Tally could answer, Marcy interrupted, "The witches have a bat signal. It can only be sounded by the most powerful witch among us, but when we hear it, we are required to answer."

A single eyebrow rose. "That's pretty cool."

"That, and I need a phone," Tally said. "I don't need three hundred witches descending on your doorstep. I'll send out the signal and add a phone number." She gave me a wink as she held out her hand. Nick walked over, set a Pack phone in her outstretched palm, and gave her the number. "After all, this is the twenty-first century. We have adapted."

"When you're done, there's a lot I need to fill you in on," I told her. "Mainly that you have a seat on the Coalition, which is forming in approximately a day and a half. Ceres wanted to take the seat for her own, which is why you were kidnapped."

Tally nodded briskly. "I figured it was something of the sort. After I sensed the change, my witch's power gathered and solidified, warning me and indicating it would protect me. I trusted it to do the job." She turned and began to chant something into the sky.

The witch signal had begun.

I glanced around for my father and found he was about to face off against Julian. They were both in their human forms, a ring of wolves surrounding them. James stood by my father's side.

The challenge was just beginning.

"This fight should be over before it starts," Ray said, stepping in line with me as I walked toward the ring.

"I agree. My father issued him a challenge earlier, and he denied it, hoping Ceres would defend him. You can see how that turned out." Her bloodied body still lay where Rourke had left it. I had no idea if she could regenerate from such an injury, but if she could, it would take time. Selene, the only other goddess I knew, had recovered from decapitation. We would figure it out later.

"If Julian wins, he'll have another challenge in front of him," Tyler growled, joining us. "There is no way he's surviving this. Either Dad finishes it, or I do."

I nodded. That was the inevitable outcome. "I just hope the fight is quick," I said. "We've got a lot to figure out."

"Honestly, Jess, all you need to do is keep those babies safe," Tyler said. "That's literally your only job. We're not going to let you do much more, so don't even think about it." He grinned. "I'm going to be an uncle. That's incredibly cool."

"Babies?" Ray peered at me. "It seems we missed more than you're letting on. We were only out cold for a couple hours."

"Ceres's winning move was to threaten my unborn children," I said. "I'm barely pregnant. It couldn't have happened more than a day or two ago at most." My guess was when Rourke and I had been intimate in the cabin the night Juanita and I had talked. I left off explaining to Ray what would likely happen to my daughter when she grew old enough. Just thinking about it, I had a lump in my throat. I was going to have to take time to process it all, and everyone didn't need to know the details. "It hasn't sunk in yet," I said. "But Tyler's right, protecting them will be my number one priority."

My father's voice boomed out as we took our place around the circle. "Do we fight as men or wolves? It's your call, Julian." Alphas had the choice to fight in their wolf form or human form. Anyone lesser fought in their human forms.

"I will defeat you in either form, so I care not," Julian snarled.

"Then we fight as wolves," my father declared. Fighting in their true form meant it would be a bloodier battle, the most intense of its kind, but quicker. The loser usually had numerous fatal wounds.

My father wanted to make a bold statement in front of Julian's wolves. It was a smart move, but would be harder to witness.

Rourke came up behind me, settling his arm around my waist, holding on protectively. He hadn't had time to undress when he'd shifted, so he'd shredded his clothes. Yet, it seemed he'd found something to wear in the bunker, at least on the bottom half. I twisted my neck and arched an eyebrow in his direction. "Your new digs are a little tight, wouldn't you say?" I said, inspecting him.

He snorted. "That's because Julian is smaller and weaker than I am. This was all I could find." He made a show of adjusting himself and grimaced. "I hope this doesn't take too long. I need to go change."

I relaxed against his shoulder, and his grip on me tightened. *I'm not ready to talk about it,* I told him. *I hope that's okay.*

He kissed the top of my head. *It's fine. We have our entire lives to figure it out,* he replied, his voice soothing. *You're going to be a wonderful mother, by the way, and I promise we will get through whatever they throw at us.*

I know.

He was right.

But I was more worried about the interim and having to make peace with everything before I met Enid face-to-face. She'd been shrewd to demand an audience with me, because, once we met, she would know where my heart lay. She would know if I was willing to give up her sister when the time came.

Rourke and I would have to be united in our decision, which would take an emotional toll on both of us. I just hoped we had enough time to process it all before tomorrow night.

My father and Julian shifted into their wolves. My father stood a foot taller than Julian, his dark coat glittering in the sun. He was imposing and regal. "On my count, you will fight to the death," James announced. "Three…two…one…begin."

My father took the first strike, his jaws breaking one of Julian's hind legs quickly. It was a tactical move that would ensure this fight didn't last long. Julian should've been expecting it, but clearly his mind was on other things. I was certain he still hoped Ceres would bail him out.

"What do you think she promised him?" I murmured to Rourke. "What could a Pack Alpha need more than what he already had?"

"It's hard to say," Rourke answered. "But I bet she promised him some sort of position of power on the Coalition. Maybe jurisdiction over all werewolves in the entire world. Who knows? Whatever it was, it wasn't worth it. He's not going to last long."

My father had Julian's neck in his jaws. Julian broke away and scuttled backward, growling ferociously, snapping at my father, blood dripping down his gray fur. They circled each other as Marcy, Kayla, and Jax joined us. Jax was back to his normal size, pants intact, everything else missing.

As the fifteen-year-old came up to me, I reached out and placed a hand on his shoulder. "You were incredibly brave today," I said. "Thank you for putting yourself in harm's way for my benefit."

He blushed and kicked the dirt. "No problem. I was happy to do it, especially since you saved me." He looked up shyly. "And, um, if you need a babysitter, you know, after your kids are born, I'm happy to help. I used to babysit back at the apartment complex when our neighbors had to work late. I'm pretty good at it."

"I'm sure you are, and I will take you up on it. They couldn't have a better friend or protector in you."

"I can't believe I missed the face-off against Ceres," Marcy said, her voice barely above a whisper. "But I can't say I'm sad at the final result. She had it coming. What I don't understand is how she knocked us all out. I mean, I should have had some way to guard myself against her. Her spells are not that much stronger than mine." She scratched her head. "I don't get it."

My eyes were on my father as I answered. "It seems Ceres had a little help from an angel named Romy. She's the one who knocked you out. Ceres mistook what she did as help. I guess it was Romy's job to see that this battle took place, but not to harm anyone in the process."

Marcy made a show of looking around, placing her fingers on her forehead. "How many angels live in this place? They're coming out of the woodwork. I've never even heard of one before now—I mean, I'd heard *heard* of them, but I didn't think they actually existed."

"I'm right there with you," I murmured. "I guess I didn't have an opinion about them one way or another before. I think they're here because their power is concentrated, and the new Coalition is forming." I thought about it for a second. "Although, Leo lives here, so that might not be right."

My father had Julian on the ground, his jaws pinning his neck.

It would take only another moment for him to snap it, which was a lethal blow for a wolf. If there was no communication from the body to the brain, a wolf couldn't survive. Though, a powerful Alpha could potentially heal from such a wound, so steps would have to be taken after the fight to ensure that didn't happen.

"This fight is fairly grisly," Kayla commented. "Are they usually this bloody?"

"This coming from a girl who plays with dead people," Marcy said. "To tell you the truth, I've never seen one either. But I think Callum is making a point with Julian. My man just better not get too close to the fray. I don't want one hair on his body damaged."

"James can take care of himself," I said. When Marcy gave me a look, I replied, "Don't give me the hairy eyeball. I get it. If Rourke was that close to the fight, I'd feel the same way."

In the next instant, it was over.

There was absolute silence for a few moments.

"The winner of the challenge is Callum McClain." James's voice carried over the crowd. "If there is any wolf who opposes this outcome, they must speak now."

No one said a word.

My father lay down and began to shift back. We watched as Julian's body did the same, as wolves did in death.

I was just about to head over to talk to my father when a figure in the distance moving toward us caught my eye.

Ray tapped me on the shoulder. "We've got company."

Sure enough, a small, hairy figure with insanely spiked hair, wearing a white robe and carrying a large book, was headed straight at us.

29

Jeb showing himself to the masses was new. This wasn't going to be a secret meeting. "It's time for Eudoxia, Tally, and Naomi to meet Jeb," I said. "After all, they're going to be interacting with him a lot in the near future."

Naomi stood off to the side with Danny. "I will go with you, of course," she replied, but her voice held curiosity.

I inclined my head at Danny. He hadn't told his mate about her position. It was time to fess up. He cleared his throat. "Um, yes, about that. I haven't actually had time to mention anything. It's been a bit of a blur since this morning." He took Naomi's hands in his, meeting her startled gaze, smiling warmly. "Love, it seems...well, it seems you have a seat on the Coalition. Eudoxia will take the place of the fae, and by default, you are the most powerful vampire in the land, so the seat is yours."

To say that Naomi was startled by this announcement was an understatement. "I...I don't understand," she stuttered. "Surely it is not my place, and there are others stronger and more powerful than I to fill it." Naomi was reserved and shy, but she was also honest, straightforward, and trustworthy. Traits I valued at the highest level. She was perfect for the job and would make an impressive vampire advocate, but she was going to need a little convincing.

"There's no mistake," I told her. "You have ingested my blood, which in turn has given you incredible power. More power than any other vampire, save Eudoxia. And too bad for her, but the Vamp Queen can't take two seats. So the power found the next logical replacement." I peered at her. "Surely you've had some inkling," I said gently. "Tally said her power tightened around her. Have there been any indications the vampire power has chosen you?"

Power was tangible, something Naomi couldn't deny.

Naomi clasped her hands. "*Oui*. A very strong surge came to me while I was being held captive, but I set it aside, thinking it was a trick of Enid's. That she was trying to urge me to break out of our space, only so she could harm us afterward. I would not risk Jax's life in that way, so I dismissed it."

"Is it still there?" I asked.

"Come on, speak up," Eudoxia demanded, walking up to us. "The ambassador awaits. I cannot believe the power chose you—someone so inept—but if it's so, we need to know right now."

Naomi leveled her gaze at Eudoxia, her former Queen. There hadn't been much respect there to begin with, and there certainly wasn't now. Naomi slowly lifted her arms. I felt a rush of power, almost like a mini-cyclone, brush by us as it rushed to her, forcing her hair to billow up. "The power is mine," she stated evenly. "It has chosen me, and now I command it."

I darted a look in Eudoxia's direction. Her face remained impassive, but I knew she was pissed. "You once wielded that same power," I pointed out to the Vampire Queen. "Do you sense its loss now?"

Eudoxia seemed surprised by my question, but that might be because she was only half listening. "Of course not," she scoffed. "When I came into my fae side, it more than doubled whatever piddly power I once had. I am stronger than ever."

I narrowed my eyes.

Sure thing, Eudoxia.

For someone who coveted power, she missed it like sunshine on a cold day. "Does that mean Naomi is now in charge of your Coterie?" I asked. "It would make sense that the vampires would follow the most powerful vampire, not the most powerful *fae*."

Eudoxia shot me a steely look, one I was used to. "I guess we will see when this is all said and done, won't we?" she said. "Once we take our vows, the rule will be clear. Until then"—she glared at Naomi—"things stay as they are."

I felt proud as I watched Naomi strengthen her resolve. "The vampires are mine," Naomi stated coolly. "I am certain of this. If you wish to challenge me, so be it. But I will meet the challenge on their behalf, as they deserve a Queen to look out for them and not one who looks out for her own interests, as you have done all your life."

Before Eudoxia could reach apoplectic, I stepped between them, spreading my arms. "Okay, ladies," I said. "This discussion stops here. No need for any more challenges today. Let's see what Jeb has to say. I'm sure he can clear up some of this. Whatever the Coalition—and the power—dictates, we agree to that as law moving forward. Petty disagreements can't get in the way of forming the most powerful leadership in the supernatural community. Especially when it's needed so badly and we've gone without for so long." Eudoxia made a move toward Naomi, and I stopped her. "If you fight Naomi, you fight us all." I flexed my power in front of her, so she would feel it.

"You got that right," Tally's voice interrupted. "Nobody has time for your little power skirmishes, Fae Queen, or whatever your title is now. Take your change in status like a woman and stop complaining about it. Once we pledge our vows, and we share power, we will all be sufficiently strong—more so than any other supernatural in the land. If that's not good enough for you, I don't know what is. Maybe we should consider replacing you. If you've done your research, you know that can happen, and the ambassador here can back me up."

Jeb cleared his throat. He'd managed to get closer than I'd thought without us hearing. "The witch is correct," he stated, his voice cracking a bit as we all turned. The pressure to keep us all in line was rearing its head. "A Coalition member can be removed, but it would take a majority vote and sufficient power to depose that person. It states right here"—his book flew open, his fingers ran along a page—"in order to do so—"

"Enough!" Eudoxia raged, her fists clenched, her pallor edging toward red. "No one is removing *anyone*. We are not even a Coalition yet. This talk is nonsense."

I grinned. "Everyone, this is Jebediah Amel, the High Ambassador to the Coalition, and apparently a secretary of sorts."

"I am most certainly *not* a secretary," Jeb retorted, offended at my careless introduction. Not a great place to start. "I am the administrative assistant to the leader of the Coalition, which is you." He glanced pointedly at me. "I am also the scryer who keeps all eyes on the community and reports back about what needs to be done. It is an incredibly important position, one that my father held and his father before him."

"And you're a keeper of the forms," I joked. "In triplicate. Because this is a business, is it not?"

"What names her the leader?" Eudoxia asked, crossing her arms, not being fooled by my lame attempt to defuse the situation.

The first of many sticking points, and we hadn't even

started. Before Jeb could answer, I did. "I already declined the position. I've informed Jeb that this will run as a democratic committee." I stared hard at Eudoxia. "I will continue to turn down the leadership position. There are five of us, which means we always have a tiebreaker. We will conduct our business as a democracy. End of story." I continued to hold eye contact with her, daring her to say otherwise.

After a moment, she nodded, and that was it.

The all-powerful Vampire Queen, now Fae Queen, had given up her Coterie to Naomi without a fight and had just given up debating me about leadership of the Coalition.

For the first time in a long time, I had hope that things would go well.

"I must meet up with my witches soon," Tally said, bringing the conversation back around. "As luck would have it, the group who has my daughter is near here. Ambassador, please let us know what needs to be done, so we can attend to other pressing matters."

Jeb rifled through some of the pages of the book. "The ceremony will take place two moons from now, at promptly three a.m., lunar time. That day marks a new moon, and the energy and power will be particularly potent."

"Should I summon the Princess of Hell?" I asked.

"I beg your pardon?" he said.

"You know, the fifth seat on the Coalition, the demon seat," I said. "I have her summoning stone. She can be here shortly."

Jeb seemed momentarily stunned as he leaned over his book and rifled through more pages.

Rourke, Ray, Tyler, Kayla Marcy, and Danny all stood around us waiting for an answer.

Rourke leaned into me. "Maybe we have it wrong?"

"Could be, but then, who fills the seat?" I said. "I thought there were five factions—werewolves, witches, vampires, demons, and fae. Who else is there?"

Jeb glanced up. A pair of round spectacles popped into place on his nose, enhancing his large, bushy eyebrows. "Demons are indeed one of the top powers, but they aren't technically part of this realm. The Coalition has always been about only this world. If not"—he cocked his head thoughtfully—"the Coalition would contain people like myself, and angels, and many others who are more powerful."

Point taken.

It seemed our world lagged behind others in strength. That was news to me, but none of us was really old enough to know who'd taken the original seats. I only knew my predecessor had one. "So, if the Princess of Hell is not who we're searching for, who is?"

Jeb bobbed his head down again, his stick-straight hair not even pretending to move. "The last spot is reserved for those who commune with the dead. It's not always one specific supernatural Sect, but in this case"—Jeb looked over his spectacles—"it's reserved for a necromancer."

His gaze moved past me and stopped over my shoulder.

I turned, meeting Kayla's startled gaze as her hand settled over her heart. "Me?" She shook her head. "I don't think so."

"I haven't known Jeb for very long, but he hasn't been wrong so far," I said. "It seems Enid knew a thing or two when she picked you to do her bidding. She must've seen this already. You are the most powerful necromancer around, right?"

Kayla was almost too overcome to answer. "Yes...at least...I think I am. But we're not like you." She glanced around. "We are solitary, independent supernaturals. We don't operate in a typical Sect."

"Then how would you know if you're the best of your kind?" Ray asked. He caught my eye and shrugged. "Just asking."

She gazed at the ground, and Jeb said, "I can answer that. You see, her father was the most accomplished necromancer the world has ever seen. He, and he alone, was able to raise armies, to command the dead on a mere thought. Kayla has inherited not only his power, but his unique genes."

Kayla was clearly overcome. I made my way over and laid a hand on her arm. "Kayla, we've already witnessed your incredible power up close. It's truly spectacular. I don't think Enid was careless when she selected you. She did it because you are meant to take this position. I know this must be overwhelming, but I am certain your parents would be incredibly proud. Your place on the Coalition will also solidify your brother's safety. There's no better place for you guys to be than here."

Kayla stilled herself, finding her quiet inner strength, which was just as fierce as any of ours. As far as keeping the supernatural world in line, her skills would be unmatched.

No supernatural could defeat an army of anything.

Jeb coughed politely. "It seems as though Fate has your favor," he said to me.

"My favor? I can't exactly agree with you there," I replied. "Since I've been born, my life has been nothing but an uphill battle."

"Your relationship with each person on this Coalition is unprecedented," he stated evenly. "Not only are they known to you—some even bonded to you—a few of their mates are related to you. A mate bond is no simple thing. It's etched into the very fabric and cell of each party. This entire Coalition was set into motion many, many years ago. Yes, there've been a few glitches," he admitted. "But it seems someone, or something, wanted to be doubly, or triply, sure that this operated smoothly and efficiently by putting their faith in *you*."

"Well, if that's the case, I'd have to assume Eudoxia is a mistake. There are likely very few people in the world I get along with less than the Fae Queen."

"We can't all be your sheep," Eudoxia declared

authoritatively. "If that were true, then you would get lazy and put us all at risk."

"I'm not bonded to you either," Tally said.

"Actually," Jeb said, thumbing through more pages. "I wouldn't rule that out just yet."

"What are you talking about?" Tally asked, alarmed. She'd said it so vehemently, Jeb arched his head back like he'd been struck.

"Well, you're not mated yet, but it is written here—"

Tally held up her hand. "Stop right there. I don't want to know. When I find my mate, I'll know it. There's no way I'd take that book's word for it anyway, so don't complicate things. Are we almost done here? I am anxious to be reunited with my daughter."

Jeb's lips curled in distaste. The Coalition was going to be run by five headstrong women who would not be pushed around by a conservative, stuck-in-his-ways warlock. "Yes, we are done here," he said. "I simply came to tell you the time and the place of your coronation."

"We got it. Three a.m., two moons from now," I said. One moon would be rising in just a few hours. That meant there was only one full day left. "Where do we meet?"

"We will assemble at the highest point in Florence, a place called San Miniato. There is a basilica there, built in the eleventh century. We will meet on the grounds outside, under the new moon. I will see you then."

The words were barely out of his mouth when Jeb popped out of existence.

We all stood there for a moment, not knowing what to do.

"Well," I said. "I think it's safe to say it's going to take the warlock some time to get used to us. He's mentioned that this Coalition is already much different than the others. He's not thrilled about the change. I think Jebediah Amel is used to certainty and routine, and he will likely get neither from the likes of us."

Rourke settled his arm around my shoulders. "Let's head back to the villa," he said. "Your father's taken the wolves back to the bunkhouse to talk about the future and settle any lingering unrest. He assigned wolves to deal with the bodies as well. Let's go decompress and figure out our next step."

"I'm not sticking around," Eudoxia declared. "As I said before, I have some pressing business to attend to. I will be at the meeting place two nights from now, but you will not see me again before then." She nodded once, and then shot up in the air and out of sight.

We all glanced at each other.

It'd been a long day.

As we began to walk, I said, "I think this is the first time someone or something hasn't been after me." I laid my head on Rourke's shoulder.

He growled, "And it's going to stay that way if I have anything to say about it."

30

It didn't take long for Tally's witches to deliver her daughter, Maggie, to our doorstep. Tally had been waiting anxiously on the veranda with open arms, Marcy right behind her. There was a lot of kissing and crooning over the toddler.

Marcy held the cherub in her arms, nuzzling her cheeks loudly, murmuring, "You still smell like baby to me, even though I know you're so grown up. I've missed you, you little goof. I'm so happy you're back."

After a few more moments of continued smothering, Maggie wiggled out of Marcy's arms and toddled toward me. She stopped, lifting her arms in the universal sign of *uppy*. I obliged and picked her up, placing a kiss on her cheek. "Maggie, I'm so glad you're okay. We were so worried."

She grabbed my face between her two chubby hands, her expression comically serious. "You have babies," she told me in hushed tones. Then she brought her tiny fingers in front of my face and flashed a crumpled peace sign. "Two of them."

I smiled. "I know," I told her. "I just found out. It's big news."

She nodded gravely and grabbed my face again. "It's gonna be okay," she said. "The baby boy will protect the baby girl, like your brudder protects you. She will have lots of friends." She proudly jabbed a single finger into her chest. "I'm going to be her friend." She sighed dramatically. "She's gonna be my *bestest* friend."

My throat was too constricted to speak.

I had to glance away from her sincere little face for fear of scaring her with racking sobs.

Rourke came to my rescue, scooping her out of my arms and tossing her into the air. She gave a delighted squeal. "Kitty, do more!" she called, using the cute nickname she'd given Rourke.

Rourke obliged, and while the child was occupied with flying through the air, Marcy came over to give me a hug. "My little cousin-niece can be one spooky little child when she's spouting the future," she said. "But don't forget, she's never wrong. I believe she might be the most powerful seer in the entire world." Marcy linked arms with me as we watched my mate continued to toss her around as her squeals got louder. "If she says your babies will be fine, I believe her." Marcy's hand reassuringly stroked my arm.

I leaned my head against hers. "But that doesn't change the fact that I'm going to have to give my daughter up at some point," I confided to my best friend for the first time. "My daughter is the sacrifice Juanita was talking about."

Marcy turned to me, her eyes wide. "Are you sure?" she asked. "Or are you metaphorically speaking? Like you're going to have to 'give her up,' as in when they turn the dreaded thirteen and want nothing to do with you, you feel like kicking them out?"

I shook my head. "My daughter is the reincarnate of Bianca, the third sister. I'm sure of it," I said. "She will most likely retain her true self and memories, but I'm not sure about the timing of when she has to leave." Tears began to creep into the corners of my eyes. "I don't know how I'm going to manage to give up my child. And I can't even talk about what it's going to do to Rourke. But it's something I must swear to do to Enid tomorrow night at midnight."

Marcy purposefully guided me into the house, and we ducked into a nearby library. She closed the double doors. "Go sit on that settee," she ordered with a gesture of her arm as she grabbed a straight-backed chair and dragged it over to where I numbly sat. "I need you to look at me." She placed both her hands on my legs and gave a squeeze. At her prodding, I met her gaze. "This isn't as dire as it seems," she stated firmly.

"How can you say that?" I said, a single tear tracking down my face. "I have no idea if Enid will even let her visit once she leaves, or if my daughter will even want to." I shook my head. "What if they demand her at Maggie's age? What if they take my baby away from me? Away from Rourke and our son? What if we never get a chance to know her?"

"They won't do that," Marcy said hastily. "Ultimately, they want their sister happy and healthy, right? Sure, she'll have some of her old memories creeping in at Maggie's age, but she won't be old enough to process them. She'll need love, stability, and understanding, and you can give her all those in spades. Enid would be foolish to rob her sister of a loving family."

"I hear you, and I want to believe it, but I'm having trouble putting all the pieces in the right box." Marcy leaned back, and I stood, needing to walk out my frustrations. "It's overwhelming to learn I'm pregnant at all, much less know that I'll have to give up my child."

Marcy turned in her chair so she could face me. "You heard Maggie just now," she argued. "She's going to be best friends with your daughter. And I can see why—they're both powerful seers. Who better to help navigate the waters? Fate is choosing to take care of this itself. If you don't believe me, ask Maggie more questions and she'll tell you herself. And, honestly, you can't take all this worry on right now. If you do, your head might pop off, and then where will the babies be? I'm sorry to inform you, but they need a mother with a head or they can't survive."

"I don't want to ask Maggie any more questions," I told her, leaning against the wall and crossing my arms around my midsection. I was fearful of what the toddler might say, that it be too hard to bear. I couldn't risk that right before I had to talk to Enid. If I couldn't convince the Hag that I would give over her sister when she asked, I would die, and my babies would die along with me. The stakes were so much higher now. "I have to let this play out without the interference. Rourke and I haven't even had a chance to discuss it." I ran a hand through my hair. "I need to get my feelings in order so I can stay strong for him."

Marcy stood, coming up next to me. She reached her arm around my waist and pulled me close. I hugged her back. "You don't need to be strong for Rourke. He's *your* rock, and he will continue to be. You two will weather this storm. It's not going to destroy you. I won't let it. Nobody will. We will rally around you both. There has to be some goodness in Enid, way, way deep down, like possibly lumped up in her baby toe. Even if she doesn't agree now, once she meets her infant reincarnated sister for the first time, she will want what's best for her. She will see that the only sane thing to do is leave the child with you until she comes of age."

I stepped back. "What then?" I asked. "She just disappears into the sunset, never to be seen again? Where do the Hags even live?"

Marcy tossed her hands in the air. "How can you be hormone-crazed already? This isn't like you, and that's not how this is going to work. People don't just gallop off into the sunset, never to be seen again. We're supernaturals, for cripes sake! You will continue to see your daughter—the girl you raise from birth. You will have an ongoing relationship. If she has to leave for extended times, you're just going to have to pretend she's off backpacking through Europe, like college kids do. Then, when she comes home for a visit, you will make the most of it. That's how this will work." Marcy's voice was adamant, and for the first time since I'd heard the news that I was pregnant and giving birth to Enid's sister, I had a glimmer of hope that this wasn't going to be as bad as I imagined.

"I hope you're right," I agreed, exhaling a long breath. "Because I don't think I could bear to sever myself from my child forever. Do you think Enid will ask that of me?"

"No, honey. She'd have to be a sadist who hates her baby sister and wants her to live a horrible life. And she's not that. Enid is going to be so beyond relieved to finally have her flesh and blood breathing on this earth after all these years that she will likely become her fairy godmother." Marcy giggled. "I can just envision ol' Enid coming to Christmas dinner with an armful of crazy gifts, like the looney cat lady aunt who still thinks giving Russian stacking dolls and hand-knit sweaters is cool."

I laughed in spite of the situation. It felt good. "I keep imagining her little brother left without his sister for all those years, feeling the loss acutely. I'm a twin, and if they're anything like me and Tyler, their bond will be unbreakable from the moment they're born. It would be heart-wrenching to have her torn from our lives."

Marcy slung her arm over my shoulders. "I hear you, Ace. It's not going to be easy, especially going into this not knowing the outcome. But I don't think it's going to be as bad as you think. Plus, you haven't factored in Juanita yet. She's always been your advocate, and she will continue to cheer you on and want what's best for her sister. Enid won't be the only one making the decisions here."

There was a soft knock on the door.

Marcy went to answer it.

Rourke stood holding Maggie, who looked happy and content, her blonde curly head resting on his broad shoulder. Rourke hesitated before he came in, trying to read my emotions. "Maggie wanted to find you," he said, his face full of concern. He felt my tension, stress, and sadness acutely. This had to be incredibly hard for him, especially since we hadn't had a chance to talk.

Are you okay? he asked. *I wish we could go upstairs right now,* he growled. *But it would be remiss of us not to talk to your dad and make sure everything is running smoothly before we disappear.*

I hear you. I want nothing more than some alone time with you. And I'm doing as well as can be expected. Marcy's helping me a lot, so I'm thankful for that.

"Jess-ca." Maggie yawned while reaching for me. I took the tot out of Rourke's arms and held her close. She angled her head into the crook of my neck, while her little palm stroked my cheek. "It's gonna be okay. Annie lubs you already." Her voice was barely a whisper. She was almost asleep. The kid had been through a lot. "She's my bestest friend, and I can't wait to meet her."

My gaze raced to Rourke's.

Annie.

My mother's name.

It's perfect, Rourke said, his voice full of emotion. *It's appropriate for her to be named after your mother.*

What was your father's name? I asked.

Aodhán, he replied. *Pronounced Aidan in modern English.*

Annie and Aidan.

I turned my back on my mate, rocking Maggie in my arms as my eyes misted. I might have to face facts and admit that the added hormones might be making me weepy.

I couldn't remember the last time I'd cried.

There was a sharp rap on the doorjamb as Tally walked in.

She'd been in Stasis for weeks, but you couldn't tell. She looked as tough and ready for battle as she ever had. "Is she asleep?" she asked, coming up to me. "Here, let me take her. The witches tell me she hasn't slept much since I disappeared. The separation has been hard on her."

I transferred the sleeping child into her mother's waiting arms. "I can imagine," I said. "She must've been worried sick."

Once Tally had her daughter back, she appraised me. "They told me what happened out there, what Ceres threatened to do." Tally's voice was stony. "That goddess has never played fair a day in her life, as she constantly griped about all the unfairness she felt was heaped upon her. I should've known all along that she was going to be a problem." Tally shrugged. "But I always maintained I was stronger than she was, so it didn't matter if she bitched and moaned and threatened, because if it came down to a fight, I would win. But when you have other people depending on you"—she patted Maggie's back—"you have to make sure you cover all your bases. I didn't do that, and I'm sorry. We paid for it. It won't happen again, I can assure you."

"You *were* stronger than she was," I replied. "You just didn't count on the fact that she had a powerful ally. Or at least one Ceres thought was an ally. Romy, the Angel of Fertility, is the one who captured you and forced you into Stasis. And although the angel didn't specify, I think it was for the greater good, because it ended up giving us this moment right here. Who knows what would've happened otherwise? I'm just sorry your daughter was caught in the middle of it."

"You have nothing to be sorry about," Tally said. "This was ultimately about the Coalition forming. And since I have a place at the table, it's my battle too. And truth be told, Maggie was muttering things about angels and goddesses and trouble for a few days prior. I ignored her because we were hyper-focused on keeping that circle open. It was a hard lesson learned." She placed a kiss on her daughter's head. "I forget that even though she's only two years old, she's still a very powerful seer who can't be ignored."

I was thoughtful for a moment. "Is it hard to juggle?" I asked curiously. Tally raised an eyebrow in question. "How do you treat her like the child she is *and* bring her into her own as a seer? It seems like it would be complicated."

"It's not terribly hard," Tally answered. "She dictates, and I follow. It's that simple. There are days when she wants to be coddled and treated like a child, and there are days when she needs me to sit and listen. I do both, unconditionally. And I can tell you, I won't ignore her again. She is living her destiny, and that's just the way it is. There's no lamenting what could've been. She knows I love her. She knows her aunt Marcy loves her. She knows all of you love her. No matter what, she's cocooned in that love. For now, she seems to be content. If that changes, I'll let you know." She rubbed Maggie's back. "Now I'm going to put her to bed. My witches have taken up residence on the terrace for the night. We'll figure out where we're going tomorrow." As Tally left the room, Marcy trailed them, arguing that she wanted to hold her little cousin-niece and that Tally was hogging her.

I met Rourke's gaze.

He opened his arms, and I walked into them.

His strength enveloped me. He pressed one hand tightly on my back, while the other twined in my hair, his lips at my temple. "We are a family, no matter what. It doesn't matter where in the world any of us are located in time or space, you will always be my wife, my lover, and the mother of our children. The same holds true for our children. Nothing will ever part us."

I nodded into his shirt. "I know, it's just hard. Everything is still sinking in. We have nine months to adjust. I'm sure we'll figure it out, but I'm worried about talking to Enid tomorrow night. Now we know why she insisted she speak with me alone. If I don't convince her that we're willing to give Annie up when the time comes, she could end my life right then and there. By doing so, she will also end the lives of our unborn children. You just killed Ceres for even threatening to do such a thing. I feel helpless, like we have no recourse, and it all comes down to if Enid believes me or not."

"Jessica..." Rourke set me away from him. "Enid isn't going to just go by your words. She's going to *see* Annie's life—whether she wants to or not. She will see her sister thrive, laugh, grow, and be loved. Just like Tally said. And you can't dismiss what Maggie told us. That little tyke told me she can't wait to do all these things with our daughter and that they're going to be best friends. I choose to believe that."

I nodded. "I want to believe too."

He encompassed me back in his arms and chuckled. "After that, she said the damnedest thing."

"What?" My voice was partly muffled by his shirt.

"Your father came through the front door"—I lifted my head—"and she called him *Daddy*."

I was stunned.

Then immediately started to laugh.

Tally and my father were perfect for each other.

Two dominant leaders, neither willing to give an inch. I didn't know why I didn't see it before. "What did my father do with that particular news?"

"The better question is how Tally responded." He started laughing in earnest. "She said something equivalent to 'over my dead body.' To which your father deadpanned, 'I don't sleep with the dead.'"

31

The house was quiet. It was a few hours before dawn. I lay in bed staring at the ceiling. Rourke had finally drifted off, both of us restless. We had talked into the night, sharing tears and love.

Before we'd adjourned to our room for the evening, the wolves had accepted my father's leadership and were grateful for it. It seemed Julian had been slacking for years, not months. Tyler had been christened temporary Alpha in front of everyone, and my father planned to leave immediately after the coronation.

He would remain stateside for the most part, busy running the U.S. Territories. He wanted the wolves here used to new leadership immediately. It made the most sense, but I was going to be sorry to see him leave.

We agreed that the villa would become our new home base, at least for a while. It was secure, and Julian's wolves had gotten down on one knee and pledged their protection to me, headed up by none other than Lucas. It seemed the sly fox had explained to them what my new role on the Coalition was and that I would need extra protection.

They had given it willingly, and my heart had been full.

I slipped from bed, giving up on trying to sleep, being as quiet as I could so I didn't bother Rourke, and padded to the balcony. We'd left the door ajar to let in the fresh air. The moon was low in the sky, but still bright.

I walked outside, inhaling the scent of fresh vines and pine trees, placing my hands on the thick stone balcony. I liked it here. My wolf recognized this area and was content. It was peaceful. It would be a good place to raise children. They would have miles and miles to run and play.

I stood, cupping both hands around my abdomen, entreating a silent plea to whoever would listen. *Please, let them be happy and healthy. Let Rourke and I be good parents. Let no danger come to them.*

Someone cleared their throat behind me, and I spun, my body dipping low, my claws already out at sharp points.

"Hold on there," Romy said as she mockingly put her hands up. "You were praying somebody would listen, and I'm someone, so I came to tell you to let some of that worry go. At least for right now."

My claws retracted as I eased out of my crouching position. "Why are you here?" I asked.

"On this balcony? Or in your world in general?"

"Both."

"Well, I was ordered to this realm, so I followed that order. If I hadn't, I'd have faced punishment. Not a big fan of lengthy jail stays, so I figured it was my best bet to show up," Romy said. "Then when I heard your plea, I came to talk to you."

I sat on the railing, facing her. "I thought you weren't a seer?" I asked. "How do you know so much?"

She shrugged. "I'm not a seer, as in predicting the future, but I am extremely good at analyzing. One gift any angel has at their fingertips is information. As much as he or she wants, whenever they want it. Not of what is yet to come, but everything that has happened up till the very minute we speak. I'm not going to stroke your ego by telling you I knew who you were before a few weeks ago, because I didn't. Where I come from, we don't bother ourselves with this world. At least not most of us."

"You're referring to Leo, aren't you?" I said. "He lives here because he wants to."

A wisp of her long, blonde hair flicked in front of her face, and she tucked it behind her ear. Her features were perfectly precise, everything aligned. "I am," she replied. "A long, long while ago, he was among the mightiest of our kind. He was sent here on an errand—I believe to facilitate one of your earliest Coalitions, which is what we angels have been tasked to do. The rumors were he became fascinated with humans and supernaturals alike. He gave up his prominent position for a quiet life here." She strode to the other side of the balcony, her dark silhouette in stark contrast to her pale face. "No one has ever understood why he did such a thing." She turned and gazed at me directly. "Until now."

"Are you saying *you* understand?" I asked.

"I'm beginning to," she said. "And my fascination starts with you."

"Why?"

"You represent the kind of strength and independence we have in abundance in our world. The epitome of it. But here, there is so much weakness. Just look around at all the helpless humans who have no recourse to combat anything you might choose to do to them. They are the lesser species. You could reign over them with absolute authority, and the innocents could do very little in the wake of your power." She sat on the railing, curling her legs beneath her. "Yet, you don't see the world the way I do. Your lens is focused on goodness, democracy, and forgiveness. Those are traits we do not value where I come from. You cause one to think."

"Thank you?" My tone was reserved. Romy was intense,

and ridiculously powerful, full of a kind of magic I didn't understand—one that didn't originate from here. "Your world sounds dark and intimidating. If your world doesn't look favorably upon ours, why come here now to help us?"

She had one knee drawn up. "You have just learned of your creator, Marinette, the goddess who first created your kind, have you not? The one who tore her soul in half to create the only female of your kind." I nodded. I was all too familiar with Marinette—the battle still fresh in my mind. My wolf howled her agreement.

"She was one of us," Romy said. My eyebrows rose. "A distant relative of the first descendants who came to this world to live by choice. So by chance—or not by chance at all, depending on how you interpret things—you are a direct descendant of my world, more so than others because you harbor Marinette's very soul inside of you. But I digress. The story is much more intricate than that. When the first group of angels came here and had children of their own, they realized their offspring had diminished powers. They'd left our fertile lands, where the very air we breathe and the food we eat give us strength." She tilted her face up to the sky as she spoke. "Over time, their children's children became gods and goddesses, finally figuring out that humans—the weaker population they coexisted with—could, in fact, keep them alive and flush with power through the energy of prayer. Once the children achieved that power, they began to create supernaturals to ensure their protection in case the humans ever decided to rise up against them. With the birth of the supernaturals, the first Coalition was born. There had to be a rule of law—some way to deal with all the new powerful creatures roaming the earth constantly in search of more power, hungering for it. Hundreds of years later, when Marinette broke the rules and created your predecessor, they found the Coalition they had established was too weak."

I hung on every word.

"The Coalition could be easily overcome by these new, powerful supernaturals," Romy went on. "It needed strength to keep everyone in line. So the elders, the first gods and goddesses, sent an emissary to our world to beg for our assistance, and in return, they would provide us with resources from this place that we had come to value, such as iron and gold. A deal was struck, and with each new Coalition, we journey here to bless it and infuse it with our power, making the council stronger than any rivals." She turned to face me. "That's the long answer to why I've come to Earth to help you. Together, Leo and I will grace this Coalition with our power, honoring the bargain we struck all those long years ago."

I had no idea what to say. "Wow, that's quite a history lesson. I don't even think my father knows most of what you just told me. It's hard to believe that, in essence, all supernaturals here sprouted from your world. But I guess it makes sense, because they had to originate from somewhere. They weren't conjured from thin air. So, in return for your continued favor of power, do we still owe you iron and gold?"

"No," she mused. "Leo has amassed great wealth in his time here, and he makes more than enough contributions to cover our needs."

"If you don't need our resources," I asked, "why would your powers that be choose to honor the age-old agreement?"

"Because Leo desires it," she stated simply, unfurling herself from the railing. She stood and gazed out over the expansive rolling hills. "You are worried about the safety of your unborn children." She turned to face me. "You need not worry."

"How can you say that with such certainty?" I desperately wanted to believe her. "You've already said twice now that you don't see into the future."

"Because even though you will give birth to a reincarnate,

she will be created from your own flesh and blood—a gene pool that has descended directly from angels. Your daughter will be the strongest, by far, of her three sisters. Enid can see this. Pandora can see this. Enid will want herself and her sisters to remain strong at all costs, for nothing is certain in this world. As Fate changes, so do our roles. They are all intertwined. Strength and power are coveted by all."

"You are the Angel of Fertility, is that correct?" I asked. "Does every angel have a specialty?"

She plucked a small stick off the railing and twirled it in her fingers. "More or less. In our world, we are all powerful, but in different ways. It takes all of us working together to make us whole." Her voice sounded distant, almost tired.

"Did they send you here because they knew I was pregnant?" I asked. "Your role was to facilitate what happened today, but also to protect me from Ceres?"

"Yes, in a way." She brought the stick up to her nose and inhaled. It was safe to say all the scents here were likely different than in her world. She turned to meet my gaze. "The elders in my world have been following the progress that has led up to the formation of the new Coalition. They know of Enid's desire to have her sister back, and when you killed the other, Ardat Lili, a dangerous rent ripped through our world as well as this one. If this realm were to fall into chaos, ours would eventually follow, as we are separate but linked. If forced to fight, angels would pick sides, leading to chaos for us all. They couldn't have that, so they sent me. If you had not conceived, Ceres could have rendered you infertile—and would have out of spite as soon as you came near enough. As luck—or Fate—would have it, you had already conceived. I stayed to make sure no harm came to you and your unborn children."

"Well, for what it's worth, I appreciate what you've done. I'm humbled by it," I said. "Knowing there are angels watching over my children brings me great peace." Leo had also pledged his protection in the church. He must've known what was at stake.

She turned toward me with fluid grace, her blonde hair swaying. We were almost the same height, but she had me by an inch. "There you go, confounding me once again." She chuckled. "If you were anything like others of your kind, you would claim that our protection is your right, that you are deserving of this, and that it's your entitlement." She made a show of looking me over. "I believe you will be a good leader, because your traits allow you to see things in a broader sense. Do not take them for granted."

"I won't," I assured her. "When this is all over, are you going to stick around? Or do you plan to go back to your...world?" Realm? Plane?

"I will linger here for a time," she answered. "I must report back, but expedition is not necessary as long as things go in the correct fashion."

"Can you answer me one more thing before you go?" I asked. "Eudoxia told us that the vampires were gossiping about white angels and dark angels, each created from a different place. Are you a dark angel? I'm only assuming that by your style of clothing, which isn't very scientific on my part."

She seemed amused by my question. "Humans love the idea of heaven and hell, good versus evil. Their pious views of my realm couldn't be further from the truth. But, for all intents and purposes, yes, I am a dark angel," she affirmed. "There are also white angels. You can tell us apart by the color of our wings. But there is no good versus evil. We are simply dark and light, two cultures sharing the same world."

It didn't sound as cut-and-dried as she wanted me to believe.

"And there is no strife between the two cultures? No struggles for dominance? Here on Earth, it's a constant battle.

Many are judged by the color of their skin and to whom they pray."

"There is certainly strife. As I've stated, our world has been on the brink of chaos for a long time. In sending me here, our elders, both dark and light, greatly hope to avoid falling into that abyss. Only time will tell if we've achieved it." She climbed up on the railing as a pair of huge gorgeous black wings emerged seamlessly from her back. They glittered in the moonlight like shiny pebbles lying just beneath the water. "I shall see you later tonight under a new moon." She leaped off the balcony without a sound. I tracked her for only a few seconds before she disappeared from sight.

A moment later, Rourke stepped out onto the balcony. He came up shoulder to shoulder with me and as we watched the sky brighten in anticipation of the new day. "I always knew you were an angel," he said.

I laughed, turning a bright smile his way. "Yeah, right. Even though I may have some lingering angel DNA, I'm far from the beauty and majesty that is Romy." I grabbed his hand and arched up to meet his waiting lips, whispering, "But I'll always be happy to role-play with you."

He growled in response, scooping me up and carrying me back to bed.

32

The sun had just dipped below the horizon. Dinner was scheduled in an hour. Lucas had insisted he keep cooking for us. I'd promised to hire some kitchen help as soon as I could find the time, but he had told me that he loved doing it and wanted to keep his position.

I had acquiesced.

For now. But only if he agreed to join us at the table.

My father had appointed him as the new Director of Communications for the Mediterranean Pack, since he had more than proven his loyalty to me. My father had chosen to keep the Pack name the same to avoid confusion. It would take time for the supernatural community to figure out that Julian was gone, and that was the way we wanted to keep it.

Once both jobs became too much for Lucas, I would hire a full kitchen staff. They would have to be supernaturals we trusted, but since Florence was flush with them, it shouldn't be a problem.

During the day, in between discussions about the future and what was set to happen later tonight, Rourke and I had explored every inch of the villa. It was magnificent, and much bigger than we'd originally thought. There were thirteen bedrooms and sixteen bathrooms. It had a walkout basement set up with a conference room and several offices stocked with high-tech gear.

Julian hadn't skimped on anything. It was the perfect headquarters.

Jeb wanted a place to file paperwork, and he would get it.

"I'm sad Marcy and James are flying home after the coronation," I told Rourke as we headed into the kitchen. "It's going to be especially hard on her, since Tally and Maggie will be staying." The Italian Witch Coven had recently lost their leader, who we assumed had been one of the witches who'd stood with Ceres yesterday. The old castle where the Coven was located was on the other side of Florence, which was convenient for everyone.

Naomi, Danny, Tyler, Kayla, Jax, and Nick were all staying for an undisclosed length of time. We figured it would take a year or two to acclimate to our duties on the Coalition, and lucky for us, the villa was more than big enough to house everyone.

Nick was put in charge of transferring the Hannon & Michaels offices over here. He would continue doing P.I. work, as needed. We figured investigating issues in the supernatural community could only help us keep the peace. Jeb could facilitate that as well, but nobody had seen him, so we couldn't ask him.

I had no idea how to summon the warlock, but I knew I'd be finding out soon.

Kayla was seated at the kitchen table as we walked in. Tyler stood behind her whispering something in her ear, both of their backs to us. She let out a soft giggle and turned to peer up at him, happiness on her face. Now that Jax was safe, Kayla had let down her guard. It was nice to witness the transformation firsthand.

I cleared my throat politely, and they both looked up, seeming startled.

It wasn't like Tyler to let someone creep up behind him, since his hearing was excellent. I chuckled. Love would do that to you. "Has anybody seen Ray?" I asked. "He left last night, and he hasn't been around all day. We need him here before dinner, so we can go over the plan for tonight one last time."

Even though I was set to meet with Enid alone, all the wolves in attendance and my entire team were going to accompany me to the location. They would stand sentinel outside. They wouldn't necessarily be able to save me if Enid chose the darker path, but a show of force couldn't hurt. Ray and Naomi would be key, as they would take positions on the roof.

Jax walked in behind us and immediately made a beeline toward the fridge. Keeping him fed was going to be a gargantuan task. The kid spent most of his time in the kitchen. "Are you talking about the vampire with the steel-cut flattop?" he asked as he pulled the fridge door open, careful not to yank too hard. "I saw him out front. He just landed. Shocked the crap out of me, but man, was it cool. Wish I could fly." He took out a gallon of milk and a dozen eggs. We all watched in silence as he poured a huge glass of milk and proceeded to crack six eggs into it. He was halfway done guzzling it before he turned and found all of us staring at him. "What?" He dragged a sleeve over his mouth. "Can't a guy eat in peace?"

Kayla slid her chair back and rose from the table. "We will, of course, help offset the cost of the groceries. Jax has to keep his caloric intake up, or he gets fatigued."

"Yep," Jax agreed. "I'm still growing. My mom said when I'm finally out of puberty, maybe in a couple of years, my appetite should level out."

"The groceries will come out of Pack funds," I assured them. "It's not an issue. Feel free to eat as much as you want,

Jax. I'm going to need a strong, healthy babysitter in the house. And, honestly, have you ever seen how quickly a pack of wolves devour food? You've got nothing on us. Now, if you'll excuse Rourke and me, we have to find Ray. Everybody's meeting back here in an hour for dinner. Don't be late."

"We'll be here," Tyler said.

We found Ray sitting in one of the chairs on the terrace, gazing out into the distance. He looked a little disheveled, his clothes rumpled. I took a seat next to him. "Where were you? We've been looking all over." I inspected his outfit. There were several dead insects splattered on his shirt. "Wherever it was, it seems you were in the air a long time."

He sat back in his chair and exhaled. "I flew home."

"Home? As in the United States *home*?" I asked. "Why would you do that?" If Ray was going to be gone that long, and travel that far, he should've run it by me first.

"I know what you're thinking, Hannon," he said. "And don't start. I didn't tell you because I wasn't sure if you'd let me go, and it needed to be done, so I did it."

"Okay." I hesitated. "Are you going to tell us why?" Rourke had taken a seat across from Ray on the railing, crossing his arms.

Ray looked a little uncomfortable, which was as close to miserable as he got. He unconsciously yanked at his shirt collar. "I went back to check on someone."

"Enough of the song and dance, Ray," I said. "Spit it out."

"I went to check on Selene."

My mouth dropped open a little. That goddess had been the bane of my existence for a long time. But she'd lost everything in the Underworld. We'd voted by a narrow margin to bring her back. She'd been badly damaged, and Ray had been in charge of her. He'd placed her with some local nymphs for treatment and healing. It hadn't been clear if she would regain her whole magical self.

"How is she?" I asked tentatively.

"Almost back to her cantankerous self," he said. "The wounds have all healed, but her magic has not fully returned, which is likely a good thing for everyone involved."

"Yes, it is," I said. "So why the trip back to see her? Why couldn't it wait?"

Ray leaned forward, sliding his hand along the back of his neck, bringing away some debris from the ride. "Because..." He stood abruptly and walked to the edge of the terrace. "Because, dammit, she is my mate."

"*What?*" I could not have been more stunned. Selene had been a horror to us, even if she'd shown some decency in the end. She was a narcissistic, spoiled, childlike-goddess who had never grown up.

Wait a minute.

Ray spun around. "I know what you're going to say, so don't go there," he snarled. "I'm nothing like her."

I kept the comebacks to myself. "I'm not going to say that you two are a perfect match. Or that you will be the most cantankerous couple who ever walked the planet. Actually, when I line everything up in the right columns, it works. Healthy distaste for authority? Check. Grouchy? Check. Can't seem to find happiness, even when it's right in front of your eyes? Check. Can't take an order without complaining? Check. It's all right there."

"Laugh all you want," he said, "but this isn't funny. As much as I want to forget about her, I can't. I'm compelled to make sure she's okay. She's a beast—but she's *my* beast."

I coughed politely into my hand. "How did she take the news?"

"How do you think?" He grimaced. "She's in full denial and won't even consider talking about it."

"You've got your work cut out for you," I said. "I do pity you. A little." I had to bite my lip. "I hate to tell you this, but

Selene can't join us here until we are absolutely certain of her loyalty to you, and to us."

"She's a viper. Jessica's right, we can't have her here unless I know for sure," Rourke said, standing. "I'm not certain she can be tamed, but if she can, you're definitely the man for the job." Rourke stuck out his hand to Ray, who grasped it. "Good luck. You're going to need it."

"Don't I know it," Ray sighed. "I told her I wasn't coming back until she asked to see me. We'll see how long it takes. It could be years. And I'm plenty content to wait."

"I don't envy you," I said. "But I am happy you found your mate. It is a wonderful thing…when it works." I walked over and stuck out my hand to Ray. "We hope it works out."

Ray shook his head slowly as he dropped my hand. "This is just what I don't need right now. I am *certain* that stubborn woman is going to make me wait for an eternity. But two can play that game. We'll see how she likes it when I don't jump at her first summons."

"Oh, you're going to jump all right." I chuckled. "I guarantee it."

"I know I am," Ray said miserably. "There's no way getting around it."

"I'll send Marcy to check in on her when she gets home. She'll work on her," I promised. "But right now we have to talk about tonight. I need you to be clear on your role."

Ray's expression went from frustrated to serious in a heartbeat.

He stood tall, crossed his arms, legs apart, classic cop pose. He was all business as he asked, "Every wolf and supernatural in the Compound are accompanying you to this meet, correct?"

I nodded. "Yes, and all of Tally's witches. It should be quite a show of force. But in the end, it won't matter. If she decides to kill me, having the greatest army in the world won't stop her. But as a tiny proactive move, I'm hoping that we can convince Leo to join you and Naomi on the crumbling roof. He can cloak you from her, and you three will be able to react the fastest if there's an issue."

"Sounds like a good plan," he agreed.

"There's only one issue," I said. "We have to locate Leo. I'm hoping you can fly into Florence now to see if he'll agree to help. That is, if he's at Accademia right now. If he's not, I'm not sure if you'll be able to find him."

"It's not a problem," Ray stated. "I'm fairly certain I can locate him. Since we met, I've figured out his signature. He cloaks himself most of the time, but he can't contain the slow burn that leaks out, and it's bright white."

"Good," I said. "I want you back in an hour, regardless. At dinner, we discuss the final plan."

"Got it. On my way," he said, grinning. "I welcome the distraction. Anything to get that woman out of my head." Before I could reply, he shot up into the air.

I turned to Rourke. "Do you think he'll find him?"

"There's a very good chance," Rourke answered. "If not, we'll figure something out."

"Can you believe Selene is his mate? I was floored. But after thinking about it for a nanosecond—it couldn't be more perfect."

Rourke shook his head, a strangled noise coming from the back of his throat. "I can't imagine being tethered to that woman for an eternity, but you're right. They're cut from the same cloth."

"Their children are going to be a mix of reaper, vampire, witch, and goddess." I let my palm come to rest over my abdomen as we began to walk back into the house. "Do you think our kids will be a mix? Like Jax? Or will we have one little wolf and one little cat?"

"Maybe they'll both be cats," he said as I swatted his shoulder.

"They most certainly will not be. More likely, they'll both be wolves."

"And, by the way, I've never been called *little* in my life. Whichever of my children takes on my traits, they will be a *big* cat."

My voice dipped. "I think it will be Annie. In my mind, I see her blonde, like you. She will be our fearless big cat."

"That she will," Rourke murmured, sliding his arm around my waist. "Accompanied by her brother, Aidan, the big, magnificent wolf."

33

The entire group was assembled outside the small, deserted church near the Abbey of San Galgano, where Enid had kept Jax and Naomi. It was ten to midnight, and the full moon was almost directly overhead. Things were quiet, other than a few wolf howls.

Tally had recruited an impressive number of witches, many of them coming in from outlying areas. She'd explained that she'd wanted them all to witness the coronation, so why not help out here first? She stood to my left, Rourke to my right. My father stood beside Rourke, Tyler beside him. On the other side of Tally were Marcy and James.

Ray had found Leo, and he had agreed to help. Naomi, Ray, and the angel were situated on the roof. They would wait for my signal, which would be a whistle.

I was due to walk through those doors to face Enid in nine minutes.

Juanita had not contacted me, so I had no idea if she was inside or not.

"We've got the entire perimeter locked down," Tally said.

"I've commingled the witches and the wolves to give us the greatest advantage. The wolves will charge, while the witches will stay back and spell. Unless Enid can teleport, if you don't come out, she doesn't come out. But even if she can disappear into thin air, I've got a few witches who specialize in that kind of tracking. She won't get away without paying the price with her life."

I glanced at the witch beside me, back in her standard gear—dark fatigues and a black baseball hat pulled down low over her eyes. Her long white ponytail hung loosely out of the opening in back, a no-nonsense expression on her face. "Tally, you were born to do this," I told her. "You're a battle captain with serious expertise."

"Yep," she agreed, her tone serious. "If I'm not slated to fill a similar role on the Coalition, I'll be surprised."

I knew my role, but now that she'd brought it up, I had no idea what anybody else's job duties would be. It made sense that Tally would be a battle captain. "Do you know any of the other job titles?" I asked her.

"Not really." She shrugged. "I've read bits about the Coalition over the years, but none of it very accurate. I'm not sure if the roles are the same every time, or if they adapt depending on which supernatural takes a seat." She turned a wry glance my way. "But if I'm not the battle captain, then something is wrong with this universe."

"Agreed." It was almost time for me to leave. I leaned around Rourke to talk to my father. "Once I give the internal okay to Rourke that everything's fine, you and Tally lead everyone out of here to the coronation location. We will follow." I was going with the best-case scenario—the one in which I survived. If I didn't, they would decide the course of action as they saw fit. "I'm heading in now."

Rourke's hand grip tightened on me.

There was no way he wanted me to step foot in that church. This might be the hardest separation we'd ever had.

He took me in his arms, leaning down to give me a long, tender kiss. My hands went to the back of his neck, caressing. I tried to pour some calm into him.

As soon as our lips parted, he growled, "I'm going to walk you to the door. I don't care if she's pissed off. I'm not moving from that spot until I know you're okay."

"That's fine," I replied. We began to walk arm in arm toward the church door.

You've got this, sis, Tyler said. *There is no way she's gonna harm my niece and nephew. We'll see you out here soon.*

Over the last hour, I'd begun to feel the same way.

And truth be told, I didn't really want to function in a world where someone could take three lives so unjustly. *If she does, she'll have to deal with our wrath,* I told my brother.

When we were almost to the door, I glanced up. A dark shape was crouched next to the chimney. It saluted me. Romy had come to watch the show. I hoped that boded well for my cause. It certainly couldn't hurt, especially knowing what I knew now about the angels and how important this new Coalition was to them.

I wondered for a moment if Leo and Romy were stronger than Enid.

My mate and I stopped at the door, the crowd behind us silent. Rourke gave me a searing kiss, holding my face in his hands. "I will be with you the entire time," he pledged. "One word from you, and I'll be inside."

"I know," I said. "It's going to be okay." I stepped reluctantly out of his arms and reached for the door handle.

Behind me, Marcy yelled, "Go get 'em, Tiger! Wait, wait! I mean, superstrong wolf. Go get 'em, Wolfy!"

I chuckled as I tugged the rickety door open, the wood half eaten away around the edges. I met my mate's gaze. "I love you."

"I love you too. I'll be right here."

The church was dark, save a few low-burning candles near the altar. I made my way slowly up the main aisle. When I was halfway to the front, Enid strode out onto the platform, wearing the same dress.

"I said to come alone, yet you bring an army," she stated, her voice clear and succinct, but not angry. I took that as a good sign.

"You said I couldn't come in here accompanied by anyone," I answered. "But you didn't say anything about out there."

"Do you think your show of force threatens me?" she asked.

I shrugged. "Not really. Threatening you wasn't the plan. You could call what's outside a show of love and support, as much as anything else. All those people out there care about this outcome."

"Indeed," she said. "Please, have a seat." She gestured to the pew on my right.

I obliged, sending a quick thought to Rourke. *Everything is fine so far.* As I sat, I cupped my belly with my right hand. I had a feeling that I was going to do that a lot more often from now on.

"I'm going to dispense with any niceties," she started, "and get right down to the details. You will agree to release my sister, the one who grows inside of you now, on my terms and my terms alone?"

"No," I said, surprising myself. Enid's expression began to change quickly. I held up my hand. "Wait, before you get bent out of shape, let me explain." I leaned forward. "You've seen her, haven't you? You've seen my little Annie being born, happy, laughing, growing up with her brother, and her best friend, Maggie. Look me in the eye and tell me you haven't seen her."

"I've seen her."

"Do you love her?"

"Of course I do! That's the only reason I'm allowing you to sit here."

"If you've seen her—*really seen her*—can you see that she will be shaped by our unconditional love? As much as she will be your sister, she will also be a daughter, a niece, a granddaughter. She will have shifter genes and questions about her life that will need answering. For that reason, and that reason alone, I cannot let you have carte blanche over when you take her from us. We have an open dialogue about it now and agree on a time frame, or there's no deal."

"You would risk your life, and the lives of your unborn children, because you don't want me to have *carte blanche?*" Enid snarled.

I stood. "No, I won't risk my children's lives for anything. That's why I'm doing this. I would never risk Annie's happiness and well-being, even for you. It's clear you're allowing fear and anger to dictate your actions. It's a reaction from missing your sister all of these years. It's understandable. But I will not allow my daughter's entire life to be decided in this moment, under these circumstances. There are so many things that will factor into her upbringing. When she's ready to leave"—I met Enid's hard stare—"I vow to let her go. Not a second before."

Enid narrowed her eyes. "She is my sister first, before she is your daughter."

"No, she's both." My voice was steely. "And above all, she's herself first and will be entitled to make her own choices. The healthiest way to do this, and ensure your sister's happiness, is for both of us to be involved in her life. As she asks questions, we can both be there to answer them. So, when she's finally ready, we'll all know."

"I do not make my choices out of anger," she spat. "I make them out of love."

"Prove it," I challenged. "Do what's best for Annie, not what's best for *you*. In the visions you saw of the future, did you see her alone as a child, without her family around her? Or did you see her with us? Don't lie."

When Enid didn't readily respond, Pandora emerged from the shadows, her simple dress flowing out behind her. "Answer her, dear sister," Pandora coaxed. "Tell her what we saw."

"The child stayed with you until early adulthood," Enid said. She whipped her head toward her sister. "But that does not mean that picture cannot change. We can change it, if we want to."

"Why would we?" Pandora countered. "We'll be in Bianca's life, just as Jessica said. We will be there to answer her questions and lead her down the correct path. After all, what is twenty years when you talk about how many years we've been without her? Would you rob Bianca of her new life?"

"Of course not," Enid shot back. "But her life is with us, nurtured by us, and it will be just as rich as the one she has elsewhere."

"I think not." Pandora strolled across the floor. "When I was born into my new family as Juanita, I experienced things I never thought possible. I saw and understood the world in a way that was remarkably different than I had ever before. Having lived that life has positively affected me and will influence the choices I make moving forward. I would not rob my sister of such a chance. In fact"—she inclined her head at her sister—"it might benefit you to go through the same transformation. It would broaden your mind in a way you've never thought possible. The world has changed drastically since we were young girls. It's incomprehensively different—nothing you could teach without living it firsthand."

Enid gaped at her sister. "You talk nonsense. I have seen no such thing in my future!"

"Ah, but I have." Pandora smiled. "It was just shown to me today."

"You can't be serious," Enid sputtered. "I do not choose to be reborn."

"Sometimes these things are left up to Fate." Pandora met my gaze. "A certain reaper vampire and a certain goddess kindled their bonds today. It won't be long now until they consummate them. If all goes as I've seen, they will have a daughter." Pandora turned to face her sister. "And she will be you."

Enid looked as stunned as I felt.

I reached my hand out to steady myself on the pew. I was flabbergasted at Pandora's words. Ray and Selene? Their baby would be Enid?

Right at that moment, Rourke cut in, *What's going on? Everything is too quiet in there.* His voice was full of worry.

It's going...fine, I assured him. *The strangest thing just happened, but it's not bad. At least I don't think it's bad.*

Jessica, you're not making any sense, he shot back. *Strange doesn't equal good. What's going on?*

I watched as Pandora paced slowly to her sister. *You're going to have to trust me,* I told him. *I can't talk now, but I'll let you know as soon as I can.*

"What you're saying is beyond ridiculous," Enid snipped. "My life is fine the way it is. This is not about me." She glared at me. "It's about getting our sister back."

"I believe this is out of your control, dear sister," Pandora answered. "Fate has shown me the way, and I believe it to be right. Just as I believed keeping Jessica alive was the only option."

Enid took two steps away from her sister, panic beginning to show on her face. "What are you talking about? My place is here...Fate needs me. Who would be at the helm while I was gone? I have kept things running by myself for all these years. There is no other to do it."

"I will," Pandora answered. "Have no fear. This couldn't have worked out better if we tried. You and Bianca will be born around the same time and will thoroughly enjoy your lives together. And then, when you are both grown and ready, we will all reunite, coming together stronger, rejuvenated, and refreshed from where we had been stalled before."

"I don't understand any of this." Enid shook her head.

Pandora placed a hand on her sister's shoulder. "You need not understand, for all the answers will be revealed to you in due time. Bianca's death has changed you. Pain and anger have steered you off of your rightful path. But Fate has found a way to fix it. All will be well. You just need to trust in me."

Enid tried to back away.

My hands slid up to my shoulders as I hugged myself. Pandora's intensity and strength couldn't be denied.

"I refuse you," Enid stated. "I will not come back to this world as a child! Forced to start over from scratch. I will not do it!"

"But you will," Pandora said. She smiled at Enid, her voice gentle. "The best way for you to enter your new life is filled with happiness. Accept what Fate has decreed, so you might shed your burdens and start anew."

"I don't know how to do what you ask—"

I didn't see the dagger until it flashed in Pandora's hand. Her strike was swift as she found true aim. Once the iron had plunged into Enid's heart, the Hag fell to the ground, Pandora bracing her close as she laid her down.

I rushed onto the altar, trying not to panic. I knelt on the other side of Enid and grabbed her hand. Enid turned to me, her face stricken. She was still breathing, but the front of her dress was red with blood.

"I believe Pandora," I told her, my voice rushing. "You will be loved and cherished. You will be a welcome part of our family. The lessons that this life can teach you can make you stronger. You will be happy. I promise."

She looked to her sister. "How…could you?" She coughed. Blood trickled from the side of her mouth.

"I can, because I love you," Pandora replied as a single tear trickled down her cheek. "Someday you will understand, and I believe you will thank me. I am content to wait until that day."

The door banged opened behind us, and footsteps rushed in.

Leo knelt beside Enid, taking my place as I stood. "There could be no other way," he told her, his voice a soothing melody. "Pandora was brave enough to make that decision, and because of it, your life will be whole again. Be well. We will meet again."

Then Rourke was beside me, taking me in his arms, his lips pressed against my hair. "What the hell happened?"

As we both stood there, Enid's body slowly disappeared, evaporating into nothing.

I tried to find the right words, but failed miserably. All I could manage was, "Ray's going to be a father."

34

Nothing that had happened over the last few hours had fully sunk in. The only solace was that Enid could no longer take my child away on a whim. That part was amazing and had filled me with incredible relief and joy.

After Enid had disappeared, I'd talked to Pandora briefly. She'd assured me all would be well. She planned to stay in our lives and help guide us. She also said we'd know when the girls would be ready for their independence—they would tell us—and not to worry.

Easier said than done.

I knew my life would be full of a new kind of worry once the twins were born.

We'd managed to make our way to the tallest point in Florence, which had taken some time. Once we arrived, we were surprised to see the place was jam-packed. It seemed that every supernatural far and wide had shown up to see the coronation.

Jeb stood on a raised dais at the very top of the hill, holding his trusty book. On either side of him stood Leo and

Romy, their wings discreetly glamoured away, their hands clasped behind their backs.

Five ornate podiums were situated in front of them.

As we women made our way to our places, Jeb bowed, instructing us where to stand. White robes, much like Jeb's, hung next to the podiums. We donned them. My place was squarely in the middle, directly across from the warlock. Tally was on my right, Kayla next to her. There was a space for Eudoxia to my left and Naomi on the end.

The Fae Queen had yet to arrive.

Jeb cleared his throat. "We will begin shortly. I will read the vows, and you will acknowledge each verse with 'I do.'" He glanced at each of us down the line. "Your vows, once taken, will be binding. Any questions?"

"Are we allowed to find a replacement for Eudoxia if she doesn't show?" I joked, trying to lighten the mood.

Jeb wasn't amused. "We must start at three a.m. on the dot. The Fae Queen has exactly seven minutes to arrive."

"What happens if she doesn't get here in time—"

I was cut off by a whooshing noise as Eudoxia landed exactly in her place. She turned to give me a look. "I keep my appointments, little wolf girl," she said, using a nickname she'd given me long ago. There was no doubt Eudoxia was threatened by my presumed leadership position on this Coalition.

"Glad to see you could make it," I said, ignoring the jab. "It would've been a shame to have to dig somebody up to fill your spot."

"There is no other. There is only me," she sniffed. I'd never asked Eudoxia where the remaining fae population lived. The rumor was they had dwindled to almost nothing and lived off plane somewhere.

My family had fanned out behind Jeb and the angels, my father and Rourke front and center, pride beaming on their faces. The supernatural crowd behind them seemed sedate and curious. I didn't sense any threats, but my wolf was on high alert. It was likely that Jeb had done something to contain the area so no mishaps would occur.

Exactly three minutes later, Jeb's voice boomed out into the night sky. "We have gathered here for a momentous occasion, one that we have not witnessed in a thousand years. Before you stands the new Coalition, five supernaturals to whom the power has chosen above all others. This is your High Court, those who will enforce our laws. You must answer to them for any wrongdoings, as they vow to protect those wronged." He gestured at Kayla. "I give you the Negotiator." Then he moved to Tally. "The Protector." He lingered on me and said, "The Enforcer." Then he motioned to Eudoxia. "The Peacemaker."

Wait, what?

He ended with Naomi. "And the Tracker."

Eudoxia's position was *Peacemaker*?

Was Jeb serious?

He couldn't be.

I glanced at the Fae Queen out of the corner of my eye. Her face was set, showing nothing.

Jeb continued like nothing he'd just said was out of the ordinary. "Are you ready to take your vows?" he asked us.

We all answered, "We are."

He walked forward a few paces, his white robes dragging behind him. He came to a stop in front of me, his finger landing at the top of the page of his book. It moved as he began to speak. "Do you solemnly swear to uphold the Supernatural Laws, created by your elders, for the good of both humans and supernaturals alike?"

"I do," we all chorused.

"Do you vow to be judicious in your sentencing, staying within the laws and their succinct guidelines?"

"I do."

"Do you vow to be overseers in this world, bringing peace

and stability to all supernatural Sects and protecting them from danger?"

"I do."

"Do you vow to stay honest and neutral, allowing each party their own counsel on matters brought before you, before you pass judgment?"

"I do."

"Do you all agree to follow the lead of the Enforcer, deferring to her as the head of this Council?"

Absolute silence.

I glanced around.

Tally appeared confused. She peered at me, replying, "Er…"

Kayla looked pensive.

Naomi bowed her head.

Eudoxia was furious. She was about to say something scathing when I cut in. "Jeb, did you just add that in there?" I teased. "That doesn't seem like something that would be written in the book."

He looked a little abashed. "I've change the wording slightly to represent the modern times, but the sentiment remains the same. The Coalition has always had one leader, and that position has been held by the Enforcer since the time of our creation. You represent the strength of this Council. With strength comes leadership."

"I've told you this before," I said. "We are running this Coalition as a democracy. With five votes, we will always have a tiebreaker. I have to believe that our creators would understand that times have changed. The eras of dictatorships are over for the supernaturals. I do not want these women swearing me in as their leader chained to that unbreakable vow. That's not how this is going to work."

"But…but…" he stammered. "Without this vow, I will not know to whom to report. The High Commander has always reported to the Enforcer."

"Why don't we amend it to something like this: From this day forward, the Coalition will operate as a democracy, and Jebediah Amel will report to all members equally, depending on the issue at hand." I smiled as I added, "That way, if you have a defense issue, you can report directly to Tally. If someone's in need of being found, you report to Naomi. If there's trouble brewing, you report to Eudoxia. If two parties are interested in solving their issues peacefully, you call Kayla. And when you have an errant supernatural in need of catching, you report to me." I crossed my arms, hoping he wouldn't challenge me. He didn't say anything for a moment, so I continued with, "Honestly, Jeb, what I just outlined is a more efficient way to do business. If you bring each and every issue to me, who knows when I'll be able to get to it?" Especially in my current condition. "We know you're all about efficiency. This way works best for all of us."

Leo bent over and whispered something into the warlock's ear. Jeb straightened. He rifled through some pages, leaning over to examine the book. His bushy eyebrows rose as he peered at me over the spine. He cleared his throat. "I...well...there seems to be something written here along those same lines. But I can assure you it was just added."

"Why don't you go ahead and read it?" I encouraged.

He cleared his throat. "Do you vow to operate this Coalition as equals, each of you having a single vote?"

All responded with a resounding, "I do."

"Do you vow to keep your place on this Coalition until your death or the power seeks another?"

"I do."

"Do you vow to share power with one another in the effort to do greater good?"

"I do."

Jeb closed his book with a flourish. It made a deep booming sound, catching everyone's attention. Then it popped out of existence. Jeb moved forward, joining hands with Leo and Romy, each bowing their head. "We bless this coronation with our combined power. Once we are done, the Coalition will be formalized. The vows spoken here today are sacred and binding. From this day forth, you will be known as the High Court."

The force of their combined power took me by surprise. My wolf howled as the two angels' strength commingled with the warlock's and shot forward, swirling inside me, entering my body from seemingly everywhere. My head arched back, my hair billowing back from the force. By everyone else's intakes of breath, they were feeling the same thing.

After a full minute, it died down. I raised my head and opened my eyes.

"Now you will come and join hands," Jeb said.

We all obeyed, walking around our podiums. We formed a circle, intertwining our fingers. No one said a word.

I was overwhelmed and humbled at the same time.

"When I give the command, push your power signatures out and don't let go until you feel your own magic come back into you," Jeb ordered. "It knows what to do and has been waiting for this." Suddenly, the book was back in Jeb's hands, and he began to murmur something in another language. My hands began to tingle, my wolf howling, ready to release our power and take in the others'. "Unleash yourselves!"

We did as he commanded.

The power threatened to overload each and every one of us.

"Don't let go!" he called. "You can withstand it. Be patient. This is what you were meant to do." He was acting like a Coalition football coach.

The magic signatures swirled in my body, each a different specialty, all of them meant to make me stronger. My wolf was frantic, channeling it away as fast as she could. I wondered for a moment how everyone else was faring without a wolf running around in their brains.

Just when I thought I couldn't take any more, I felt my power re-enter my body.

"That's it, just a few more moments!" Jeb coached. "Okay, drop your hands."

I shook my arms out, tingles racing along my body. I felt electric. My children were fine. The power had not infiltrated my womb. Supernatural bodies apparently safeguarded against such things, and mine had done it naturally.

Jeb turned his back on us, facing the crowd. "I give you your Coalition!" His voice boomed louder than I'd thought possible.

The crowd erupted in cheers.

My family rushed in, surrounding us, Rourke hugging me, followed by my father, then Tyler. Marcy drew me into a bear hug, then separated us by an arm's length. "How do you feel? Any different? You looked so regal up there. You guys seemed to glow a little bit there at the end. Come on, spit it out! The world is waiting for answers, and by the world, I mean me."

I laughed. "I don't feel that much different," I admitted. "But I do feel strong." I knew I could call up the different signatures and use them to help me when I needed it. We all could.

The Power of Five.

Danny came and gave me a hug. He exaggeratedly sniffed me. "You smell like a drunkard," he joked. "Like you've been to the well one too many times. Your power scent is overwhelming. I would wager your liver is about to burst."

"If I smell this way," I said with a chuckle, "I'm certain your mate does too."

"That she does, but her true scent is never far from my heart," he said, draping his arm around Naomi, who had come to stand by his side. He leaned over and gave her a kiss on the cheek, murmuring, "You look utterly beautiful, love."

Nick and Lucas came up next, each giving me a quick hug.

"Jess, nothing could've prepared me for this moment," Nick said. "All those years ago as kids running through the woods...I can't believe it led to this. I'm awestruck."

I nodded my agreement. "It's hard to believe that all the harassment and pain we endured back then made us into what we are today."

"It most certainly did. It made us stronger," Nick said. He glanced at Lucas and smiled. "We're going to head back to the villa and get some food ready for when you guys get back. I hope that's okay."

I nodded. "Sounds good. I don't think we should be too long. The sun will be up shortly, and that means the humans will be waking. Even though this area is spelled, we have to make sure all these supernaturals have time to get out of here without notice."

Jeb came over as Nick and Lucas left and reached out his hand. I smiled as I clasped it. "Welcome to the new democracy, Jeb. I think you're going to like it. It will be much more efficient. I promise."

"I will adapt," he agreed affably. "My father weathered change, as did his father before him. I must admit, being able to take my cases to all of you will speed up the proceedings."

I was proud of Jeb for coming to terms with this so quickly. "And everyone can share in the paperwork," I said. "Surely that's a bonus. By the way, when does work officially begin for us?"

"Right now," he said, opening the book that popped into his arms. "The pages are filling up fast. The first assignment has to do with a reclusive band of banshees. They are encroaching too close to the human world. We must send an emissary to reason with them." He ran his finger over the top of a page. "And there's more."

"Okay, okay," I said, holding up a hand. "It's going to take us some time to figure out how we're going to run things. There's a large conference room in the villa. Let's meet there tomorrow at nine a.m. Are we allowed to appoint other supernaturals to specific positions? As in, if we send an emissary to deal with the banshees, does it have to be one of us?"

"Oh, you're allowed an entire staff if you want one," he said, his head bobbing, hair unmoving. "The actual capturing and arresting must come from one of you directly, but leading up to that, it can be anyone in the field."

"Good to know," I told him as Jax came up to us.

The blue giant engulfed me in one quick hug. "Congratulations," he said. "It's pretty badass you're on the Coalition. I mean, I didn't even know it existed before yesterday, but it's still cool."

"Thanks," I answered. "Jeb here was just telling me that I can appoint people to be on my staff, and I'm thinking you'd make an amazing sentry in the field. That is, if you're interested in a job like that. Not right now," I added hastily, "but eventually, once you get a hold of your powers."

"Like a bounty hunter?" he asked with wonder in his voice. "That would be totally awesome. I'd be up for that."

"More like a bouncer," I corrected. "You'd be the muscle. Your sister is the Negotiator, so I'm figuring she's going to need someone to back her up when she goes in to help supes work out their issues. Who better to do that than you?"

He nodded thoughtfully. "Not as cool as a bounty hunter, but still pretty great. I'm in."

"Good, I'm going to have you work with Ray starting soon. He'll have you in control of your skills in no time."

"What're you signing me up for now?" Ray complained as he stuck out his hand. I shook it, smiling as Jax moved to the side. "Nice going up there, Hannon. You looked like the queen of the world. You're going to do a helluva job."

"Thank you. I think. I was just signing you up to work with Jax. He needs some guidance, and you're just the guy for the job." I hadn't mentioned a word to Ray about what Pandora had told me. I had no idea if he'd overheard, but so far he'd said nothing. There was a chance that Leo had masked the conversation from him so the news didn't interfere with Fate's plan. I was going to let him have some free time and let things fall where they may. Trying to rationally explain that he was, in fact, going to make Selene his mate sooner rather than later, and that they were going to give birth to a baby Enid, would send him over the edge.

One baby step at a time.

"I'm happy to do it," he said, eyeing the large fifteen-year-old who grinned at him. "We'll have you police-force ready in no time."

"That's what I'm counting on," I said. "By the way, Ray, I'm making you my chief officer. Not only will you go out in the field on my behalf, but I want you at all the meetings. I value your input, and having an experienced cop at the table will be invaluable. A lot of the issues that will come our way will be of the 'supernaturals interacting with humans' variety. Those will be your specialty."

"I'm honored," he said, giving me a little bow. "It seems like you finally get to do what you do best—solve cases and catch the bad guys."

"It does feel kind of right," I agreed. "Before we start, however, I want you to take a few days off. You've earned it. You've had your hands full and have been working hard."

He raised a single eyebrow. "I'll take you up on that." He looked off into the distance, preoccupied. "This will be a good time to shore up all my loose ends at home. I left the police force abruptly, told them I was taking a long vacation. It's time to clean things up before somebody files a missing-persons report on me."

And meet up with Selene, I murmured to Rourke, who stood next to me. *And make some babies.*

If he knew what we know, he'd be enraged, Rourke confirmed.

Maybe, maybe not. Love is a strange thing, I said. *I think Leo blocked him from hearing what Pandora had to say, so it's important he stay in the dark.* Angels were smart. "See you in a few days, Ray."

He gave us a small salute and backed away.

I was just about to ask Rourke if it would be okay if we snuck out, when I spotted Eudoxia marching toward us. I smiled sweetly at my new Council member. "If you're about to try your peacemaking skills on me," I told her, "you might want to try another day. By the look on your face, I'm thinking yoga might help you find your inner Zen."

Instead of taking the bait, Eudoxia kept her expression grave. "Something has come up. It will require me to be gone for a month, maybe longer."

I balked. "What are you talking about? You can't leave right now. We have to figure out how the Coalition is going to run. The five of us being together is absolutely necessary."

She snatched my arm and dragged me a few paces away. "I'm only going to say this once, so listen up. My people are in trouble. My fae ancestors, that is. There are only a handful of us left here, but in the last day, I've received word that a large population of fae were taken off plane against their will hundreds of years ago. Plans are already in place to retrieve them. I have no choice."

"Isn't this something the Coalition should discuss together? This is the kind of thing we're supposed to deal with. We can allocate resources to you and figure out together how to move effectively."

"There is no time." She shook her head. "The people who have enslaved my ancestors have found out that I am in a powerful position. We have to move now. Without a surprise attack, we have no hope."

I'd never seen Eudoxia so worried. "Okay, but you're going to have to find a way to send us word, or we'll have no choice but to come after you."

She nodded. "I will do my best. I've also given my proxy vote to your pet vampire, for now. I've already confirmed this with Jeb."

"Ray? You're giving your voting rights while you're gone to *Ray*?"

"Yes, please try to keep up," she replied, irritated. "While I'm away, if there are matters that need my judgment, the male vampire in your service may cast a vote for me. He's the only one of you with any sense, anyway."

I snorted. "That's fine by me. I wish you well, Eudoxia. How are you planning to accomplish this mission?"

She narrowed her eyes. "By being a Peacemaker."

I began to laugh, but stopped abruptly when I realized she was serious. "Honestly, I didn't think Jeb was in his right mind when he gave you that title. I thought it was some sort of ironic selection."

"There are many things you don't know about me," she snapped. "He was not wrong. How do you think I managed to run the largest Coterie in the world?"

"Fear and blood sport?"

"Wrong," she asserted. "I've been a diplomat since I was a young girl. My father was the Tsar of Russia. I will carry out my mission. I'm sure I can find a solution for my kin's release."

"And if you can't get there by peacemaking?"

"I'll rip their throats out," she snarled. She didn't bother to say goodbye. She just shot up into the air.

"Good luck, Eudoxia," I called. "Send us word when you can."

Romy was headed toward us, Leo at her side.

Once they stopped, they both bowed their heads. I returned the gesture. "When I vowed to grant my protection to your sacrifice," Leo said, "I meant it. Your children will find a guardian in me."

Rourke reached out to shake the angel's hand. "We appreciate that more than you will ever know."

"Are you sticking around Florence?" I asked Leo.

He glanced at Romy before answering. "It's come to my attention that there is some unrest in my homeland, so for the time being I am leaving my options open."

"Same for you?" I asked Romy.

"Yes," she said. "The news has reached our realm about this coronation. I will wait to see how it all plays out."

"You are welcome to join us at the villa, for however long you choose," I told her. "I'd love to learn more about your realm and about how an uprising in your world will affect us here. That is, if you can spare the time."

She grinned. "I will stop by and keep you abreast. It's unknown what the implications will be, but I understand from the position you're in now, it will be important for you to know all the facts as they unfold."

"I appreciate that," I told her as they turned to leave.

Danny and Naomi stepped in. "We're going to head back," Danny announced. "My beautiful Tracker is going to expedite our leaving by flying us out of here."

Naomi leaned in to give me a kiss on each cheek. "I look forward to serving on this Coalition with you, Jessica." She smiled. "You've done so much for me. I cannot begin to thank you. I will plan to continue paying my debt forward by doing my job to the best of my abilities."

I was so incredibly proud of Naomi. This was the first time in a long time that she hadn't addressed me as her queen. We were equals. I watched as Naomi wrapped her arms around her mate, his face joyous, and they took off into the air.

My father and my brother came forward. My dad embraced me again, holding me for several seconds. "I cannot tell you how pleased I am," he said, his voice breaking. "I knew from day one that you were special. I just didn't know how special. You and Tyler are the light of Annie's and my life. I wish your mother was here to witness this. She would've been your biggest supporter."

Tears pooled in my eyes. "I know she would've been. I think about her often. My daughter will bear her name." My father rarely spoke of my mother. Not because he didn't love her, but because it was just too hard. Tyler and I had never met her, as she died in childbirth.

He nodded. "I approve."

Tyler reached out to give me a big hug. "I love you, sis. We're in this together. Never doubt that."

"I don't," I said.

"I'm going to be the best uncle in the entire world," he said. "Your kids will beg to play with me." Kayla joined him, and he wrapped his arm around her. She gave him a warm smile.

"You're going to have some competition with Jax as favorite uncle," I told him. "You're going to have to up your game."

Tyler laughed. "It's on."

Kayla leaned over and placed a kiss on my cheek. "Thank you for everything you've done for me and my brother. I will never forget it. This is going to take a while to sink in, but you have my word that I will be a fierce participator in this Coalition. I will always have your back."

"And I'll always have yours," I told her. "Never doubt for a moment that you're supposed to be here, Kayla. The power chose you for a reason. You will live up to—and surpass—your potential, I'm certain of it."

"I've got a van waiting for us," Tyler said. "Let's head back. I don't know about you all, but I'm exhausted."

"My mate needs more sleep than usual." Rourke grinned. "And I'm going to make sure she gets it." Without warning, he swept me off my feet.

I laughed, kissing him soundly. "Take me home," I told him, my arms entwining his neck. It felt good that we actually had a home to go to, and even better that nobody was after me.

This must be what heaven must feel like.

"It'll be my pleasure."

Three months later...

I rolled over, my pillow pressed firmly over my head. "Do I have to?" I mumbled. "How about five more minutes?"

A familiar laugh penetrated the feathers over my face, as two warm, firm hands caressed my legs, slowly inching up my thighs. "I can think of a few other things I'd like to do rather than let you sleep, but unfortunately you don't have any more minutes left. The dark angel just arrived, and Ray is back. Jeb's meeting with Tally as we speak. You need to get moving. We let you sleep in."

I tossed the pillow away and sat up, my gigantic belly beating me to the edge of the bed. "What time is it?"

"Ten."

"Ten?" I gasped. "Rourke, I told you to wake me up at seven!"

He grinned. "I tried. You're like a zombie when you sleep. The consensus was to let you be. The babies are going to come sooner rather than later, and you need your rest."

"You're telling me," I mumbled as I got up and waddled to the bathroom.

There'd never been a pregnant female werewolf before, so we had no idea what to expect. Apparently, my gestation was going to be half as long as a human's—if that.

Carrying two supernatural children had proven to be an incredible feat thus far. They were always active and kept me up most nights. I had no idea how my human mother accomplished such a thing.

She was my hero.

I brushed my teeth quickly. "I'm just going to wear this," I told my amused mate as I walked back into the bedroom. I had on one of his oversized T-shirts. "Don't make fun. It's the only thing that fits." I snatched a pair of sweatpants off the chair and stuffed my legs in, managing to cinch them at the bottom of my hip bones. A place I hadn't been able to see in well over a month.

Rourke kissed me, still grinning. "You look beautiful, and everyone is used to it. Come on, Lucas made breakfast and I saved some for you."

I followed him downstairs.

Maggie was perched on the kitchen counter, chatting with Lucas, who loved indulging her. She immediately stretched her arms out to Rourke, who scooped her up. She didn't bother to try that with me anymore, as there was absolutely zero room. "Annie and Aidan will be here soon," she cooed. "And Auntie Marcy too!" Marcy was flying in for the birth. Her words had been, *Just try to stop me.*

"That's what you keep telling us." Rourke chuckled. So far the little cherub hadn't been any more specific than *soon.* "Is your mommy downstairs?"

She nodded vigorously. "Yes, the warlock is *willy* upset."

When wasn't he?

It was taking more time than I had hoped for Jeb to acclimate to the new structure of the Coalition. Since my pregnancy was going so fast, others were taking meetings with him in my place. Jeb had taken a certain umbrage to being passed around, but so far it was working as well as it could. We'd had no immediate issues that had been too hard to handle.

I grabbed a few pieces of bacon, a muffin, and a glass of orange juice. "Is Romy in my office?" The dark angel stopped by once a week. She had kept us updated on what was happening. Unfortunately, her world, a place she called Vail, was very close to total unrest. It was worrisome for all of us.

"Yes," Rourke answered. "I'll be down as soon as I can get rid of this little kitty cat." He tickled Maggie, and she giggled.

I padded through the house, taking one of the two stairways that led down to the basement. My office was in one of the bigger rooms, complete with a set of French doors that led outside. The view of the countryside was amazing. I enjoyed living here. "Sorry to keep you waiting," I told Romy as I walked in. She was lounging on a leather sofa, but stood as soon as I entered.

"Nice outfit," she snarked.

"Yeah, my choices are a bit limited these days." I set my glass and plate on my desk. "Doesn't make sense to stock up on a bunch of maternity clothes when I'm about to give birth." I tried to ease behind my desk with some grace. It wasn't easy. My belly ended up knocking most of the things off the desk. I shoved the juice glass and food out of the way in time. When I was finally situated, I asked, "What's up? You were just here on Monday. Have things changed?"

"Yes, I'm afraid they have. And I fear chaos in our world will leak into yours."

"How can we prevent that from happening?" I asked.

"I'm not sure yet," she admitted as she began to walk around my office. "I have a meeting with Leo later today. We will likely have to leave for Vail soon." I was still trying to

BLUE BLOODED

understand all the nuances of the different realms and how they worked. It was complicated.

"I want to send someone with you," I said. I'd gotten to know all of Julian's wolves over the last few months. "There's a wolf with a special talent who might be an asset."

"What talent is that?" she asked.

"His name is Dag, and he can heal any wound with speed. Some wolves have healing skills, but I've never seen anything like this before. I'm pretty sure he could've put Ceres back together if he'd wanted to. If your world is as harsh as you say it is, you will be in constant danger. I don't think Dag would mind accompanying you. On the contrary, I actually think it would be right up his alley. He's enormous, imposing, gregarious, and is always up for adventure. You could present him as our emissary. I wouldn't mind sending representation along with you."

"That might be useful. I'll let you know," she said.

Tally stuck her head in the door. "We have a problem. I need you in the conference room."

"Got it," I told her. I turned back to Romy. "Is there anything else I can help you with right now?"

"No," Romy said. "I just wanted to let you know that I'll be leaving soon."

She hesitated.

"What is it?"

"There is a chance once I leave I may not be able to return to this realm," she said.

"Why not?"

"I haven't been completely honest with you." She paced toward the French doors and looked out. "I was actually ordered home months ago."

"Why didn't you go when you were summoned?" I asked.

"Because my sister had been taken hostage by white angels."

I wasn't following. If Tyler were in trouble, I would've

rushed to him. "Why wouldn't you have gone home and tried to get her back?"

Romy sighed, turning to face me. "My sister is a very powerful angel. She holds a prominent position in our parliament. They wanted me home to trade my life for hers. There was no plan to break her out, only to give me to them in hopes that they would set her free."

"That almost never happens," I pointed out.

"Tell me about it."

"So what's your plan?" I asked.

"Leo has decided to help me, which is unprecedented, as he is white and I am dark. But, whatever the outcome, I may not be able to return. I could be jailed for failing to do as they asked, or worse. I wanted to let you know because I've come"—she paused—"to call you a friend. I wanted to give you a proper farewell."

I made my way out from behind my desk, managing to aim my belly away from anything breakable. We embraced as well as we could. "I've come to call you a friend too," I told her. "Let me confer with the other women, but I'd like to send Dag with you at the very least. If your world falls, I want ample warning, and Dag can also provide you with protection. He's a fierce wolf. You told me before that there are many ways in and out of your realm. If they lock you up, Dag can alert us, and we can help you."

She nodded. "Your offer is very generous. I'll send word after my meeting with Leo."

"Be well," I said, kissing each cheek. "I hope you find your sister and that everything works out."

"Me too." She walked to the French doors and opened them. "Give those beautiful babies love from me." She glanced over her shoulder. "You will be a wonderful mother."

Then she was gone, her long, blonde hair flowing out behind her.

I picked up my juice and plate and walked into the

conference room. Tally sat at the head of the table. Naomi and Kayla were also already there, Jeb pacing behind them. The first thing I noticed was Kayla's pale face.

I eased myself as gracefully as I could into a chair. "What's wrong?"

"It's the gargoyles," Tally started before Kayla could answer. "The ones after Jax. We've gotten some intel that they're planning to strike against us."

"When?" I asked. "Why would they do a stupid thing like that?"

Jeb had his book out. "It will happen within a week," he read from the pages. "According to what is written here, they have a good chance of winning their prize if they're allowed to arrive in Italy. We must preempt them, ideally somewhere in Austria, as they're coming from the Czech Republic."

"Any word from Eudoxia?" I asked.

Tally shook her head. "No, nothing."

We'd heard from her only twice in the last three months. I glanced at Kayla. "They must want Jax pretty badly to come all this way and try to fight us for him."

Kayla's gaze was pinned to the table as she fidgeted. "They need him for a specific reason."

I leaned forward as much as my belly would allow. "And what's that?" I asked.

"To procreate," she said. "Their numbers have dwindled far lower than I'd thought before. They believe Jax to be fertile. They will likely stop at nothing."

I turned to Naomi. "Can you track this band of gargoyles?"

She nodded. "I believe so. It shouldn't be too hard." She glanced at Kayla. "Do you have anything one of them might have touched? Maybe something of your families that you kept?"

"I might," Kayla answered. "When they attacked, they brutalized my mother. I have her things. I can search through them after this meeting."

"Okay, we send Naomi to scout their exact location," Tally said, coming up with a directive. "Then we send Kayla in to negotiate terms. If that doesn't work, we send in a battle battalion full of witches and spells to break them up."

We all nodded.

"I'll go with Naomi," Ray announced as he walked into the room, yanked out a chair, and sat. "Sorry I'm late."

My eyebrows rose to my hairline. "You look like hell. Did you get Selene settled?" There was no way the goddess was going to live here with us, so she and Ray had gotten their own place. Because Ray could fly, they'd picked Rome. Apparently, Selene had acquaintances there.

"More or less," he said as he sighed. "This mate business is a bunch of malarkey."

I laughed. "Well, it is when you're mated to somebody like Selene." That was a circle of hell I didn't want to know about. "Hang in there. If her pregnancy is anything like mine, your baby will be here soon." He had announced she was pregnant a few weeks ago. I hadn't had the heart to tell him about Enid yet. There would be time for that *after* he bonded with the baby.

"Back to the business at hand," Jeb announced with a sniff. "As Tally was saying, Naomi and Ray will go scout the location. After that, we send in Kayla."

"Let's add Danny and Tyler to the list," I told Jeb. "Since this is Naomi's first official tracking duty and Kayla's first negotiation, both mates will want to accompany them." I addressed the women. "I'm assuming you want them with you?" I smiled. "If it makes it any easier, I don't think you need them there to do your job. But when I get back into the field, Rourke and I will go out as a team. Every time. I believe it makes us all safer in the end. But the choice is yours."

They both nodded. "That works," Kayla answered. "The gargoyles will be hostile, so I'd like to take ten to twenty wolves with me."

"And some spell crafters," Tally announced. "Just to be safe. We don't need to go into these meets blind. I'll have my witches research spells that work on gargoyles. They are resistant to most things, but I'm sure we can drum up something."

"Sounds good," I said. "If the gargoyles don't back down, we can always send Jax off plane." Everyone stared at me blankly. "What? It's not the craziest plan in the world. If they can't find him, they can't take him."

Kayla crossed her arms. "And where exactly would you send him?"

"That depends on what happens with the angels and their civil war and how dangerous it becomes," I said. "Romy has described Vail as welcoming to other supernaturals. If that's not an option, there's always the Underworld. I've been in contact with the Princess of Hell a few times, and we're on good terms." I leaned forward. "Do you have a better plan? Our duty is to keep Jax safe, and I'm willing to do whatever it takes."

Kayla was quiet for a few seconds. "I am too."

Tally stood, placing her palms on the table. "This meeting is adjourned."

Jeb was about to say something when a small voice interrupted him. "Auntie Jessica?"

I turned to find Maggie in the doorway with Rourke. "Sorry to bother you," he said. "She insisted we come down." We'd all learned to listen to Maggie when she had something to say.

"What is it, baby?" Tally crooned in a voice she reserved for her daughter.

Maggie met my eyes. "It's time."

The moment the words tumbled out of her mouth, a gigantic contraction ripped through me. I moaned as my nails gouged the conference table.

Everyone jumped out of their seats.

Tally took Maggie, and Rourke came to my side. "I'll call Genevieve," Tally announced. "She's the best midwife we have, and I've had her on call for this. You won't feel a thing." She disappeared out the door.

Another searing pain washed through me, and as I tried to stand, my knees buckled.

Rourke caught me and scooped me up into his arms. "Are you okay? Is this normal?" His voice was full of concern.

"I'm fine," I told him, wrapping my arms tightly around his neck, right where they belonged. "It's just time for us to meet our babies."

He rested his forehead against mine. "I can't wait."

The BLOODED WORLD continues…Stay tuned.

For up-to-date info please stop by my Facebook page: http://www.facebook.com/authoramandacarlson

Or simply sign up for my newsletter and get new releases in your inbox: http://www.amandacarlson.com/newsletter-sign-up

NOTHING IS CREATED WITHOUT A GREAT TEAM.

My thanks to:
Awesome Cover design: Rob Shields
Title Font: Chad Roberts
Photographer: Shirley Green
Digital and print formatting: Author E.M.S
Copyedits/proofs: Joyce Lamb
Final proof: Marlene Engel

About the Author

Amanda Carlson is a graduate of the University of Minnesota, with a BA in both Speech and Hearing Science & Child Development. She went on to get an A.A.S in Sign Language Interpreting and worked as an interpreter until her first child was born. She's the author of the high octane Jessica McClain urban fantasy series published by Orbit, the Sin City Collectors paranormal romance series, and the contemporary fantasy Phoebe Meadows Series. Available everywhere. She lives in Minneapolis with her husband and three kids.

FIND HER ALL OVER SOCIAL MEDIA

Website: amandacarlson.com

Facebook: facebook.com/authoramandacarlson

Twitter: @amandaccarlson